What I Found Out About Her

THE RICHARD SULLIVAN PRIZE IN SHORT FICTION

Editors
William O'Rourke and Valerie Sayers

1996 *Acid*, Edward Falco

1998 *In the House of Blue Lights*, Susan Neville

2000 *Revenge of Underwater Man and Other Stories*, Jarda Cervenka

2002 *Do Not Forsake Me, Oh My Darling*, Maura Stanton

2004 *Solitude and Other Stories*, Arturo Vivante

2006 *The Irish Martyr*, Russell Working

2008 *Dinner with Osama*, Marilyn Krysl

2010 *In Envy Country*, Joan Frank

2012 *The Incurables*, Mark Brazaitis

2014 *What I Found Out About Her: Stories of Dreaming Americans*, Peter LaSalle

What I Found Out About Her

PETER LaSALLE

University of Notre Dame Press

Notre Dame, Indiana

Published by University of Notre Dame Press
Notre Dame, Indiana 46556
www.undpress.nd.edu

Manufactured in the United States of America

Library of Congress Cataloging-in-Publication Data

LaSalle, Peter.
[Short stories. Selections]
What I found out about her : stories of dreaming Americans / Peter LaSalle.
pages ; cm — (Richard Sullivan prize in short fiction)
Includes bibliographical references.
ISBN-13: 978-0-268-03392-7 (pbk. : alk. paper)
ISBN-10: 0-268-03392-7 (pbk. : alk. paper)
I. LaSalle, Peter. What I found out about her. II. Title.
PS3562.A75246A6 2014
813'.54—dc23
2014020882

∞ *The paper in this book meets the guidelines for permanence and durability of the Committee on Production Guidelines for Book Longevity of the Council on Library Resources*

For FAITH, NORMA, and GLENNA

The whole life of an American is passed like a game of chance . . .

—De Tocqueville

CONTENTS

ACKNOWLEDGMENTS

The stories in this book originally appeared, sometimes in different form, in: *Antioch Review* ("In the Southern Cone," "Tunis and Time," "What I Found Out About Her"); *Ecotone Journal* ("Tell Me About Nerval"); *Hotel Amerika* ("Additional Notes Concerning the Elevator in the Dictator's Palace"); *Missouri Review* ("Oh, Such Playwrights!"); *New England Review* ("The Saga of the Irish in America"); *Ontario Review* ("The Dead Are Dreaming About Us"); *Southern Review* ("The Manhattan Lunch: Two Versions"); *Yale Review* ("The Dealer's Girlfriend"); *Zoetrope: All-Story* ("A Dream of Falling Asleep: IX–XVII"). "Tunis and Time" also appeared in *The Best American Mystery Stories 2008,* edited by George Pelecanos (Houghton Mifflin Harcourt). The author is grateful to the editors of these publications.

WHAT I FOUND OUT ABOUT HER

1. I found out that she had always been tall, skinny when a kid and now as slim as a runway model, even if she wasn't a runway model but some sort of copy editor (I'm not sure I quite followed that, exactly what the position was) at a fashion news service in what I imagined as a blue-tinted glass skyscraper somewhere around Herald Square. Her voice was whispery, a certain softness to it.

2. I found out that she smiled a lot, and that when she smiled her top lip flattened over her upper teeth that did protrude a bit, slightly bucked, but there was something right about that, the pouty overbite, and lovely, too.

3. I found out that she had always hated the whole idea of going to a gym, all those strangers so sweaty, so she considered herself lucky to be naturally tall and slim, even if it had meant being gangly as a kid. The big green eyes and the lustrous black hair, which she wore like maybe a French schoolgirl, just parted on the side and with a single yellow plastic barrette to hold it across her forehead, weren't any secret, anything you had to find out, or the fact that she dressed well, maybe because she did work at that fashion news service, perfect when she met me for drinks in a short straight black skirt and satiny emerald-green camisole shirt and shoes with braided gold straps that looked expensive.

She was twenty-seven and very lovely, and we spent the night together in my room at the Pennington Hotel on Forty-eighth Street. That's when I found out these things, in the room high up with a balcony. We would be together just a dozen or so hours, which in a way makes the truth of our being together—when put up against the whole matter of what eventually happened later, that big darkness—

seem negligible, but in a way so much more important, too, even frightening, I suppose.

4. And, hell, it was hot that Sunday night in late June in Manhattan, and Room 1411 in the Pennington Hotel—a nice older place—was on the building's back corner. It had the balcony perched above the humpy black roofs of several Forty-seventh Street theaters below (the Biltmore, the Barrymore, the Brooks Atkinson), and that balcony was what turned out to save us, you might say, seeing that the air conditioner itself didn't pack much of a punch; we ended up keeping the twin doors to the balcony open, the big windows on the corner's other side open, too, windows overlooking Eighth Avenue, then tenements and glistening street lights and lime-green puffs of summer treetops, clear to the black Hudson and silhouetted New Jersey across the way.

The whole week and then the weekend had been breaking June records, and before we finally got together, met for drinks and then dinner on that Sunday night, before we eventually went up to that room, 1411, I had asked myself why I had been so crazy as to linger in the city for a weekend when I had already finished up by Friday just about everything I had to do in the city during my stay of several days. And New York on a summer weekend was too crowded to even think about the Metropolitan Museum or the recently reopened MoMA, altogether too hot to just walk and contentedly walk, which is what you're supposed to do in New York, the only city of that kind in the whole of America, a world city, where you can just walk and walk and walk, no?

5. But to backtrack some, I had met her at a dinner party in Los Angeles, a couple of months before. She was visiting L.A. then for a long weekend.

I was simply supposed to look her up if I was ever in New York, so I did just that. And we talked over drinks in the quiet bar where we met on Ninth Avenue that she suggested on the phone, then talked some more at dinner in the good pasta restaurant on Ninth Avenue that she also suggested. (She said she knew the area a little because she had friends who lived in the orange-brick high-rise of Manhattan Plaza nearby—two struggling actors, a couple—and she explained that Manhattan Plaza was basically subsidized housing for theater people, having been locked into forever being such when an overaggressive developer in the seventies was too far ahead of his time in figuring out that because Hell's Kitchen was so close to midtown, it would one day be upscale and in demand; she said the city had to bail out the developer back then, buying the high-rise and setting up that subsidized-rent deal with the theater union, she said her friends were set for life, with their rent being based on what they made, and—she laughed—they both made damn little.) We walked back to the hotel in the heat, and when we talked out on the balcony, a fine view of the definitely lurid show for a sunset in the haze over New Jersey, she said she wished she had brought her pot to smoke, it would have been perfect, which made me realize how young she was. And still out on the balcony, smooching some by then in the darkness, we watched in a nearby high-rise an odd scene of some little kids rolling around on the carpet in their lit, air-conditioned living room, wrestling with one another, thumping one another solidly with sofa pillows, and we both laughed; it was terrible but pretty funny, too, to see that, and when she laughed she did put her hand over her teeth that were a little buck, like I said, a gesture that seemed entirely girlish and made me also realize again how young she was.

A dozen years between us, though maybe that isn't all that much. I'd just turned thirty-nine.

There was eventually lovemaking that neither of us had expected, certainly, when I had called her that week after getting into the city from L.A., when she had told me she was tied up most of the weekend, Friday night and all day Saturday, but Sunday evening would be fine for her if it was for me. So I decided to stay for the weekend, and, after all, the agent I had met with that week was paying for everything, this trip to New York.

6. Her mother had died when she was seven, and she said it probably affected her sister, a few years older, more than her. With her

father assigned to so many places in his consular job with the State Department (Egypt, Barbados, Senegal), she got used to being on her own in the other countries, which was more or less what being raised by a nanny felt like, she said, and by the time her father remarried, she was already off in boarding school in Switzerland. She said her time at the school in Switzerland was now kind of a blur to her, the same for taking the last year before college at a prep school in Providence called Moses Brown, where she said that, granting it was a Quaker institution, there were an awful lot of serious drugs and not just pot, because rich American kids like that had money for all the drugs they wanted. She said there had been some experimenting with girls sexually, at the boarding school in Switzerland, or at least one girl. She said the girl was a pale and lisping and skinny girl at the school there, a girl named Nicole, who she never knew what happened to. She said she would like to have an address even now to email her, to see what became of Nicole in life.

I mean, I was finding out an *awful* lot about her.

7. I learned that she made forty-one thousand dollars a year on the job as a copy editor for the fashion news service (I had asked her only out of curiosity and she was direct), and I learned that she had been wooed by a similar operation that apparently did about the same kind of thing, but it was located in New Jersey, across the river, so she didn't take the offer, though they wanted to give her almost fifty thousand, a deal where she might get Fridays off as well. She said she really didn't want to take that step, working in New Jersey and not actually be working in New York, she didn't like the idea of that. She lived in Williamsburg in Brooklyn.

8. I don't know exactly what I told her, and I suppose there was equally as much talk about me, probably more than her own talk about herself. But you never remember all of that, or much of that, what you yourself said, when you do look back on one of those first times together with somebody, do you? I mean, it's all a matter of what the other person has to say to you, isn't it?

In truth, I have no real idea what I said to her, what I told her. I suppose she did ask me about my screenwriting work in L.A., I suppose I did tell her about my bust of a brief marriage, no kids. And I don't want to make it seem that she was going on and on with her own story, because all of what I found out about her just came out in the course of conversation, in the restaurant, then on the balcony, then in bed after the lovemaking, and I suppose I gently asked her things the way you do when you first get to know somebody, especially when both of you immediately feel so attracted to each other that way.

9. And even now I would like to be able to say that there was some clue in the course of it all, something she said, even in our brief time together, to indicate what eventually did happen to her might happen to her. (Months later I finally got a long-distance call back in L.A. from her sister, a few years older, as said, who told me that she herself was married with kids, lived in Connecticut. She had taken it upon herself to carefully go through all the phone messages that had been left with her sister's answering service and finally reply the best she could to people, and the sister was the one who told me what had happened, that's how I got word of it, but only after my leaving several messages following the beep, which I—knowing what I do know now—lately hear as so haunting; but I had given up leaving messages for her after a while back then, had decided then that for some reason or other the young woman I spent the night with was obviously dodging me, even screening the several calls I made when back on the Coast.) Yes, now, to think that we were together for only what amounted to hours and there was *so much* I learned, there was *so much* that I found out about her—though, I should emphasize, our conversation was completely relaxed and casual, all of it natural enough, when I found out these things.

10. I found out that there really hadn't been that many boyfriends, or as many as I would have expected, anyway.

In college at the University of Arizona (she was an English major, said she went there because a lot of other kids from the prep school in Providence were going there, and she later decided that she maybe should have thought more about what college to attend, picked a place more serious), in college there was a hippie-retro guy her age in the student co-op where she lived with a lot of other hippie-retro people, and she dated him for most of her sophomore and junior years (she laughed, saying that she personally hadn't been a hippie, retro or otherwise, and the co-op turned out to be pretty crazy—it seemed a bunch of them there gave the pet Scottie that she had gotten at an animal shelter a magic mushroom one night while she was out with the boyfriend at a movie, and the poor little dog apparently wandered off thoroughly stoned, she never saw it again), and then when she was a senior she had a job working as a waitress in a Tucson brew pub, which I found myself picturing, all that polished copper and polished mahogany you always find in any brew pub, and she dated a grad school dropout studying Latin American politics who was a bartender and perpetually trying very hard, she laughed, to get back into grad school, not turn out to be a lifelong Ph.D. dropout; she still heard from him occasionally, married in Tucson now with three kids, no Ph.D. (when I seemed surprised to learn that she had to work during college, the waitress job, she explained that maybe I had gotten the wrong impression from what she had told me about being at the Swiss boarding school and then what surely was the expensive prep school in Providence, she explained that tuition for such places was a perk her father got with the foreign service, and he actually didn't make that much money as a consular-section staffer and simple government employee, was saddled to the usual step-by-step raises and not much more than that). I suppose it was very surprising that there hadn't been more men in college, more men now, when you considered how attractive she was, how soft-voiced and pleasantly engaging she was.

11. She laughed and said she wanted to have kids some day. Of course, she wanted that, she *really did* want that.

12. She said she lived in Washington right after college (her father now lived there, but I'm not sure whether I quite followed that

either, if he was retired or simply assigned there before retirement), then she moved to New York to share a place with pals from college. In New York she met a young Wall Street lawyer not long after getting her first job, and they dated for two and a half years, but that was thoroughly over now. She laughed that though he had a good degree from Columbia Law and though he worked for a large and important firm, was very successful, he was also convinced his career would eventually be doomed by the fact that his last name was Cruk, pronounced "Crook," certainly not the name any lawyer would want. (I think I was more envious than curious about that, and I knew what kind of money big-time lawyers made in Wall Street firms, even young lawyers, money for Porsches and summer houses out in the Hamptons, that sort of thing, and my screenwriting career was middle income at best, that best being when one job did lead to another, which I, and especially my own wise-cracking agent in L.A., always hoped would be the case.) More recently, for about a year, there had been somebody named Jack, who she said was a welder and who she had known for a long time, he had gone to prep school with her, that Moses Brown School. And then rather than laughing she seemed to express a remembered and quite real concern about the fact that there was genuine danger to the welding he did, and sometimes he would out of habit tip up his mask too soon, before he should tip up the mask, and a stray spark or two would flick toward his eye, she was always nervous about the danger of that for him, always told him he had to be more careful, he could injure himself for life. (I guess that raised questions as I lay there listening, and I also felt envious with mention of him, the welder, to think of some surely muscular and handsome young working-class guy, but maybe he wasn't such, because hadn't she said that she had known him from prep school, and then I felt even more envious, to think that possibly he was a welding artist not only muscular and handsome, but somebody masterfully handling the eerily glowing blue torch, wearing a mysterious, almost primordial mask, to wrestle with heavy steel slabs and energetically construct, no doubt, huge and acclaimed art installations—but I didn't ask her to elaborate, so

I never really knew what kind of welder that boyfriend had been.) I listened.

She laughed and said that maybe she wasn't good with relationships.

13. "Are you seeing anybody now?" I asked her.

Hell, it was hot in that room, our naked bodies glazed and the two of us lying there side by side, facing each other, the doors to the balcony and the windows thrown wide open to the night, or possibly *more* than wide open like that, so the outside was inside, maybe. You could hear the traffic and horns below, somehow distant, you could imagine all the people down there in the heat, perhaps getting out of the theaters now on a Sunday evening, out on the sidewalk and themselves amazed by the sultry deep-blueness of the evening, people still half in the other world of whatever pantomime of life they had been so caught up in for the last couple of hours there under the roofs of the theaters directly below the balcony of Room 1411, and she reached out to push my own forelock up from my brow, look right at me with the truly green eyes, flecked with gold like autumn leaves, very lovely, and say:

"I'm seeing you right now."

I looked right back at her, smiled, and I suppose I thought what a rare surprise it was, how I wasn't even going to linger in the city for the extra couple of days—face all that heat, all the usual summer weekend crowding, plus my knowing that I should have been back in California and tending to things piling up there, I could have booked a flight out on Friday evening—and now everything had turned out like this, so right, so wonderful, you might say.

14. "I'm seeing you right now." That was the exact line, maybe the only exact line I could quote from her for the entire night even if I do remember so much, and it sticks with me. "I'm seeing you right now," which she said as she looked at me that way, as she did *see* me right then.

15. The horns continued to sound, softly, very far below, lulling and pleasant in the night, like distant surf can be lulling, like a thunder-

storm heard rumbling a couple of towns over can be lulling. From the sheets, creased and lumped from our tumbling before, you could look out through the open balcony doors of the hotel so high up like that and see the giant red-and-white neon *M* atop the yellow brick pile of the very old Milford Hotel, the letter almost floating untethered in the night sky of a hot Sunday in late June, you could see now and then a faraway jet swooping up, taking off from maybe LaGuardia into what must have been the set ascent path for takeoffs, a silver speck making no noise at all, but very much there, getting smaller and smaller as it gained height, as if it was something you almost knew, something you were trying to think of, but then it somehow got away from you the more you did try to think of it, the more you tried to concentrate on it, determine what *exactly* it was.

"It's crazy hot in here, isn't it," I said to her.

I remember my saying that, probably more than once, the joke of the air-conditioning getting nowhere against such record-breaking heat, and, in fact, I had learned by my second day in the room that week that it was worse to keep the doors and windows shut and try to let the AC do its job, which it obviously really couldn't do.

And maybe when I talked about the heat, she didn't say anything, still looking at me. She just smiled, there was that pouty overbite.

16. And what was it that she had said before, the exact quote? "I'm seeing you right now."

17. I found out that the apartment she had over in Williamsburg was shared with two other people her age (not the original roommates, there had been understandable turnover); she said the place was a bit absurd, in that it was divided-up loft space in an old factory and was located right above, wouldn't you know it, a recording studio for an independent rock label. She said the noise could be loud sometimes, even rattling the dishes, and she said that recently, in the last month, there had been the even more absurd situation of some construction going on across the street (I was trying to picture it, knowing about Williamsburg only from a couple of L-train trips there over the years maybe to see art in small galleries, but also knowing that Williamsburg nowadays was unquestionably "in" with

younger people, the old Hasidic neighborhoods and block after block of brick factories giving way to more loft space, lately very hip and with too many, surely, galleries and restaurants and trendy new dating bars, that sort of thing), yes, with the construction across the street, there suddenly seemed to be a fleeing of mice from the demolished building there and a resulting mass invasion of them now into her building. She said she was going to get a cat, even if a single girl having a cat was a cliché, did sound stupid, she admitted, and she said she had already looked into it, how you could go down to the Brooklyn Animal Shelter for a kitten—getting a cat, everybody told her, was the only real way to solve the mouse problem. When I asked her about the noise from the recording studio, she said that for her it wasn't bad at all, because it coincided with her own schedule, the music always knocking off by midnight, and she never went to bed before midnight; plus, she said, there pretty much was none of it on the weekends. She said the location of the place was great, the rent really reasonable for that much space, too. And I told myself that her being completely accepting of such annoyances, that alone was electric in a way, youthful, to think how much somebody could put up with at twenty-seven; I remembered what I mentioned before, how when I first showed her the balcony and the view, the first thing she said was that she really wished she had brought her pot to smoke, it would have been perfect to have it out there, she said.

18. I suppose that after I heard nothing from her once I returned to L.A., got no answer to my messages left, I didn't think of her much before long, and I was eventually in what you might call a very serious relationship, the kind of relationship that I really wanted to work at, that I really wanted to develop. I didn't think that much anymore about how it had been so good to be with the young woman that night, how unexpectedly enjoyable were the dozen or so hours we spent together.

Which is to say, when her sister did call me from there in Connecticut—to tell me the big sadness of it all, to talk to me honestly, because it was obvious that the woman thought I was somebody more important than I was in her sister's life—not only was

I caught off guard by the unexpected call, the terrible news she gave me then, several months later, but, very definitely, it threw me for a loop for a while, to the point that I found myself thinking again and again about the young woman, thinking a lot about her.

I had some dreams about her, or two dreams, anyway.

19. In the first dream we were indeed there as we had been in the hotel that night, but somehow I had to go out for a bit.

Or—yes, this is it—I had to go out for a bit to get something from the deli on Eighth Avenue, diagonally across from the hotel there on Forty-eighth, which made sense, that such a detail should figure into the dream. I myself had been using a deli on Eighth often during my week of business in New York. (In New York that week I had to meet with a big-money novelist and his agent for a few sessions, seeing that they were interested in tapping me to do a screenplay adaptation of what was this writer's new novel that really didn't interest me all that much, yet another so-called psychological thriller that was anything but thrilling, though, as usual, I could use the work; the trio of us got together in the overpriced Monkey Bar, off Park Avenue on East Fifty-fourth there in the swank Hotel Elysée, the agent suggesting the spot and he himself seeming to want to impress the writer, his own successful client, more than me, obviously; I had tried not to appear too wide-eyed about the place, not fazed that a very dry, crystal-clear martini with its staring eyeball of an olive cost a flat twenty-five bucks there, I had tried not to be too obvious in my looking around at the paintings done in tasteful muted colors on the carefully preserved walls of this the Monkey Bar I had often heard of, the famous murals depicting celebrities of the day—the 1930s?—as monkeys in a very leafy jungle; and when I noted as an aside somewhere in the ongoing conversation that I thought it was here that Tennessee Williams spent his last evening, boozing in this very bar before dying upstairs in his hotel room later that night, the other two didn't seem very interested, and when I added something I just thought of, that it was amazing that in addition to Tennessee Williams's beautiful, beautiful plays there was a large body of short fiction he had written, enough to establish a solid career on that count alone, neither of the other two seemed interested in hearing about that either.) Anyway, and as said, in my time at the Pennington Hotel I had been using the deli a lot, the way you do use a deli a lot when in a hotel in New York, heading across the street for a coffee in midmorning, let's say, while working, trying to do at least some writing on the laptop set up on the dresser/desk, or in the evening heading across the street for a couple of cold tallboys to take back to the room, to sip (one can in hand and the other buried deep in ice in the insulated bucket) while reading or watching some news or sports on TV. But in this dream it was all somewhat different. It seems that I was with the young woman in bed, then I was getting dressed to go across the street to the deli for something; or maybe she had sent me out to buy her something, maybe cigarettes, and though she didn't smoke cigarettes, to my knowledge, possibly that detail stemmed from her mention of pot before, another of the shards of reality rearranged some in a night-imagining. Dressed, I left her in bed, and as soon as I was out into the wine-carpeted, pink-wallpapered hallway—yes, it was definitely the Pennington even in the dream, that hallway—as soon as I heard the door latch behind me, it seemed that I realized I had forgotten the electronic key card to get back in again.

I knocked, but I got no answer, I knocked again and still got no answer. And when I went downstairs to the lobby, I tried calling up from a house phone and I *still* got no answer; panicking, I had one of the guys from the front desk accompany me upstairs, a handsome guy in the gray flannels and dark-green blazer and regimental-striped tie of the hotel staff's uniforms (it seemed that he suddenly wasn't just an attendant but my own brother, though I was so scared, so panicking, that I didn't let that reinterpretation of a detail jar me, cause me any surprise, except for me to acknowledge that my older, brighter, handsomer brother Pete had always shown such concern for me ever since I had been a kid), and when the door was opened for me, of course she wasn't there.

20. I apologized to him (the attendant? my brother?) for causing so much trouble, and I then said that maybe there *hadn't* been a woman

in the room with me, maybe I had merely been *imagining* that, and picking up the key card from the faux-mahogany night table, it being right there where I had left it, under the faux-brass lamp glowing, I went downstairs again. I walked over to the deli and bought a six-pack of red-and-white cans of Budweiser, calmed by then, asking myself why I had been so crazy as to believe there had been a beautiful young woman with green eyes and lustrous dark hair, a woman who worked a job as a copy editor in the fashion business, in my room.

21. The second dream was much more literal than that. I was back in my apartment in L.A. Or maybe it wasn't exactly the apartment I live in now, but one of those I have lived in on my own over the years here, as interrupted by the few years of marriage, when I made the largest mistake that probably any freelance screenwriter in L.A. can make, mortgaging myself up to my flapping gills to buy a home, a pretty costly tiny pink bungalow in Santa Monica, during the marriage. No, which of the many apartments it was, or even if it was the bungalow, didn't matter, but what did matter was that in the dream I seemed to be sleeping. Then I seemed to be hearing the agonized and repeated chirping ring of my telephone in the front room where apparently I did my writing, and in the dark I seemed to have gotten up to answer it, to be standing there, just woken, looking at the telephone that was very much the yellow console one with an answering machine that I do have on the desk in my present place; I seemed to see that the caller-ID was showing in its stick-formed black digits on shimmering silver a phone number that I somehow knew was a Connecticut area code even if I had no idea of any Connecticut area code, and I already knew it was the young woman's sister calling me to tell me what she wanted to—or, more exactly, *had* to—tell me. The phone kept ringing, the band of the caller-ID display kept glowing brighter in the dark, kept showing the number that I somehow recognized, and I almost took satisfaction in the fact that I wasn't going to be tricked, I wasn't going to fall for the trap of answering it and hearing what the sister had to tell me. I knew the answering machine was turned off; I smiled to think that I was in control, way

ahead of the game, and all I had to do was *not* answer it, because if the sister (and somehow I also already knew what her voice sounded like, mature and even-toned, not as vibrant and whisperingly pleasant as the young woman's), yes, if the sister didn't tell me it, then it couldn't be true, because if I didn't know it, then for me it wouldn't have happened, so for all intents and purposes the young woman there in Williamsburg hadn't done what she had done. I told myself I was in *total* control, and, to repeat, that second dream was quite literal, no Freudian depths there and it clearly expressing my deep hope against hope that I wouldn't learn what I eventually learned. But I guess that the first dream, of the forgotten key card, was equally—or possibly more—literal, and for me in that first dream, to discover after considerable panic that there was no young woman in the hotel room was to fully assert a wished-for evidence that there never had been any young woman in the hotel room—so, again, what happened to her never would, in fact, happen to her.

22. But it did.

23. That night in the Pennington Hotel with her, I suppose I slept in snatches, she seemed to have slept well. She had explained that she would have to be up very early, to take the subway back to Williamsburg, change into clothes more suitable for work; she would then take the train back to her company's offices, around Herald Square. If I did sleep in stolen grabs, I woke before her, got up to look out the big balcony doors still wide open and to see the sky lightening, and when I eased back to the bed with her, adjusted myself beside her without waking her because it was still only six or so, I looked right at her face, marveled again at her loveliness—and then I watched as she opened her eyes with a smile and that overbite, looking right at me again, not actually saying it then but almost as if what she had said before was the first thing of her own day, "I'm seeing *you* right now." We talked, smooched some, and when the digital clock on the night table showed that it was getting late, that she should get going, I myself got up, took a quick shower, and I guess there was some comedy to the rush of the whole scene—how we had lingered there

in bed too long, that it was *really* late and we had to get moving, dress quickly. With my own limited knowledge of this pocket of New York from having spent the week there, I tried to determine which subway stop would be closest for her, tried to remember which trains ran through which stops, too; she would have to make just one change to get back to Williamsburg, though one change meant time as well.

But it was out in the early sunshine of what would be another hot but entirely splendid June day there in Manhattan that maybe the strangest thing of all happened. Stranger, in a way, than either of those dreams I did eventually have about her, the young woman I found out so much about.

24. And even now, more of what I found out about her comes back to me. It's close to crazy how much I found out, one thing leading to another about her, so much piling up of the talk during that night together.

I'd found out that she wished she had more money for travel, and to her—she put on a mock frown—it seemed almost not right that she had been in so many places when young, with her father being assigned all over the world, unfair that she had gotten such a bug for travel early on and that she didn't get to go more places now; also, she was given only two weeks vacation each year, blew most of that, she laughed, in missed work days here and there, or perhaps on a long-weekend trip somewhere, like going out to L.A. to see friends, as when I had met her at the dinner party. I found out that she really would like to go to India, see the ancient golden Hindu temples, see the continual happy madness of a massive city like Bombay, especially, though she said it was true that for a long while in her life she had wanted to go to any place *but* India; it seemed that when her father had been posted in Barbados and she went to a Catholic grade school there, a school chum originally from India—surely in the school uniform of knee socks, blouse, and properly dark, pleated skirt, I pictured the girls talking—a chum had regaled her with stories of the horrors of the dirt and disease in India, and because of that she had never thought about travel in India—until recently, now, when just the idea of India began to intrigue her so. I found out that she also would really like to spend some time in Rome, even if she knew it could also sound rather a cliché, every young romantic's dream of spending time in Rome. But in one of the few real "events" in her life, which didn't seem like an event at the time, she said, she and her sister were traveling alone and had stopped over in Rome on a flight back to the U.S. from Egypt, where her father had been posted for several years. The girls stayed a few days with a couple who were both friends of her father from the foreign service, and the couple managed to wrangle through protocol to bring the girls along to some sort of reception at the Vatican in honor of Mother Teresa herself; there among the abundance of exploding color that is Michelangelo and the Vatican's endless creamy marble and gilt upon gilt, she actually was kissed at age ten by the little withered woman in her simple coarse nun's habit, and so, as trite and affected as spending a vacation in Rome might seem, she admitted, Rome would always be a special place to her, somewhere she really wanted to return to, if only to get back again the feeling of what had become for her a very special event in her life.

25. I found out that for her, Mother Teresa's kiss on her cheek felt like . . . felt . . . I found out that it felt . . . that it . . .

But why go on? Except to say that even as I reconstruct it now, I am struck yet again by how much I got to know about her in such a short time, how much I found out about her, how even now one detail just leads to another and that to another . . . and . . . and . . . but, as I said, enough of that.

26. True, the strangest thing of all, or what seems so strange now, was what happened outside the hotel that morning. We both dressed, admittedly very quickly so, we went down the elevator together (the brownish mirrors in that little chugging elevator, the gleaming polished brass), and then through the lobby (it was empty, and I had been in the hotel long enough, a full week, that the desk staff in the dark-green blazers and the various doormen in the dark-green blazers had gotten to recognize me, and they certainly noticed that I, always alone before, was now with this woman, tall and slim as a

runway model, radiant even if mussed), and we went out the big brass-and-glass doors and into the Monday morning on Forty-eighth Street. The day had the particular softness of a summer morning well before the heat, honey-hued. A workman with a hose was sudsing down the length of sidewalk in front of the rather whimsical, maybe Moorish facade of the Walter Kerr Theater—old patterned brown brick and frilly iron arabesques—there across the street, and he seemed very happy to be doing it, starting his day; going toward Broadway, there was one of those coffee carts, polished aluminum, parked in the street along the sidewalk, office workers in summer dresses or in shirtsleeves and ties lining up to buy from the reliably solid selection of displayed danishes and donuts, and there the people in line, they, too, seemed fresh and even happy to be starting their day, while the Latino guy who was the proprietor and the woman who helped him with orders in the cramped little box of a trailer (I had gotten coffee there a couple of times myself, remembered them and their cheeriness) appeared completely happy themselves to be getting everybody started for the day. There was that aroma of the city, a little bit asphalt and a little bit exhaust and a little bit just the strong, flat metallic something that *is* New York, what speaks the whole hugeness of it, the whole importance of it, the whole uncontrollable rush of it, like nowhere else in the country, definitely, possibly like no place else in the world. Walking along on the sidewalk, she looped her two bare arms around my arm, leaned close to me like that, as if to emphasize what she had told me earlier as we dressed, as we started out from the hotel, what I had told her was the same for me as well—that the night had been nice indeed, that we'd both had a lot of fun. (And she had laughed so much, I could get her laughing so easily, scrunching her shoulders, girlishly putting her hand over her mouth that way, doing that as if embarrassed about laughing, yet it, too, was perfect.) It seemed that I had figured out which subway stop was the closest, taking into account the change she had to make to Brooklyn, and from what I knew, as I had decided and already told her, going over to Seventh Avenue was probably better than heading up Eighth Avenue, where there wasn't a stop until a few blocks north, on the far, opposite side of Fiftieth Street, I was pretty sure. Though she had spent time around the area herself, she admitted that she wasn't too familiar with the stations.

We stopped at Broadway at the traffic light, we would part there when the glowing white walk signal showed. I assured her that I would call her from Los Angeles, I assured her that we definitely had to see each other when she did come out to L.A. again to visit her friends, or see each other when I was in New York again, and we kissed. And then the walk signal blinked on, and everything got very rushed. I mean, after all, she was quite late, she had to go all the way out to Williamsburg to change from those clothes, the rather dressy outfit of the short black skirt and the satiny emerald camisole and the shoes with the braided gold straps, beautiful shoes. We kissed again, the people crossing now out in the four one-way lanes of Broadway, hurrying, moving fast themselves, because there was the back-up of cabs and trucks and brightly shining cars of any early morning on Broadway waiting to jump ahead when the light changed, to race off once more to who knows where in the floating toss of the dice that does pass for what is commonly known as our time on this planet, go to wherever their own day would soon enough take them. I stayed on the sidewalk, she was still crossing the street when the walk signal went back to red, with her having to speed up for the last few strides of those wonderful long legs. I stayed there and watched her go.

I watched her head to the other side of the short block across the diagonal of Broadway, then it seemed she was totally confused, in a quandary and trying herself to remember, from her own knowledge of the area, which way, in fact, the subway station was, which way that she, in fact, should go. I saw her take a few hurried steps toward downtown, her big red leather shoulder bag bouncing and her holding onto it lower down to keep it from bouncing too much, reaching up once with both hands to adjust the single yellow plastic barrette parting that lustrous black hair to one side like a French schoolgirl's, then I watched her stop, almost freeze, look this way and that, and finally decide that she had gone in the wrong direction for the station—then, more hurried, her somewhat flustered steps in the uptown direction after that.

Then she was gone, beyond the rise of a mirror-windowed skyscraper on the corner of Seventh Avenue, beyond my vision, my watching her. And standing there, a man in a city that wasn't his own city, a thirty-nine-year-old man who had thought that his entire week on this other end of the continent had been a waste, really, nothing would come out of those foolish sessions in the famous and overpriced Monkey Bar lounge with a self-satisfied hack novelist and that creepy, even more self-satisfied agent of his (at least my L.A. agent had a sense a humor, was a clown, actually), on that sidewalk was a man, me, who had just ended up a week thinking about too many things when alone in a hotel room, the bust of my failed marriage, the bust of my career in Los Angeles, having to hustle so at this stage of the—indeed—game, having to try to line up enough work to support myself for another six months, another year, yes, standing there in loafers and slacks and open-collar dress shirt half unbuttoned in anticipation of the coming heat of the day and before I would fly out on the red-eye that night, the sleeves of the shirt pushed to the elbows—continuing to stand there and thinking of a lot of things, also knowing that the trip had been well worth it if only for the single night with her. Right then, and *very strangely,* I felt a strong urge, even a need, to just dodge the speeding cars out there on Broadway, do some of those broken-field-running moves through the horn-honking, brake-screeching traffic, palm flattened for the old backfielder's classic straight-arm like you always see in the movies, run hard across that tapered island of the half-block on Broadway and catch up with her on Seventh Avenue, *make sure* that she was going in the right direction, *make sure* that she did get to the station, and the right station at that, descend the steps myself into the cool dimness, the glaring, bare-bulbed lighting there, to put her safely on the right silvery train and to help her not lose any time getting back to Brooklyn, so she could change clothes and then return to the city to be at her work cubicle by eight-thirty. She had told me in the hotel, laughing again, that she'd been late altogether too often recently and that she really *couldn't* be late anymore.

27. But, of course, I didn't go after her. I stood there a minute longer, told myself once more what I had been thinking ever since when first in the restaurant with her the evening before, what I'd told myself

after the lovemaking—that staying the weekend had thoroughly salvaged what otherwise would have been the *utter* waste of a week. I was feeling good.

I headed back along Forty-eighth street, thinking I could maybe even write a little that morning in the hotel room. I could work on the project of my own, an original screenplay that I suddenly found myself believing in again, before taking the airport shuttle van out to LaGuardia later that afternoon. I saw the little coffee cart, its quilted, polished-aluminum sides gleaming in the sunshine that was fuller now, stronger, and I waited in line, told the cheery guy within who ran it that I would have a large coffee with milk, no sugar, and maybe a cinnamon donut (I pointed to it behind the glass—I never ate donuts anymore, but, what the hell, I was in New York); the woman who worked with him put the lidded, green cardboard coffee cup and the donut into a small brown paper bag, carefully placed in the bag a few white paper napkins, too, and she told me in what seemed very earnest tones, as if she truly meant it, "Have a great day, sir."

I went back to the hotel, did sit down at the little Mac PowerBook set up on the dresser/desk, did write well until noon.

28. And I am still thinking of more things, what I found out about her.

And I am still thinking, trying to discover some clue in what she did tell me. Was there a haunting sadness in her mother dying when she, the young woman, was only a child like that? But then I tell myself that she herself had said she probably wasn't affected as much as might have been expected by the loss, she was only seven and not at the age where you would be affected, it had been worse for her sister, three or maybe four years older. Was it one of those ex-boyfriends? I tried to think what she had told me about them, the welder, or the young Wall Street lawyer with the name Cruk, but even when she had talked about them at my prompting in bed that night, it seemed as if there was certainly no sadness or even bitterness there either. I mean, she laughed about the lawyer having a tough go of it with that defeating name of his, Cruk, and she seemed concerned that the welder (a genuine workman? a daring sculptor? I would never know which) might catch an errant blue spark in the eye when the mask got slowly lifted yet another time. I am still thinking that there could have been some clue, that there should have been something, and, after all, I am a writer, even if only one of lousy second-rate movies and lousier TV episodes, I should have some understanding of the heart and how it works. (The sister gave me only a few details about what had happened, what the young woman had done, when I asked her for details in the awkward phone call, which turned more than awkward when the sister herself seemed to sense before long in our conversation that I wasn't anybody with any large role in her own sister's life, the several messages I had left perhaps having given her the wrong impression, making the sister believe that I was somebody who should eventually and in time be, well, "notified," I guess is the word.) *I still want to believe that I should have detected something.*

But I hadn't, I didn't. From what I could see, it made no sense, *no sense whatsoever,* and, I will admit, it is foolish to think that in but a single night of talking and lovemaking and talking I should have any idea on any of it.

29. *But what I found out about her, so much of her life, there was so much I had found out about her. And, also, there was how she looked right at me, how she had said, "I'm seeing you right now."*

30. To be frank, I had found out nothing about her, and maybe none of us ever does find out anything about anybody else, nobody ever really does *see* anybody else, there is no clue or no revealing detail or any valid sense to any of it, really. And I suppose all that can be said is that to be with this young woman, you never would have known that what did happen to her would happen to her. And, I mean, she was so entirely lovely, so ready for the wonder of the world and her life ahead of her, Rome and faraway Bombay, smiling, laughing, so honest with herself at twenty-seven, she seemed so very, very rare.

31. Which is to say, I had found out nothing, absolutely nothing, about her at all.

IN THE SOUTHERN CONE

A man feared that he might find an assassin;
Another that he might find a victim.
One was more wise than the other.

—Stephen Crane

I. San Telmo

Win Shapiro had originally come to Buenos Aires to research a master's thesis on Borges. It was supposed to be a month-long project, done with a grant from his school, the University of Pennsylvania. He ended up staying in the city for what was now close to two years. Or, to put it another way, he found himself totally enamored with the place.

It wasn't just that B.A. was as beautiful as everybody always told you it was—the stately boulevards downtown with that half-dreamt white wedding-cake architecture, French, the shading emerald plane trees and the sidewalk cafés—it was maybe more so the very texture of the city. And how Buenos Aires could also look a bit shabby, especially in the hot weather of February in the peak of the summer like this, when the cloud of purple exhaust from the buses and seemingly millions of taxis hung rich in the humid air, and when walking along the sidewalk was never letting your guard down—you kept watch for broken tiles that could trip you to a stumble, always knew, too, to dodge any puddle of wet ahead, seeing that it meant another cheap window air conditioner was hosingly dripping on everybody passing by below. Indeed, such faded luster was a big part of its charm, and, better, Buenos Aires possessed a certain cultural something that you simply couldn't find in America. There were all the bookstores along Avenida Corrientes and the dozens of art-house movie theaters; or possibly, Win Shapiro thought, it could have been that ultimately the place wasn't thoroughly Walmart-ized (people still shopped and chatted in small downtown shops) and it wasn't thoroughly Oprah-ized (or Ray Romano-ized, or, worse, *Entertainment Tonight*-ized—in Buenos Aires the television was no better than that in the States, but most people weren't obsessed with it, unless there was a soccer match on, and they saw TV for what it was: crap). Win Shapiro lived in San Telmo, a decidedly funky enclave south of the Plaza de Mayo.

He liked it there. San Telmo had cheap enough rent in the crumbling low high-rises or the more crumbling, and often genuinely colonial, older houses, the masonry frilled and painted bright pastels; San Telmo was an artists' pocket, too. Win Shapiro had first got to know it some because it was important in Borges's work, pretty rough back when B. as a young man had meticulously explored its narrow streets. Actually, Win Shapiro abandoned his graduate work before long, deciding (dreaming?) that he would write a lengthy book on Borges and Buenos Aires for maybe a quality mainstream trade publisher like Knopf or Farrar, Straus, forgetting the back-biting academic rat race. He did work on that for a while, turning out over a hundred pages of text, before he met the Argentine girl Silvina; having a girlfriend like Silvina, beautiful as she was, was almost a full-time occupation in itself, leaving little time for *any* major writing project, Win Shapiro realized. Not that Win Shapiro wasn't working. With his Spanish fluent and being an English speaker possessing a prized American accent, it was surprisingly easy to find employment teaching classes in English.

At the Wall Street Institute, a language school, the guy handling applications didn't even ask him to fill out anything and said he could use Win Shapiro for a class starting that very evening. The guy also said not to worry about the work-visa complications, he could take care of that himself for Win Shapiro in a week or so. And he did, such documentation for a foreigner in a city like Buenos Aires, with its reported twenty-percent unemployment, a real prize. Win Shapiro moved on from there to teaching English classes for business students in an office building being used temporarily by the Universidad John F. Kennedy over by the Congreso, seat of the Argentine legislature. The Universidad Kennedy was a private university and also second-rate, at best, and the big red, white, and blue placards advertising it, complete with a picture of mop-topped, ever-smiling JFK himself, were all over town, particularly thick in the ornately tiled Subte stations. (So perhaps the Argentines weren't utterly sophisticated in everything—considering those hokey names like Universidad Kennedy and the Wall Street Institute, the latter an international company, actually—but, of course, icons were icons when it came to selling education or anything else.) With his classes in the late afternoon and early evening, Win Shapiro never had to get up early in the morning at his San Telmo flat, which meant he could indulge in the city's nightlife with Silvina. As for Silvina, she was used to that nightlife, because certainly any hip, beautiful Buenos Aires girl of twenty-two was entirely used to it. There were the jazz clubs in San Telmo, as well as the stretch of British and Irish pubs (though Win Shapiro never liked the places) up on Calle Reconquista, a couple of blocks over from the very posh Calle Florida and its designer boutiques. Yes, Silvina was used to it, even if she did have to be back at work at the Office of Tourism kiosk on Calle Florida by nine-thirty every weekday morning.

Win Shapiro admitted that he was in love with Silvina. There was no denying she was a knockout—five-nine, that striking combination of olive skin and honey-blond hair, long, which maybe you do only find in Argentina; brown eyes and full lips and posture so erect that just walking across a room her long legs seemed to be rhythmically leading the way, an alluring strut. Though she relaxed at night at the clubs in jeans and T-shirts, she had to dress up for that job on Calle Florida. Win Shapiro also admitted that on the two or three nights a week he stayed over at the apartment she shared with another girl in San Telmo, he absolutely savored just, well, *beholding* her after she was done with her showering and blow-drying and putting on her makeup (which she really didn't need) in the morning, dressed chicly indeed in maybe a silk blouse and short skirt, always high heels. He often fantasized about a future with the two of them together back in the States, where he would eventually return to wrap up the master's and then get a Ph.D. in literature (the plan of writing a more popular book had completely passed, and he again wanted to do something truly significant regarding the critical study of postmodern fiction—Borges, naturally, and others). Eventually with a tenured job, in his imagining, he would be gossiped about as the renegade professor, the one who had chucked it all and lived in Buenos Aires when younger, marrying that Argentine girl who he brought to the faculty parties, a breathtaking beauty ready for professional fashion modeling, his envious colleagues would agree. But it wasn't *only* her beauty. Win Shapiro knew that Silvina with her soft laugh and with her wonderful "Silvina way" about so many things (Silvina observing how intricate was the pattern, let's say, of the rain pouring off a tiled roof during a thunderstorm, Silvina stopping on the sidewalk to give all the change in her purse to a woman in ragged Indian dress holding her two babies and begging), true, Win Shapiro knew that she was special. And she seemed intrigued with the whole idea of possibly going to live in America with him.

The way Win Shapiro found out about her seeing the rich young Argentine lawyer, Bernardo, wasn't subtle. The guy drove a perfectly restored maroon 1950s Triumph TR-3. And he was well connected enough politically (via his family that owned a chain of successful dairies throughout the country) that he didn't care if a conscientious member of the PFA ticketed him when he parked illegally right there on the pedestrian mall that was Calle Florida, to go into the air-conditioned little stainless-steel drum of an office, the tourism kiosk, and chat with Silvina some more; for Bernardo, with his connections, any parking ticket could be easily fixed. Tanned, slim, always wearing a good summer suit, he was a few years older than Win Shapiro, who actually was introduced to him by Silvina one afternoon when Win himself stopped by the kiosk. Silvina seemed relaxed around Bernardo, and apparently Bernardo's family and Silvina's family had long known each other, the two families even had neighboring beach condos in Mar del Plata. For weeks after that, Win Shapiro made it a point of walking by the kiosk, though not going in, before hurrying over to his first afternoon class at the Universidad Kennedy, and he got visibly dizzy, near enraged, to spot the smug and gleaming maroon British sports car, all that chrome trim, parked there illegally still another time. He would hurry down into the cool darkness of the Subte at the Bolívar station, and he couldn't concentrate whatsoever on his teaching. Soon everything started unraveling with almost inevitable predictability. Silvina was often not at her apartment when he phoned, her roommate making hollow excuses for her; or Silvina herself, if home, would tell him she was too tired from work to have him stay at her place that night—she needed a good night's rest. He finally confronted her with it at her apartment:

"It's because you've been screwing that sleazy rich bastard, isn't it."

Which she didn't deny. Win Shapiro should have acknowledged it was over then, but he kept pursuing her. He loved her so, he thought only of her all the time; he slept poorly, his teaching suffered to the point that he began to dread leading the usual sad party through the routine of spitting out the harshly angular English syllables there in the grim classrooms in the ramshackle office building used by the Universidad Kennedy. Silvina did concede to sitting through repeated sessions of having a coffee with him and listening to him pour out how much he loved her, how hurt he was, how anybody could see that her Bernardo wearing his expensive suits and driving the ostentatious restored Triumph was—wasn't it *obvious?*—a bourgeois pig, Silvina only softly saying that she never wanted any of it to happen this way. She cried some, and he continued with his talking. Until one afternoon she seemed to have steeled herself for his performance beforehand. And she appeared quietly angry as she listened again. They sat under the sky-blue-and-white Quilmes beer umbrella on the terrace of their once favorite café on the Plaza Dorrego in San Telmo; there was the racket of thumping tango music leaking out of a music store nearby. Flushed, as if she couldn't stand another second of his talk, in her Spanish she blurted out:

"Will you please, please just *stop* it—stop being such a fucking whining Jew!"

Of course, anything between them immediately ended with that. Actually, one of the most painful moments in Win Shapiro's life had been when he was a kid at Conestoga High School out on Philadelphia's Main Line and he tried to rally the other guys on the track-and-field team to go in with him on formally complaining about their coach; the coach, a phys ed teacher, was a known drunk who nipped Seagram's 7 in his cubbyhole office in the rear of the gymnasium and who was making everybody's life on the team miserable with his erratic behavior. Behavior that most of the guys seemed to agree was over the top, though a certain shot-putter oaf named Dolf DiBiasio said he didn't care—he said he got a kick out of it, the coach's loopiness, adding that he was tired of Win Shapiro going on about it, "like a whining Jew." Understandably, the incident with Silvina now brought back that particular pain full force, maybe doubled it. And it triggered in Win Shapiro his admitting to what he knew that he had surely ignored in Buenos Aires too long, the underlying and rampant anti-Semitism. The way that there had been the terrorist bombing of the Israeli Embassy there ten years before, killing at least twenty, and the federal police had never properly investigated it or brought anybody responsible to justice; it was as if the lives of Jews didn't matter. How, in fact, there had been throughout Argentina deep and vocally expressed sympathy with the German and Italian fascists during World War II. Perón, on the rise to power then, was a chief perpetrator of the sentiment; early on in his career, he wasn't averse to delivering speeches that encouraged hooligans to stomp into Jewish neighborhoods to bash heads, showing again the dictator's masterful ability to tune in on the mindset of the general population—to say what they wanted to hear, prompt them in what they themselves wanted to do. Why, Argentina never officially declared it was with the Allied Powers until 1945, a scant couple of months before everything finally ended in Europe.

Suddenly Buenos Aires looked *different* to Win Shapiro, and he just wanted to be *out* of there. Out of San Telmo, especially, where strolling amid the old pastel architecture that he had once admired so, he might run into Silvina—was bound to run into Silvina. The summer session courses finished at Universidad Kennedy in early March. He had already contacted the English department at the University of Pennsylvania concerning grad school readmission, and while he waited for word on that and before eventually going back to Philadelphia, he thought he might spend a month in Uruguay. Occasionally, he actually wept to think of how much he still loved Silvina—how *beautiful* she was, how *observant* of the world around her she was—but that maybe would start to heal, he knew, with a change of scene. (How could she have said that to him, called him a whining Jew, and he had, of course, told her that one of his own grandparents had been murdered in the camps—what could any Jew be *but* whining with the lousy hand of cards that history had dealt this people!) He couldn't be out of Buenos Aires too soon.

After selling off most of his books and the cheap furniture he had accumulated, he shipped what remained of his belongings back to Philadelphia. He had only a single black nylon flight bag when he boarded the white ferry at Dársena Norte for the two-and-a-half-hour trip across the choppy Río de la Plata the color of Coca-Cola. He thought he would set himself up for a while—using the money he had put aside from teaching—in the small Uruguayan town of Colonia del Sacramento, the port for the ferries from Buenos Aires, rather than large Montevideo.

II. Colonia del Sacramento

Hans Krüger had been born in Marburg, not far from Frankfurt, seventy-nine years ago. He didn't think of himself as old. Once a month he drove the three hours from Colonia del Sacramento to Montevideo for a weekend, which always included time with a young prostitute who worked as sort of a B-girl at a nightclub called Friday's, and so he fancied that others didn't think him that old either. Still wide-shouldered and imposing at over six foot, even if he did have a sagging paunch, he was rosily florid rather than tanned, his surprisingly thick head of silver-white hair cut in a short, functional brush style. He could be seen around the streets of Colonia in the afternoons in his Bermuda shorts and sport shirt, plus casual boat shoes, in from his ranch in the white Ford pickup truck and doing errands at the banks. Later in the evening, Hans Krüger was almost always to be found at the Centro Unión Cosmopolita. Centro Unión Cosmopolita was a social club that supported a local soccer team and maintained the center proper, a big, stark expanse of a dozen tables and plenty of extra chairs for watching the giant plasma screen and the soccer games. With the cable hookup, you could find a match of one sort or another on the many Argentine and Uruguayan stations, even ESPN Latin America; Centro Unión Cosmopolita was right in the middle of the town, on its leafy little main street, Avenida General Flores.

Hans Krüger had been in Colonia for over fifty years and Hans Krüger had seen it grow. When he first came there from Germany in 1947—after a short time in Brazil, then Montevideo—it was little more than a minor river town, and then not even busy with the ferries from Buenos Aires. (It certainly had been an important port in other centuries, and the Portuguese colonizers who once controlled the Uruguay region had developed it as a trading center to rival Spain's recently founded Buenos Aires, which itself was slow to grow early on.) True, when Hans Krüger purchased his ranch outside of the town, near Real de San Carlos five kilometers away, Colonia remained a very quiet outpost, if a very beautiful one, seeing that it had so much of its original colonial architecture. But the new ferry port thoroughly changed that, along with the two-lane road to Montevideo being rebuilt as a modern expressway. Now boats didn't have to make the long sail from Buenos Aires to Montevideo. The crossing of the Plata to Colonia was less than three hours, then only an hour when hydrofoils started to be used on some runs, and sleek, comfortable buses could transport passengers onward for the subsequent three-hour ride from Colonia to Montevideo; it made for a much faster connection than the old overnight trip completely by propeller ferry between the two capitals. Still, most travelers never got beyond the pink-painted ferry dock north of the little green finger of the peninsula that was the town, and though they could see from the boats the pillar of the handsome white lighthouse and how the peninsula was neatly ringed with a fringe of sandy beaches, see the solid old Portuguese fortifying walls, too, few people ever bothered to perhaps catch a later bus to Montevideo—the buses were waiting at the pier—and walk the several blocks from the dock, explore the place. They never saw the picture-perfect nineteenth-century *ayuntamiento,* the town hall, facing the central square with its bandstand and antique cast-iron benches, tall palm trees, or strolled even farther than that and into the Portuguese Old City itself. There the original small masonry houses, painted bright pink or yellow or white, still remained in abundance, the crooked narrow streets, cobbled with blue river stones, offered magnificent views from atop the neighborhood's hill to those long sandy beaches both north and south of Colonia; the simple, twin-turreted colonial church in the Old City was the very oldest church in the entire country, an indisputable cultural landmark. Actually, *some* travelers must have eventually made that walk and discovered the rarity of the town, because in time Colonia del Sacramento became a resort; well-to-do Porteños from Buenos Aires vacationed there, expensive sailboats were moored in an expanded separate yacht harbor on the far side of the peninsula. Guidebooks recently called Colonia a pristine gem of not just Uruguay but all of South America. And Hans Krüger capitalized on the changes over the years.

With his wife long dead and his one son living in Europe—the son late middle-aged now—Hans Krüger scaled back his cattle raising and eventually sold off more and more of his ranch land outside the town; it adjoined a good beach groved with eucalyptus and was very attractive to Argentine developers. He was content to simply monitor his capital at the local banks, go nightly to the Centro Unión Cosmopolita and drink liter bottles of Doble Uruguaya pilsner, watch the soccer and exchange views on the world with his cronies there. But this summer of 2002 a lot of people in Colonia were already talking about Hans Krüger's behavior, especially after he had been drinking Doble Uruguaya for three or four hours at the club.

That Hans Krüger had served in the German army during the war was no secret, yet it was never seen as anything out of the ordinary. Countless Germans had come to Uruguay—and more to Brazil and Argentina—between 1945 and 1947, so there certainly were many others who had such a past with the Reich. In fact, if Hans Krüger had any local notoriety, it was that he was known to wield a definite streak of independence. He supported the first attempt at unionization of ranch workers in the sixties and heartily encouraged those working on his own ranch to organize and join the national union, and he turned outright vocal against the corrupt Uruguayan military regime of the seventies, when the infamous crazed generals took over the republic's government and declared a more or less permanent state of siege in the capital, convinced that every middle-class university kid was a trained Marxist terrorist and disposing of most of them accordingly. Even this far from the capital, not many people were willing to speak up against any of that back then, but Hans Krüger did. In truth, Hans Krüger's own time as a dedicated Nazi often seemed to him something that had happened in another incarnation, or at least in some watery and repeatedly dissolving bad dream, always gone by morning's waking. Nevertheless, records were on file in Frankfurt to show that he joined the party while an engineering and architecture student. He was commissioned by the time he was twenty-two and made a full lieutenant, and as an exceptionally young—some would say "brilliant"—architect and officer, he moved in important circles and occasionally with the top brass, contributing to the design of factory buildings and, later, several new German air bases; he had once received a written personal commendation from a personage no less than Goebbels himself for his service. However, his military career wasn't such that he had to flee the burnt carcass of Germany in 1946, and he left because there was just no future there at that time for a young man with a wife and son to support. After working rather humbly as a draftsman in the office of an architecture firm in Rio de Janeiro, then doing much the same in Montevideo, briefly, he started looking for better opportunities, eventually buying the cattle ranch outside of Colonia; it was managed well for him by the leathery foreman, Rodríguez, who had also run it for the former owner, and Hans Krüger became prosperous. All of which is to say, Hans Krüger's behavior was *quite* surprising that summer at the Centro Unión Cosmopolita, his constant railing about Jews. It was surprising to his cronies, and it was probably surprising to himself, if he was honest about it.

There was little soccer of consequence that summer. The Uruguayan and Argentine leagues wouldn't be fully into their championship play for a month or more, and on the big screen at the Centro Unión Cosmopolita the men sometimes were content with just watching a televised taping of a hard-fought European match from the night before. Admittedly as good as Real Madrid was, even Manchester United, Hans Krüger knew it was still not the same as watching the favorite area teams. Hans Krüger poured refills from his tall, sweating brown bottle of Doble Uruguaya, talked with his gray-haired or glossily bald old *compadres* at the long tables in that large room with fifteen-foot ceilings and functional black linoleum—the usual conversations, no doubt, about the continuing devaluation of the "floating" peso over in Buenos Aires then in 2002, or the comparative abilities of potential recruits for the local team sponsored by the social club. If the televised European match wasn't all that interesting, one of the younger guys there might get up to ask everybody if it was OK to switch to the nightly news from the station in Montevideo, and after perfunctory nods, that was done. The news of Middle Eastern trouble was major that summer. And merely seeing more clips, in the few minutes of international coverage, of the Israeli tanks growling into the Palestinian-controlled West Bank once more, going after suspected suicide-bomb terrorists, was enough to start Hans Krüger off on it. Because somewhere deep down, in either memory or conviction or possibly the ultimately inherent essence of himself, Hans Krüger felt again an unbounded rage and hate against Jews, any and all of them, in his opinion—the Jewish bankers who had ruined the fine Germany he had known as a very young man, the Jewish sleuths from the new Israeli state who in the fifties had hounded and pestered good German emigrants trying to lead productive lives in various South American cities (he had a close friend from his university days, Ernst Heinzelman, who committed suicide in a São Paulo hotel room during the Eichmann trial), also a specific "hijo de puta, un rusito!," a banker named Aronberg in Montevideo, who—Hans Krüger would have sworn this to a judge—had tried to later alter the paperwork that the banker and Hans Krüger had already legally signed concerning a loan Hans Krüger had taken out to expand his ranch holdings in 1974 (like some Argentines, Hans Krüger often used "rusito" generically for a Jew—a "little Russian"; the phrase "hijo de puta" was—of course, and for him very much so—the equivalent of "son of a bitch"). He could get loud in his rage, his German-accented Spanish bellowing:

"Goddamn Christ-killing Jews!"

His business-executive son came over from London, where he lived, for a visit that summer, and the man, frankly, was amazed and painfully embarrassed by his father's actions. The son confessed to others that this was a side of his father's temperament he had never seen or known about before, considering that his father, even if he had been in the German army, was a man who had been so brave in his independence over the years, taking unpopular but surely noble public political stands in Uruguay on several occasions. In Colonia during the summer, the teenage kids, bored and more than eager for high school to start up again, congregated around the balustrade along the winding seawall in the evening, at the very tip of the peninsula there in the Old City. The pretty girls in their hip-hugger jeans and tank tops, the noisy guys in their baggy surfer shorts and T-shirts, they goofed around; they watched, with boredom, the sun setting spectacularly orange yet another time, and they watched the last, seven-thirty white ferry for B.A. moving but not moving out there on the muddy Plata, which for once, at that hour of the day, was the silver hue of its name and handsomely sparkling. They, too, had heard word of Hans Krüger's behavior at the club, maybe from their parents. And as they dispersed from the seawall when the first stars started to ignite over the shaggy-headed palms—walking back in loose groups to dinner at their own homes, or riding off on tiny buzzing motorbikes—often they saw on the street the tall, wide-shouldered, rugged old man, noticeably florid, in Bermuda shorts and a sport shirt, yes, they spotted him. Granting that some of them had German surnames themselves, they taunted him, shoutingly addressed him as "Herr Commandante!" or gave him the stiff-arm Nazi salute. Laughing.

And Hans Krüger kept on with his nightly performances.

It was a very slow time for the Centro Unión Cosmopolita, to be honest. The four octagonal card tables covered with green felt for ladies' canasta play off to one side, which were always busy in the winter's rain, were now empty, and with the ongoing currency problems in Argentina, the summer business had been bad (the club wasn't a private affair by any means, it encouraged tourists to come in). A sign board was set up outside on the sidewalk advertising a *promoción*—a small pizza and a full liter bottle of Doble Uruguaya for fifty Uruguayan pesos—and that must have been what originally attracted the young American guy one evening. A few of the younger local guys at the Centro Unión Cosmopolita had talked a bit with him before, seen him around town, and they told the others that they had learned he was some kind of scholar; they said he had lived in Argentina for a couple of years, teaching English, and was now staying at the pink Posada del Rio guesthouse by the old rowing boathouse, located there until he went back to the States to maybe resume either study or teaching. He was from New York, one said, though another claimed that it was definitely Philadelphia in the state of Pennsylvania where he was from. The young guy was lanky, with a shag haircut more fit for the sixties than today, when a buzz-cut seemed to be what Americans favored at that age; he had perfectly round steel-rimmed glasses, which reinforced the assumption that he probably *was* a scholar, even a young university professor. Before long, the American was showing up there every other night. He always brought a few books and a notebook with him, sitting alone at a table in back and drinking his single beer slowly, reading and taking notes, waiting for the pizza that Natalia, one of the two girls who worked there, always made a big production out of serving him. She smiled and unwrapped a fork and steak knife from the paper napkin the utensils were rolled in. She set them on the black sponge-wiped table top, carefully arranging the fork and the long, very sharp knife beside the napkin, lining up everything; Natalia knew that this young American would leave her a decent *propina,* while the regulars often didn't give her as much as a forced "Gracias."

One night on the news (CNN Latin service this time) there was a particular clip. It showed the bloodily mangled bodies of a Palestinian family—or at least the mother and two young daughters, maybe eight or ten and clothed in what looked like ripped party frocks—pulled from a torn-apart automobile. It all happened after a rocket from an Israeli helicopter, reportedly zeroing in on what was thought to be the vehicle of two known bigwigs and organizers in the suicide-bombing attacks, hit the wrong car in the Gaza Strip. The captions gave the translation of the father who survived it being interviewed; he was sitting on the ground in front of the smoking wreck along a seaside road and weepingly asking how people could *do this* to other people. Even before Hans Krüger reacted, those with him at his table winced, anticipating his bellow:

"Hijos de putas!"

Which was just Hans Krüger's preamble, his full-blown railing soon going on for five minutes. "Hijos de putas, estos rusitos!"

According to Hans Krüger in these tirades, the globe had gone crazy because of Jews, the World Trade Center disaster itself had happened only because of U.S. support of Israel in the Middle East.

Some of those who on other nights had noticed the young American guy reddening whenever Hans Krüger began it again, they knew that the situation was bad. They could now see the American eating his usual small wheel of a cheese-smeared pizza, slowly, a fork in one hand and in the other, tightly gripped, the steak knife with its thick wooden handle and sturdy serrated blade. In measured whispers Hans Krüger's friends told him to keep it down, he was embarrassing himself and them; they had told him the same night after night. Old Alfonso Benetti told him, old Rafa Casares told him. They all said to Hans Krüger that something terrible might happen, and they reminded him how the American kid himself didn't look right. Why, this night, as on other nights, the kid definitely looked outright strange, they said, even if he had consumed only half of the one brown bottle of Doble Uruguaya that was served along with the pizza. In short, Hans Krüger had been warned repeatedly that something *very terrible* might happen.

And something very terrible certainly did happen.

A DREAM OF FALLING ASLEEP: IX–XVII

Difficulties arose: events I could not fathom seemed to conspire against all my good intentions.

—Nerval

IX.

. . . but in this dream of falling asleep I am awake, and I keep telling everyone I meet up with in Paris (yes, it is Paris and when I lived there in 1987, the labyrinthine ways of those empty streets as I walk alone back to my place past the closed cafés late at night, the watch-dogs half-heartedly barking from within when I pass, and sometimes there is the lavender rain in the Marais during the day, sometimes the brighter-than-brightness of sunshine on such a fresh, even blanket of snow almost spilled from the alabaster dome of Sacré-Coeur), I keep telling everyone I know in Paris, it seems, that I keep having this dream.

X.

"It's what I guess you'd call recurrent," I tell Cohen-Doré.

"*Récurrent,*" Cohen-Doré says, the French word that is all but the same as the English, yet his pronunciation has full Gallic intonation, to give it a roll (those *r*s) and a definite presence (the hollow kettledrum thump of the stress on the last syllable); he nods, acknowledging what I have told him, says the word again: "*Récurrent.*"

And Cohen-Doré looks at me. He's a handsome guy in middle age, and there's something very theatrical, even swashbuckling, about him, sort of a French Sir Laurence Olivier, not averse to wearing what he is wearing now, a paisley silk ascot with a tweed sport jacket and the dark-blue cashmere overcoat draped across his shoulders like a cape; he is my departmental chairman at the campus of the university in the suburbs where I am on a faculty exchange from my own university in Ann Arbor for the year, and when we first learned that we had Saul Bellow in common (Cohen-Doré the leading French scholar of the American master, and I once Bellow's graduate creative writing student in Chicago), true, with that shared something between us, we hit it off immediately. Cohen-Doré's extended family is in the garment business in the Sentier, and he studied literature at the Sorbonne, the professor in that family, while his several brothers work for the clothing-finishing operation founded by his father; his wife is an opera singer, and his two young daughters, eight and ten, are lovely, so entirely melodic and polite. I spend a lot of time at their admittedly glitzy apartment in a new high-rise in the Twelfth Arrondissement, almost part of their family it sometimes seems, laughing with them at meals, listening to smiling Cohen-Doré—concerned about my still being a bachelor at thirty-nine—more than once pronounce that, most definitely, he will find a wife for me in Paris.

Yet somehow late this Saturday afternoon, we are not at his apartment, but we are on the way to fix a broken window in the cubbyhole room—a few streets from his place—that the Cohen-Dorés keep for the teenage Portuguese girl named Rosa; diminutive and curly-topped, the ever-grinning Rosa works as an au pair for the family. He told me the week before of the problem; he said he was going to hire a glazier to repair the window, and I assured him there was no need and I could do it. (Cohen-Doré died several years ago, killed in an Autoroute car crash while he was returning from visiting his elderly mother, who was in a rest home in the south of France; even now, in what is 2005 and this long after my time in Paris, I exchange letters with his beautiful opera singer wife every year or so, she gives me news about the daughters, both having completed university and married, one a doctor, the other in the diplomatic service.) I explained to Cohen-Doré that I had plenty of experience with odd jobs when younger, glazing included, paying for at least some of my college bills at Harvard and what my ice-hockey scholarship didn't cover by working as a carpenter's apprentice during summers back in Rhode Island.

We enter a *quincaillerie* on Rue de la Brèche-aux-Loups (now that I think of it, forget about a common word like *récurrent,* and there indeed is utter airy transport in so many French words—*quincaillerie* for hardware shop, or a street called Brèche-aux-Loups, meaning Wolf Run, having its own somnambulistic message very fitting for a dream of falling asleep), and we deal with the proprietor wearing a blue smock; in the course of the transaction, the proprietor seems to be looking mostly at me and not Cohen-Doré, even as Cohen-Doré explains to him the job at hand with words that might be beyond my own reasonably fluent French vocabulary, which is understandably limited when it comes to something like this. Cohen-Doré has measured for the size of the pane needed, and the proprietor, amid the wonderfully heady smell of nails and iron itself that is any hardware shop anywhere, he scores and cuts—carefully, crunchingly—a suitable glass slab on his worktable, which he then wraps in crisp brown paper. We follow him behind the counter. From underneath it he slides out on the oiled wooden floor a large blue metal canister, lifts off the lid, and with a plastic scoop produces a suitably sized dollop of aromatic glazing putty, wrapping that in waxy white paper. Quietly, as if an aside, I tell Cohen-Doré that I like the fact that this hefty, smocked *quincaillerie* proprietor will sell just enough putty for a single job and not require that we buy a pint or quart can, as would happen in the States, and Cohen-Doré nods, approvingly. The proprietor next counts out exactly a dozen of the little blue-black triangular steel "points" to be tapped into the window frame to hold the pane in place before spreading on the putty, and I tell Cohen-Doré that the man's doing this is good, too, so we don't have to buy a whole package of them; Cohen-Doré again nods. The proprietor asks me if I will need a putty knife, and he holds up a large red-handled spatula for putty, then a smaller one, and I ask Cohen-Doré in English if there might be a butter knife at Rosa's place. He tells me that surely there is, she has some utensils and dishes for her meals cooked on a hotplate when she doesn't eat with the family, and when the proprietor realizes that I'm not going to be buying one of his spatulas but can improvise easily enough for a single small job of this sort, he is the one who nods, finally looking to Cohen-Doré as if to say: *This man knows what he is doing.*

We leave the shop and head into the cool winter air of the Twelfth Arrondissement, where somehow it is no longer the bruised blue of late afternoon when we entered, but it is suddenly and thoroughly night, black and with big stars like matches flickering; the two of us continue through lumpily cobbled side streets to the old baroque stone building with Rosa's tiny single room.

"Tell me again about the dream," Cohen-Doré says, returning to what I spoke to him of earlier, moving along with that coat over his shoulders like a cape. I carry what we have bought at the shop.

To be honest, I get a little scared to think that there is no way I can let him know that this itself is part of the dream, a dream in which I am telling him—like everyone else who is one of my dear friends in Paris in 1987, very much so—how I keep having a dream and in it I am falling asleep, about to begin some dreaming.

XI.

But maybe I am not walking with Cohen-Doré along a street called Brèche-aux-Loups that time we did go to fix the window in the tiny room of his au pair, Rosa.

And no, Cohen-Doré has not yet found me a wife in Paris, as he has jokingly assured me he would. Actually, he pronounced it the very first night he invited me to dinner with his family. The subject of my never having been married came up while we sat at the big dinner table in the spacious apartment with its books and sleek furniture and abstract art, the loudly marbleized wallpaper (glitzy, bordering on gaudy?) showing a shimmering gold in the design.

However, there is a woman I have been spending time with in Paris since the beginning of the semester, Françoise, cheery and pleasant. And I inevitably see her out at what passes for the university's campus, a forlorn expanse of once hopefully futuristic reinforced-concrete buildings just beyond La Défense and the western limit of the city proper. Built in the 1960s, the buildings are now more or less crumbling, splattered with graffiti and broadsides, nothing about them, in fact, having stood up to the future very well. Françoise seems to station herself in the Salle des Professeurs whenever she knows I will be there in the afternoon, right before my two classes taught back-to-back on Friday. (Considerate Cohen-Doré intentionally scheduled my teaching that way so I will have to be on campus only once a week and can concentrate on my own writing, the first class in creative writing in English and the second a seminar on Faulkner.) The Salle des Professeurs, despite its elegant appellation, is a cluttered, linoleum-floored room with a modernistic light-mahogany meeting table and a dozen or so matching chairs, everything marred and rickety; there are pigeonhole faculty mailboxes and high stacks of old yellowing mimeograph handouts atop the sill of a long row of windows on this the third floor of the functionally named Bâtiment B, home of the department that Cohen-Doré chairs, Études Anglo-Américaines. On Friday afternoons, when the campus is near empty, few students around, I will walk into the big Salle des Professeurs (it serves the entire department, in France faculty have no individual offices) and lately always see Françoise sitting at the table alone, grading translation papers and possibly dressed too, well, *sexily* for an instructor, even a part-time one like Françoise; she gets regular work teaching several sections of an elementary translation course and also supports herself writing music and drama reviews for the Paris newspapers, chiefly *Libération*. Pudgy, she has a pretty moon face, a mane of wavy dark hair pushed back from her forehead, startling amber eyes; she wears loose beige slacks and strapped high heels, a sort of lacy, very low-cut white bustier, revealing a considerable amount of cleavage as French women do, with a tight, single-button miniature wool cardigan over it, red. She is buoyant, and especially sexy when she speaks her English. It is English with an endearing French accent; the words come out with a touch of almost baby talk, pouty and songlike, and there's no trace, thankfully, of any of the very properly enunciated British English that many French academics—subjected since childhood to summer language camps in the U.K. and such—forcibly intone when speaking the language, sounding comically pretentious, like maybe a parody of minor British nobility on a bad day.

"*There* you are," Françoise says this particular Friday afternoon, smiling brightly.

She is looking up from the pile of translation exercises written on the loose-leaf graph paper used for writing assignments in France, Françoise pretending to be surprised to see me—which hurts me a bit, to think of sweet, ever-hopeful Françoise having to put on like that and make it look as if she just happened to be there on a Friday afternoon, her outfit itself most likely for my benefit. She wears too much eyeliner, as French women also often do, something you'd probably see only on a sixteen-year-old back home. I can smell her perfume, perhaps lilac.

"Here I am, all right," I say, letting out a sigh. "Ah, Friday afternoon, and my work week is just beginning. What a life."

"I enjoyed our date last Sunday evening. It was thrilling."

She speaks this with a certain naïveté to her acquired English—as good as that English is—not realizing that "date" isn't quite the right word in English. Actually, we simply got together to go to a play she had to review at a small experimental theater in the Palais de Chaillot arts center, Françoise bringing me along under her press pass, and I know she doesn't realize, either, that "thrilling" is too exuberant a word for two friends seeing a play together, implying the wrong thing entirely. At thirty-eight, Françoise is husband-hunting, eagerly, and this new turn of her speaking of a "date" being "thrilling" in reference to what I assumed was just our casual relationship surely makes me uneasy. I don't want Françoise to get the wrong idea.

Despite Cohen-Doré's concern, I myself am not looking for a wife at the moment. Or, to put it another way, having had my share of problems with girlfriends in recent years, failed relationships, I've been rendered temporarily a very confirmed bachelor. I have even told this to Françoise. (Finding out that Françoise had died was somewhat complicated, and while in Paris two summers ago, I tried her old phone number only because, passing through the city on my way to Istanbul to do an essay for a literary magazine on the French writer Théophile Gauthier and his time there, I remembered that Françoise herself had written a master's thesis on Gauthier; I was staying in a stark one-star hotel near the Gare de l'Est, waiting to fly out of CDG to Turkey early the next morning, and it was all a long shot, admittedly as much a product of my being bored and killing time in the hotel as anything else, unable to concentrate on my reading and staring too long at the blank yellow walls and the brown-enameled single chair and table in that cramped one-star; I suppose I never really expected to get through to her after so many years, using such an old number, too; the man answering the phone turned out to be her cousin, who had long ago taken over Françoise's apartment in the Fourteenth, and I explained in French who I was and the man eventually explained that Françoise had passed away, a victim of breast cancer only a few years after I lived in Paris in 1987.) The way I see it, our relationship is so casual that I have often joked with Françoise about Cohen-Doré's vowing to find me a wife in France. I told her about the time he gave me a ride back to the city from the university during the transit strike, and how coming into Paris in his suitably dashing Alfa Romeo sedan, after the Bois de Boulogne, we passed a huge billboard high above a building, some department store's ad that showed a row of hollow-cheeked, flowing-haired models, svelte, in skimpy lingerie and all brilliantly illuminated and larger than life in the early evening's darkness, Cohen-Doré smiling and asking me to select which one of the models I would like for a wife, assuring me he could easily arrange a rendezvous; and when I told Françoise that story, she laughed about it. And after I met a bright, lovely young woman just two years out of University of Michigan and working in Paris now as an assistant at a gallery near the École des Beaux-Arts—we'd got to talking in the Village Voice bookstore one evening at a reading by an American novelist, a guy my age who had once taught with me at a summer writers' workshop in Vermont—I found myself the next day in the separate office that Cohen-Doré does have in Bâtiment B as chairman, an expanse as big and modernistically bleak as the Salle des Professeurs. He asked me if I had found a potential wife yet, and I casually told him that, though she was certainly much too young for me, I had met at the reading a *very* lovely American, with whom I later had drinks at the upscale Brasserie Lipp; I added, to deter Cohen-Doré—who didn't seem to mind that she wasn't French, and if I secured a wife of *any* sort in Paris, it would be fine with him, his mission fulfilled—I added that, alas, the young woman was already spoken for, had a Swiss boyfriend. And when I told him that, Cohen-Doré, in a silvery double-breasted suit that day and appearing more dapper than ever, slowly stood up from his big free-form desk; he walked around the office some, finally pausing to stare out the long row of unwashed windows that overlooked the endless ramshackle and rusting railway yards there in Nanterre, the winter sky above striped gray and white like a huge feather—Cohen-Doré thinking, even pondering, and then turning to me still sitting there, Cohen-Doré motioning in the air with a forward brush of the fingers, his hand held low and downturned, like somebody shooing away an annoying fly, his brow wrinkled in French masculine condescension: "Swiss," was all he said. It was as if the very word was vaguely distasteful to him, Cohen-Doré dismissive to the degree that the implication was I shouldn't as much as ever entertain any concern of a *Swiss* male being an obstacle when pursuing a beautiful woman. And when I told Françoise that story, she laughed, too.

And now, flopping down on one of the chairs at the oval table, nobody else but Françoise in the Salle des Professeurs, I smile and assure her that I also had a good time at the play, a small production of an avant-garde work by a young African dramatist who—polite, shy—came over to speak with Françoise in the theater afterward, while she took copious notes for her newspaper piece. I heap my book pack onto the table, tug off my jacket. I let out another sigh and tell her outright the same thing I told Cohen-Doré, admitting I might be rather tired at the moment, my sleep uneasy lately.

"I keep having this dream," I say.

She tries to make a joke of it, flirtingly in her pleasant singsong: "You are a dreamer, all Americans are such very busy dreamers."

"No, it's this dream I keep having of falling asleep."

"What?"

She says this with a jangling little laugh, putting down her red pen on the pile of papers. I wonder if she actually has been grading them or if they're merely a stage prop in her stationing herself here to see me again before the weekend, hoping we might line up another "date" that will prove to be quite "thrilling." She uses both hands to adjust the single red button on the tight short cardigan, fiddling with it as she looks down her snub nose to it, and I look, too, at Françoise's wonderfully ample breasts displayed atop the lacy trim of the white bustier, a tiny satin ribbon tie smack in the middle; Françoise says something else, even before she looks up: "How can you have a dream of falling asleep, when a dream itself is already something that happens when you are sleeping? It is very daft, no?" Then she does look up at me again. That pretty moon face, those pretty amber eyes with altogether too much black eyeliner, Françoise smiling in this year 1987, and Françoise using the word "daft" for "crazy," which I realize is at least one Britishism she's picked up in her English. Intelligent, and always ready for inquiry and energetically applying any subject at hand to a discussion of literature, Françoise goes on:

"But it is a good paradox, also, I think. And as with most paradox it is daft, which is what makes it very good, an ambiguity. You see,"—and there is something about the way she can say "you see," bobbing her head, cheerier—"I have been reading your favorite, your Melville, the novel that is all paradox, the novel that Melville himself says in the *sous-titre* is all ambiguities, *Pierre*."

I don't say anything. And she's right, the novel's subtitle is *The Ambiguities.*

I sit there at the table, me back then, tall and my hair too shaggy. I am wearing black corduroy jeans, an open-collar blue chambray work shirt, and glasses with the lenses tinted purplish—more or less my usual outfit back in Ann Arbor. I know it is what I think is hip, what will make me look like anything *but* an English professor, and therefore, with my being a so-called creative writer in my department of literature, I'm at least taking some stand in dress, if nothing else, against the fact that most of what goes on in that department—the perpetual rote busywork of plodding academics—has little to do, really, with *literature.* And I don't look at Françoise, who is waiting for me to reply, and in a way it hurts me, too, to think that she's gone as far as making this effort to share my interests, reading *Pierre* now. I remember the first night we got together and had dinner at a couscous place by her apartment in the Alésia neighborhood; it was a small restaurant with the usual travel posters depicting maybe a white Tunisian village alongside the blue Mediterranean, and the usual dignified mustached Arabic waiters approaching only when they sensed you needed them, and the usual, but also very deliciously *un*usual and near magical, aroma of the spices for that stew of meat and vegetables heaped high on steaming semolina. (Is there *anything* like a good couscous in a cheap Parisian corner place?) I talked to Françoise then of my own personal twin giants when it came to American literature, Melville and, of course, Faulkner. During the meal I went on about the novel *Pierre,* such a beautiful—and admirably failed—performance, with its rare, ghostly insight about the biggest of any conundrum, the paramount baffling puzzle of what we're told is our supposed time on earth, which can sometimes feel like little more than the merely dreamt. (I remember how on one rereading of *Pierre* I marked with a pencil-check every time Melville used the word *phantom* and then counted them up, I did the same for the other equally spooky word he employed again and again, *metaphysical.*) I suppose that in the couscous place I also went on about my theory that Faulkner was Melville, and Melville was Faulkner, for me the two eerily identical, as each sought to discover exactly what he could do—what new territories he could explore and what big barriers he could shove bravely aside—by employing the sheer force of words in wild overabundance, with language itself becoming as ultimately explosive for each of them, when you think of it (or when you think specifically of *Moby-Dick* and *Pierre; The Sound and the Fury* and *Absalom, Absalom!*), as any full and thundering detonation of the split atom itself. And in the Salle des Professeurs, I remember that first dinner at the couscous place with Françoise, and to hear her now talk of reading *Pierre* does mean that she is trying hard to make *my* interests *her* interests. That really hurts me, seeing her need.

In the Salle des Professeurs I stare out the long row of aluminum-framed windows, the sill stacked with the old mimeograph handouts, and I see the sky spreading above more of the endless Nanterre railway yards and (this is very odd) again striped gray and white like a huge feather, precisely the same as the sky had been the winter's day I was in Cohen-Doré's office and telling him about the girl from University of Michigan with the Swiss boyfriend.

Françoise is still looking at me, she says:

"But what exactly is it?" She tilts her head, then adds, "Tell me about this, what you say is the dream you have. How do you call it, your dream of falling asleep?"

An electric clock is hung above the bulletin board behind me, which has notices of teachers' union meetings and big sheets announcing exam schedules from long-forgotten past semesters; the clock, trailing a squiggly cord for its plug, is a stark office-issue thing with a bright red minute hand looping around and around, the low hum audible.

I try to keep staring out the line of windows, at that sky.

XII.

I keep staring out those windows, hoping the scene will change.

XIII.

I don't dare look up. And what if I do look up, what if I find that to look up is to see that cheery Françoise—with her low-cut bustier, her tight cherry-red sweater with its single button, her pouty smile as she talks about Melville's Pierre*—she isn't even there? Or that I am dreaming that Françoise simply isn't there?*

XIV.

"French women," Vanderwaal tells me, "now that's a different story altogether."

"Françoise is a good heart," I tell him, as we walk along.

"But she's already lectured you," Vanderwaal says, "about your father, which proves my point."

"It wasn't any lecture, only an opinion. We were out after I went with her on an assignment she had, to cover some pretty lousy jazz up at a small club near Poissonnière. We were just having a drink afterward, before she took the Métro home to write her review. And of course I have been calling my father long-distance a lot lately in Rhode Island, he's on his own and his heart isn't any good, getting worse all the time. Maybe I *was* freaking out about it, because he'd admitted he hadn't been feeling at all well when I'd last called him, and when I told her then that I'd been considering flying back for a week to see him, she told me what she did—that I had to be careful of parents getting the whammy on you as an adult."

"My point exactly," Vanderwaal pronounces, grinning in his minor triumph and obviously satisfied that what I just said does prove his point, *exactly*.

Wiry, ruddy-cheeked, beak-nosed—that's Vanderwaal. We are heading in the direction of the Périphérique freeway that rings Paris, on another steely winter afternoon. He's a couple of years older than I, definitely looks like an outdoorsman this day in a short gold parka, puffy, and ski cap and jeans and lug-soled hiking boots, plus the small day pack over one shoulder, his standard outfit for tramping around Paris.

I never knew him while we were in college at Harvard, though apparently he knew of me and what passed for my ice hockey notoriety there (in my freshman year the campus newspaper referred to me, predictably enough, as the "highly sought-after high school recruit," somebody who might single-handedly render Harvard a team at last ready to compete with archrival Cornell once I joined the varsity squad the following year); Vanderwaal himself played hockey in prep school, though he has assured me, "I was always a joke, never of your caliber." Which actually seems to define the difference in what you might call our Harvard experience—truly blue-blooded Vanderwaal, of old New York Dutch stock (Roosevelts, Van Rensselaers, Vanderwaals, etc.), from a top-notch prep school and with membership in an exclusive final club at Harvard, the Fly Club on Mount Auburn Street, where even in those late sixties he dined formally a couple of nights a week in coat and tie with similar blue bloods, all male; and me, a hockey recruit on scholarship and from a Catholic high school in a mill town in the wooded hills of northern Rhode Island, where I was raised by my widowed father who ran a Sunoco gas station and where I finished among the top five scorers for three years running in the state schoolboy league's Class A division, which became my ticket to college. But once I got to Harvard there was only that one notice in the campus paper loudly touting my potential and then a lot of time for me in the dreamt-of crimson-and-white uniform on the bench when I did play varsity in my sophomore year, the level of competition turning out, despite my reported promise, to be way beyond me; by my junior year I had abandoned hockey completely and immersed myself in literature courses and creative writing courses—probably I held some kind of record for the number of the latter taken at Harvard at the time, seeing that back then the staid English department didn't allow you to count them toward the English major and you had to slip them into your schedule entirely on the sly, extra credits.

Vanderwaal lived on a modest trust allotment after college, soon taking up a decidedly alternative lifestyle for somebody of his upbringing, a complete reversal—though perhaps not such a reversal in the late sixties, when 180s were more the norm than oddity. Eventually gravitating to the West Coast and living in a commune of crafts people in San Francisco, he carved ocarinas and sold them on the street for a while and then married a French woman he'd met there, moving with her to Paris, where the marriage quickly dissolved, no kids.

Currently, Vanderwaal has some vague, sporadic employment at the American Field Service offices off the Champs-Élysées. And on his own for the last half-dozen years, getting by with the cushion of the small trust, he has recently taken an apartment, cramped and inexpensive, across the street from the big steamship-style air vents behind the funnybook-color trestling of the Centre Pompidou, fixing up the place with furniture bought at the Marché aux Puces and also sometimes salvaged from stuff left out on sidewalks. Smiling, Vanderwaal has told me that it's a good thing he's a sound sleeper, because huge, sleek German tour buses park beside the Centre Pompidou with their engines idling loudly throughout the night directly below his bedroom window, the German tourists themselves dozing away in the comfortable reclining seats and then having breakfast served to them right in the bus come morning. Vanderwaal marvels in approval: "German efficiency is something, though, isn't it?"

Besides the spotty American Field Service employment (AFS is the old volunteer ambulance-driver service that attracted many notable young Americans in World War I, including a grand uncle of Vanderwaal, and now in 1987 AFS is basically involved with high school exchanges and organizing group summer bicycling trips for U.S. students, through the castle country of the Loire Valley or the vineyards of sunny Provence, that sort of thing), yes, besides some office work two or three mornings a week, Vanderwaal is at the moment deep into an ongoing quest not just to know Paris, but to *really* know Paris. In his apartment he has a big three-volume folio set bound in maroon leatherette that identifies every building in the city, street by street, fine print providing each building's complete history, and he studies those volumes constantly, tracks down the various sites he reads about. In other words, it isn't a tourist's Paris that interests Vanderwaal, though upon request he can offer, say, a full recounting of events having occurred in, and every architectural detail associated with, all six Paris train stations (those sculpted statues lined up above the entry doors to the Gare du Nord, Vanderwaal knows the names of the Belle Époque French politicians who actually, and vainly, had their mistresses pose for the figures in flowing togas, seemingly from ancient mythology; or, the story of the assassination of a renowned nineteenth-century journalist that once transpired at the top of the marble steps of the ritzy Le Train Bleu restaurant inside the Gare de Lyon, Vanderwaal has found the spot where the blood apparently stained the white stone and never disappeared, etc.); no, not just a tourist's itinerary whatsoever, and Vanderwaal knows his way around the shabby outer arrondissements as well, like the lost Nineteenth and Twentieth, maybe the more lost Thirteenth (once you get into its grim far reaches beyond the big traffic circle and cluster of new high-rises at the Place d'Italie, anyway).

I first met Vanderwaal while standing in the long, disorganized line at the central Préfecture—where *cartes de séjour* are obtained and renewed and, overall, begged for in dealing with the haughtily bored *fonctionnaires* pretending to be working there—and now, with my schedule of teaching only the one day a week, he often calls me in the morning to ask if I want to join him on whatever project he has lined up for the day, as he continues in his quest (or happy Sisyphean plight) to *really* know Paris. A phone call from Vanderwaal usually begins with his saying, "Do you ever think what it might be like to go through life without having _____?" and then the blank filled in. Once it was a matter of going through life and not having marched in the May Day Parade, so we joined the phalanxes of banner-bearing union workers heartily tramping to the beat of drums and distortedly blaring loudspeakers from Place de la Bastille to Place de la République, the sky a rare blue above the first fragile budding of puzzle-barked plane trees on the wide boulevards closed to traffic that balmy, brilliantly sunny day. Another time it was a matter of going through life and not having seen what had once been an odd little village within the city, the Entrepôts de Bercy, where for a couple of centuries wine was unloaded from barges arriving from throughout the country and distributed to Paris via warehouses there beside the Seine, all of it abandoned several years earlier and developers arguing lately for immediate demolition in the name of urban rehab. Following Vanderwaal in his sturdy hiking boots, I climbed, wobblingly, over the high chain-link fence that walled it off now, signs everywhere saying PASSAGE INTERDIT, and I wandered with him through deserted narrow lanes, past hastily vacated little stone cottages with peaked, red-tiled roofs that had for so long provided the offices for prosperous wine merchants, the windows smashed and open to the elements; in the rooms, achingly empty, furniture was overturned, wind had swept the strewn old sales records into piles like drifting snow, and faded company calendars still hung on walls, very ghostly.

But the thing with the tunnels under Paris, where we are heading this day, has been different for me—I have been consciously avoiding it for weeks. (Vanderwaal's death was just last December, which I saw a notice of when flipping through the obituaries section in the Harvard alumni magazine; I knew he had been back here in the States for a long while, traveling in a camper around the country in recent years with his third or fourth wife and cataloging their adventures in a spirited online blog; that he was on his own again at the end, without any wife, and that it was a suicide, Vanderwaal shooting himself in a trailer park in New Mexico, I got not from the magazine but from an old pal from the Harvard hockey team I ran into in the Grand Central lobby one day, a guy who had known Vanderwaal in prep school; the idea of suicide for Vanderwaal—ready to swallow the entirety of Paris and probably the whole world, an inquisitive, lifelong student of sorts, always so energetic and upbeat and *more than alive* when I was with him in Paris—seemed to me to border on the patently absurd, as suicides too often do.) We talk as we walk in Paris this afternoon, now closer to the elevated freeway.

"Did you tell her about it, your Françoise?" he asks me.

"She's not my Françoise," I say, "and, yeah, I've been telling everybody about it."

"A dream of falling asleep," Vanderwaal says, almost tasting the idea, a wine on his palate, deciding: "You know, I think I like it."

"I keep having the dream, *récurrent,* as Cohen-Doré would have it," I tell Vanderwaal, employing the French word with suitably emphatic pronunciation. "I'm watching myself fall asleep, go into dreaming."

"You know, I also really like that Monsieur Victor Cohen-Doré," Vanderwaal says, "and we should have lunch with him again. There's something flamboyantly elegant about the guy, loopy but grand, a real intellectual, too, like a character straight out of one of the Saul Bellow novels you say he's an expert on, not your usual uptight, colossally nerdy and boring academic type."

"And there goes your theory about family, or the French family, anyway," I say.

I remind Vanderwaal of what he was speaking of only moments earlier on the walk, concerning how there's no understanding French women sometimes, and how Vanderwaal said that he had his own issues of cultural difference with his vanished French wife on many fronts, including totally different concepts of family; in Vanderwaal's view, Françoise's chiding me—telling me to be careful about worrying too much about my aging father back home and to lead my own life as an adult—was valid proof of his argument, all right, and for French kids, he claimed, it's often a battle with parents from day one, some lingering, collective 1789 Revolution of their own. He speaks more of it now:

"French parents will criticize their kids constantly, rudely correct them constantly, they hide their kids away when guests come for an evening. And all the while the kids just stew. They plot and wait till they're old enough and can say they've had enough and can at long last get back at them, no love lost once they're out on their own. The whole scenario too often turns one step short of that tried-and-true, catch-all French slogan, '*Je cracherai sur vos tombes*': I will spit on your graves."

"Cohen-Doré, he's the happiest man I know with his family," I say. "When he let me stay with them at their place, that one week when I had to change apartments and was moving to Rue de Sévigné, we'd all sit around in the big living room in that high-rise after dinner at night, Cohen-Doré reading and his wife listening on a Walkman to her opera tapes for a rehearsal and his two angelic little girls doing their homework, occasionally asking *Maman* or *Papa* to help them with this or that. It was all so happy, so perfect, so much love everywhere in that family, like nothing I've ever seen."

"That's your man Cohen-Doré," Vanderwaal tells me, and he explains that ancient culture trumps modern culture in this regard, Cohen-Doré being French but also Jewish, and if you're Jewish, family is everything—*wonderfully* so, Vanderwaal emphasizes. "Which is why Cohen-Doré is concerned that you, at your age, don't have a wife yet. He might seem like he's joking about it, but I suspect he isn't. He wants you to have what he has, a happy family, the entire wonderfulness of that. He's become a wise and concerned father for you here in Paris."

Sometimes it seems that Vanderwaal—with all his goofing around, with all his laid-back existence of sheer, uncut, indulgently idle curiosity and never really having done very much in terms of what might be called being productive with his Harvard degree—he seems to know things that I—the hard worker ceaselessly writing my fiction and somebody who luckily landed a tenured, safe-for-life university job on the basis of publishing a couple of novels—will never know, or things that I will never have a *chance* of understanding.

We keep on walking.

XV.

"Relax," Vanderwaal tells me a few minutes later, as we get closer to our destination.

"Easy for you to say," I tell him. "And I don't know why I decided to go along with this. I should be writing, I should be preparing for classes tomorrow, Faulkner, I should be doing *anything* but this."

Our breath puffs like cartoon balloons in the sooty air, and we are moving along bleak Rue Watt, where Vanderwaal tells me there's an easy enough entrance at a manhole cover, often used by kids who go down to explore the tunnels. The way I understand it, the network of tunnels is part of the ancient infrastructure of the city, spreading far below it, once connecting subterranean quarries and later used for pipelines and early power cables; it's rather secret and not like the legendary sewer system, which Vanderwaal considers only another tourist attraction. In his backpack Vanderwaal has a huge electric light, its boxy case blue plastic, along with a coil of rope and a spelunker's spike-ended hammer, implements I don't even like to think about the more I do think about them, and he doesn't appear to be listening to my qualms. Vanderwaal in the red ski cap and gold nylon parka is just looking around as we walk, savoring the carcasses of the sootily blackened old buildings in this forgotten industrial pocket of empty Rue Watt, nodding in appreciation, whistling some bouncy tune a little, until he eventually says:

"This is a great part of the city, authentic. It's all slated to go, as well, leveled or rehabbed like those Bercy *entrepôts* we wandered through. They're going to build a giant library complex or something around here, I read, it will become the new Bibliothèque Nationale."

"You didn't listen to what I just said," I tell him, "because what I just said is that I don't know what possessed me to as much as answer the phone when I knew it was you calling to get me to finally agree to this."

It takes no seer to predict the reply from Vanderwaal:

"Look at it this way, Will, can you imagine what it might be like to have sailed through life without doing something like this when given the opportunity, gone *below* Paris and to where few people ever have gone *below* Paris, a whole other world?"

"You're nuts, you know that, don't you?"

"Been so for years," he laughs, dimples showing fully.

And I'm that much more apprehensive when, before turning down the cobbled alley where the manhole cover reportedly awaits us, Vanderwaal stops at the corner, looks this way and that for maybe gendarmes, nobody else, in fact, around. When we get to the rusted metal disk, the size of a shield, he shows me where the kids have chiseled away the welded-on hasp and padlock recently affixed to it, probably by the city, the metal now mirror-shiny and scarred from the kids banging at it; apparently, the tunnels provide sort of a sport for the kids, who do consider themselves spelunkers exploring this forbidden honeycomb of passages usually at night, perpetually playing a spirited cat-and-mouse game with the pursuing cops. A couple of times I've been with Vanderwaal in a Métro station and we've seen a pack of those tough teenage boys puffing smelly Gitanes and their clothes covered with dried gold mud, themselves with coiled ropes and hammers and boxy electric lights, waiting for a train, as Vanderwaal nudges me knowingly when he spots them, tells me: "They've been down there."

Vanderwaal wedges the pick end of the hammer under the manhole's lid, pries it up like opening a massive clamshell, drops the hammer to the pavement beside him. He spreads his feet for balance, stoops again, and uses both hands to lift the heavy thing and tug it clankingly aside. Trying not to step too close, I lean over and look down, for that little rush of vertigo you get when peering into the darkness of a well, perhaps wanting to drop a coin into it and marvel at the full few seconds it takes (the *forever* it takes? the *eternity* it takes?) before you hear the faint plunk of the coin splashingly hitting the black water below—which only intensifies the vertigo, a nest of baby lime-green grass snakes slithering away in the stomach. With the big light tugged from his backpack and its long, buttery beam directed into the darkness, he shows me the steel ladder leading down the cement-walled cylinder, and I ask him possibly the only thing there is to ask him:

"How far?"

"Fifty feet straight down, I'd say, maybe sixty."

"OK," I tell him.

Because what else am I supposed to tell him? That I am in Paris and it is 1987, that I am younger than I am now in 2005, *so much younger,* explain to him again that during the entire year in Paris I keep having this same dream, a dream in which I am falling asleep and into a dream of what is *actually* happening to me in Paris. I say to Vanderwaal more firmly, suddenly with no doubt whatsoever about any of it: "OK, let's go."

"That's the spirit," Vanderwaal says, his attitude so casual that—as he descends the long ladder first, then I follow, firmly planting one probingly lowered, crepe-soled suede desert boot and then the other on the moist, ferrous-smelling metal, rung by rung, my staggered fists tight on the rungs above me, monkey-like—yes, Vanderwaal so casual that he makes small talk in the course of our descent and asks me how that window ever did come out that I was supposed to fix at the cubbyhole room of Cohen-Doré's au pair named Rosa. I don't answer him, only ask him, Vanderwaal now standing below and looking up at me, "How much farther?" and he tells me, "You're almost there, home free as the breeze at evening, as they say."

I dangle one desert boot, making hesitant arcs with it, and finally touch the bottom.

We begin moving through the tunnel, walking fully upright and having to crouch only now and then, the box light throwing fan-shaped illumination on the rough gold stone carved away for the little thoroughfares. There is the strong aroma of mud—clayish, moldy—and the cave-heavy dampness itself is tangible, as I follow Vanderwaal in what could be nothing more than a dream of falling asleep, Vanderwaal moving deeper and deeper into the maze; and there are intersections with other tunnels, there are nooks almost like chambers and littered with beer cans—blue and silver, red and gold, some crumpled—and Vanderwaal tilts the beam into one of these grottoes, explaining how the teenage kids love to party here on weekends, bring booze and boomboxes. Sometimes I see pipes, crusted with the gold mud, and elongated tangles of cabled wire, too, equally crusted, all of which must be the remnants of whatever municipal services the tunnel network was once used for, maybe still is used for, then for a while it's not just a matter of dampness, but scummed, milky green puddles, and it appears that somebody—the kids or city workmen—have laid planks for walking on in this stretch of wet. I gently place one foot down and then the other, careful as I was on the ladder, testing for stability on the planks as if heading out onto a newly frozen pond, something I often did, in fact, playing hockey in those surely dreamt woods of northern Rhode Island when young.

Vanderwaal once in a while says to me, his words echoing far below the entire City of Paris above us: "Something else, isn't it?"

I suppose I say, "Yeah," or I suppose I tell him that it is all "Really amazing," and I do mean it. What a marvel it is to think of the city above going on with its life of cars and cafés and *boulangeries* and the coming of twilight, as squawking birds flock like pepper thrown to the wind in the melon-tinged late afternoon sky stretching wide across Paris, which could just as well be far-off Rome or Buenos Aires or Beijing for all we know down here in the silent darkness, Vanderwaal and I for all intents and purposes a million miles away, or more, from everything else going on anywhere else—and then it happens.

I have made the major mistake of letting Vanderwaal get too far ahead of me, Vanderwaal enlarging the distance between us, with my being slow and so cautious in stepping on the thumping planks, sometimes arms out for balance, tightrope-walker style; I have let him get far enough ahead of me and into this tunnel we turned into a hundred yards back—a very long and very narrow corridor—that the electric light and his own shadow moving behind it are becoming dangerously small and distant.

And Vanderwaal does it.

Up very far ahead of me, turning around to face me with the beam staring right at me like a glowing diamond, Vanderwaal is smiling, I hear him say:

"Do you want to know real darkness?"

Which is when he simply puts his stubby thumb on the button atop the box light's blue plastic handle there in his fist, when he simply presses the button and clicks it off, adding, "I mean *real* darkness."

Neither of us says a thing for a few more seconds (for maybe a few hundred years?), and I am still standing there—not moving a muscle, frozen.

I finally shout for him to turn the light on, I stand blindly lost in the utter black and I tell him I'm not kidding, "Turn it fucking on, Vanderwaal!"

But he doesn't; there's no reply.

And while I will try to joke about it later when we have a coffee at a workingmen's café on Rue Watt afterward, early evening by then, a place filled with gruff laborers at the end of their day, and while I will try to deny the fact that I was scared as hell in the tunnel, lying about it all to Vanderwaal as we sit in the warm café—amid the pinging, light-flickering pinball machines and those guys at the genuinely zinc bar longing for complete anesthetizing in their indulgence in alcohol after such long hours of muscle-aching work, a group performance in inebriation that I really hadn't seen exhibited before anywhere in France—none of what I will later say or deny in the café matters now, in this swallowing, overwhelming black in the tunnel; tensed-up still more, feeling so absolutely *alone,* I shout louder to Vanderwaal in the tunnel, "I'm serious, turn it fucking on, do you hear me!"

XVI.

And even though I want to somehow pull a trump card on him, flatly tell him that he can't taunt me like this, "*You're already dead! This isn't happening!*"—let him in on the sad-but-true news that he can't do something like this to me because, unlike him or sweet Françoise or even my dear good friend Cohen-Doré, I myself am different, I am *alive* and not dead, so stop acting like a total bastard—I refrain from doing so.

There's nothing from him . . . until I hear him just say the same thing slower in the black, as he actually did say it that day, stretching out the syllables: "Re-al dark-ness, man."

XVII.

Then he does switch the light on, my eyes taking a bit of time to re-focus and adjust to the illumination, my lungs wheezing out the dank underground air at long, long last in Paris those many years ago, 1987, to be exact, and then in the tunnel of such dreams, the dissolving reality of my life there in 1987, I next seem to be walking along once more, and . . .

THE DEALER'S GIRLFRIEND

Celia was pretty high, coked up, the night she called the toll-free number for Christian International Children's Fund and became the sponsor for the child in Rio de Janeiro named João. It all gave her something to do, and if she used to start crying for no reason when sitting around alone at the condo there in Austin at night, not interested in any more TV, not interested in any more coke, she had a reason for crying now, she told herself—poor João.

Every month that summer she used a credit card to send the money to Christian International, and sometimes she would just stare at the photograph of João they had sent her. It showed João, almost too scared to fully smile, eyes very big, teeth very white, standing in green flip-flops and dirty red shorts and a white T-shirt on a street of dun-colored dust and a few stucco buildings at what seemed an intersection in the *favela* where he lived; there were a couple of overgrown palm trees in back of him and also a guy on a motorbike who seemed to have stopped in the street to watch the kid, little João, being photographed like that.

She had looked at that photo—it came in a sort of corny greeting-card folder, edged with gilt—who knows how many times, who knows how long, to be honest. She didn't go to the clubs with Tommy anymore, and, in truth, Tommy told her that he had to do his work at the clubs, often meeting "clients" there, and she should understand that. It was what paid the bills for their condo in Northwest Hills, and it was what allowed her to shop at the ritzy Arboretum Mall with its Saks and designer boutiques—though buying a five-hundred-dollar red silk dress didn't really make any sense if you weren't going to wear it to one of the clubs on Sixth Street. (She had met Tommy when she was still a student and before she dropped out of the University of Texas, an English major, and Tommy had always assured her that, of course, he had made his "move" on her that first night at the club because she was the "knockout of a blonde" she was, tall, willowy; but later he told her, very seriously, that it was something else that kept him pursuing her at first, how she seemed so much brighter than other girls he had known, also shy in a good way, he would say. Tommy had begun dealing when in high school, and after some classes at Austin Community College that didn't add up to much and then working unsuccessfully for a fly-by-night new homes builder as a salesman, he went back to dealing full-time. Tommy had a pretty good regular clientele that included lawyers and brokers, even one Austin city councilman, though once Celia moved in with Tommy, he assured her it would be only a matter of time before he got out of the business; he said he knew it was a dead end—Tommy told her he would give her a better life.) In any case, buying another new red silk dress or not, Celia really didn't want to go to the clubs anymore.

Occasionally she would have her sister over and cook dinner for her when Tommy was off doing what he had to do. And there were two other girls, Melanie and Amanda, whose boyfriends were dealers, too. They sometimes showed up to watch a video movie on Saturday night, the three of them talking and doing some coke; with dealer boyfriends, they were essentially in the same situation as she was, Celia knew, and they knew the importance of being careful. At least Tommy wasn't as paranoid as Melanie's boyfriend, the tall, handsome Mexican guy Wilfredo, who looked like a leading man right out of one of those Univisión *telenovelas* and who made it a point that Melanie shouldn't spend too much time with *anybody* who might be suspicious about her lifestyle; Wilfredo told Melanie that the girlfriends of other dealers were safe enough.

But spending time with those girls, even cooking dinner for her sister she had once been very close to, didn't interest Celia as much lately, now that she had João to think about and to, well, take care of. Sometimes, late on a weekday night and at home by herself once more, she admitted to herself that she only wanted to wait for midnight on the nose, when the cable station would run the half-hour infomercial for the Christian International Children's Fund again.

A soft-spoken middle-aged man in khakis and a loose sport shirt, somewhat broken-down with his longish gray hair but with very kind blue eyes, narrated; he was shown strolling through the slums of various cities in other countries—Madras, Lagos, and what might have been the *favela* in Rio—and he would point out the poverty in which the children lived, stopping now and then to sit down on a low stone wall, let's say, and speak to one of them, getting him or her to smile, explaining to viewers that for only twenty-eight dollars a month somebody could sponsor a child and provide three good meals a day, a *chance* in life. When Celia started sending fifty-six dollars a month, doubling it for João, the woman on the 800 line misunderstood her, as Celia fumbled in her purse for a credit card to give its number; the woman thought that Celia wanted to sponsor a second child—but Celia assured her, no, she wanted the whole amount to go to João. The woman finally did seem to understand; she said she knew that Celia clearly was a good Christian, that the Lord would bless her for her kindness. Of course, Celia overlooked that part of it, and while growing up on various military bases, with her father being a practical career-Army man who had retired in Austin as a lieutenant and her mother an elementary school teacher, equally as practical, church never figured much into her family's life—but Celia didn't want to explain that to the woman on the telephone, and the important thing was that she was helping João.

Not that it was all she thought about during those strange months that hot summer in Austin. (Yes, right from the start Tommy had promised her that he was going to try to get out of the business eventually, dealing, and the fact of the matter was that at heart he was just a quiet country sort, from East Texas. Tommy *was* a good man, Celia knew, somebody who liked simple things like bass fishing, and he surely did long for a normal life himself. He told her that she had changed everything for him, he loved her more than anything in the world, he had indeed never met anybody like her, so bright, so curious about things, so special, and he wanted so very much to someday give her that normal life so they could marry—he told her repeatedly she wouldn't have to live like this forever, shying away from people who might be suspicious, Celia even dropping out of college around that time. But after two years with him she started to doubt that, or wonder when anything would, or could, ever change. Six months before, Tommy had gotten a tip on a possible job working for a guy who was launching a new company selling customized hologram business cards, and Tommy, having worked before as a salesman, thought it might be his break at last, a fresh start. However, when he went to the downtown Austin office for the interview, the guy, smug and looking right at him from his big swivel chair behind the slab of a modern desk, he flatly told Tommy that, forget employment, he expected Tommy to pay *him* for what would only be a cover to account for his drug-dealing income when reporting to the IRS; it seemed other dealers used the bogus job of selling something as absurd as hologram business cards as a cover. That Tommy had taken it seriously made him feel like a fool, and it was an embarrassment that triggered almost a new darkness in Tommy. His drinking—Tommy never touched coke or even pot, part of his dealer's code—grew worse, and not long afterward he had an accident when his month-old "Z" sports car, cobalt blue, floated into a roadside phone pole when he was drunk late one night and returning to the Northwest Hills condo from the clubs downtown—he suffered only bruises, yet later Celia would admit that she should have known then how bad things were for him, how much he blamed himself for letting Celia down, and perhaps Tommy was suicidal.) True, Celia didn't spend *all* her time obsessing about João that summer, and she had some vague plans about returning to school at last. She went over to the campus on a hot late-August afternoon and spoke with an adviser in the English department, who worked for a full hour at the computer, figuring out just how many credits Celia had. A pale young woman with black-framed thick glasses, cheery, the adviser told her that with solid grades like hers, Celia probably could even test out of some of the requirements, and, all told, Celia might be able to put together a package that would let her finish her degree in three semesters, four max. And while it was too late to enroll for the fall, the adviser said, Celia could enroll for spring-semester classes during the next registration period coming up in October. Nevertheless, almost as soon as Celia left the English department building on the university's sprawling, impeccably groomed campus, all flowerbeds and gurgling fountains and stately Spanish architecture, yes, as soon as she got back out into the scorching, heat-rippling afternoon, she knew that she wouldn't do it. She wasn't ready yet.

The cocaine did help pass the time, and at night, the air-conditioning softly hissing, Celia alone as usual, she called her mother sometimes to assure her she was fine, called her sister sometimes to assure her she was fine, but all she really wanted to do was to think about little João.

She looked at his picture for long hours. Actually, she studied it. His dark eyes, his bony arms, his attempt at a broken smile.

She wondered about what João did when it rained there in the *favela* in Rio, when those hillside slums turned to mud, the flimsy wood-and-tin shacks surely about to slip into the sea at the foot of the mountains. She wondered if João had good clothes to wear now that she was sending more money, and sometimes—really high, doing more lines off the glass-topped coffee table—she called over and over again the toll-free number for the Christian International Children's Fund and, weeping uncontrollably, asked whoever she got on the line to please check for her, please make sure João had all the food he needed, please make sure he had good clothes. He was *only* a child, *only* six years old, he had not been responsible for the sad life that had been dealt him, she tried to explain on the phone.

All of which is to say, when Melanie's boyfriend, the vainly handsome dealer Wilfredo, did call to tell Celia what had happened to Tommy with the thugs (enforcers?) for Tommy's supplier—they were up from Nuevo Laredo on the Mexican border and had come to Austin to "talk" with Tommy about some problem in his latest payments to the supplier—Wilfredo couldn't get through for almost an hour because her line was busy and she simply ignored the beep that signaled another caller trying to make contact.

And, even then, when Wilfredo did speak on the phone, none of it made any sense to Celia at first, and again pretty high, coked up, she didn't listen to Wilfredo. She talked only about João to Wilfredo, Celia rambling, weeping some more, Celia telling him the same thing, how the poor child, João, was *only* a child, he *couldn't* be blamed for what his life was like—until Wilfredo himself, out of frustration and knowing that he had to make her understand what had happened to Tommy, the gravity of the news he had to tell her, more or less lost it, and he shouted:

"Will you just shut the fuck up for a minute and listen to me, you crazy bitch!"

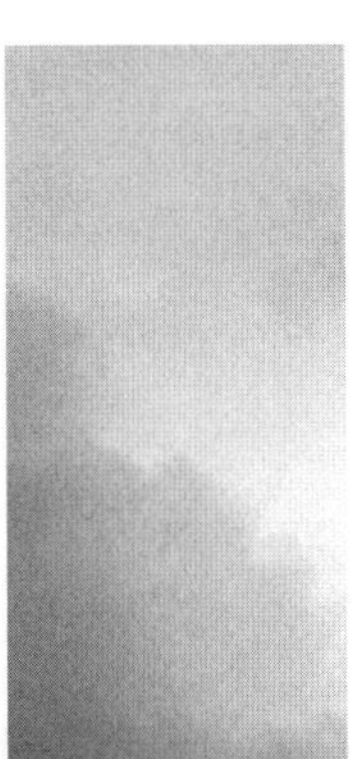

THE SAGA OF THE IRISH IN AMERICA

His soul swooned slowly as he heard the
snow falling faintly through the universe . . .

—Joyce, *The Dead*

Aidan grew up in a government row house in Dublin's working-class Kimmage neighborhood. And, of course, there was the sadness of his mother dying young, leaving his father, a clerk for the city, to raise six children on his own. But looking back on it, Aidan never thought of his childhood as bleak.

▮ ▮ ▮

Sure, he understood how hard it must have been for his father to rise at dawn to make breakfast in the dim kitchen for the lot of them and start them off to school.

But how much fun they had in those days, especially the weekend outings with his father at the oversize wheel of the faded red Volkswagen Beetle, the half-dozen offspring packed like a troupe of clowns in the tiny thing; they would go out to see his aunt and uncle in Lucan, or head to swim, and shiver, at what passed for a pebbly beach up by Howth. Actually, Aidan sometimes even remembered the odd beauty of it all, and there was one particular scene that remained, which seemed like a framed painting. In his school uniform of short pants and hand-me-down blazer, he was coming home late from classes one afternoon, not long before tea. He turned the corner and came upon his street, where he lived indeed, and he stopped to savor the so-rightness of it, the particular scene that always snagged in his mind. The older boys were playing soccer in the cramped street; springtime, the sky was strikingly blue above the uneven slate roofs of the stuccoed housing, the skinny trees pushing forth their first lime-green buds; and, yes, this was the best part, what he never forgot—floating from an open window somewhere was the virtually patented double-track guitar of George Harrison, specifically on "My Sweet Lord," the song's title itself perhaps giving a holiness to the whole thing.

Aidan took naturally to mathematics as a child and in school. He went to University College Dublin and was the top student in several of his engineering classes. He even put in a summer in Amsterdam as a brick carrier on a construction site with some of his university pals, not managing to pack much muscle on his skinny frame but succeeding in—his brother who worked in the postal service had predicted it, or, more so, guaranteed it—losing his virginity to one of the city's chubby prostitutes.

▮ ▮ ▮

If Aidan had for years been watched and admired by Norman Cleary, as Norman later loudly claimed, told anybody who would listen, Aidan for one had never had any particular sense of that back in Kimmage.

▮ ▮ ▮

Even for an honors graduate in engineering who had distinguished himself, won prizes, there was little employment in Ireland then in the 1980s.

Aidan did manage to get contract work with a company for six months, and then with another for four, and though the second firm assured him they would certainly take him on when a permanent slot opened, one never seemed to materialize; he returned to work for the first company, but they soon reduced his status to a lower-salaried week-to-week position. When he read an ad in the business pages of the *Irish Times*, a call for electrical engineers for the large American electronics company based in Chicago and expanding its telecommunications manufacturing to the upcoming high-tech center of Austin, Texas, he applied. He figured the long-distance call came the very day they received his mailed resume. The manager in charge of personnel said that, naturally, they would need letters of recommendation from his university professors or past employers, yet, the way Aidan also figured it, the second call, hiring him, came before they even received those letters. The agreement would have him on the job within two months, which would allow him time to arrange for moving, along with the necessary visa paperwork.

Granted, Aidan was a bit scared of pulling up and leaving everything familiar to him, but he was definitely excited, too. Thanks to the bragging about Aidan from that older brother who worked for the PTT, Aidan became sort of a minor celebrity, not only in Kimmage but also in the pubs downtown that were frequented by classmates from UCD. People heard word that Aidan was emigrating, going to Texas, no less; everybody knew about Texas from the American movies over the years, knew about it most emphatically from the show *Dallas*, which had been re-running on Irish TV for what seemed forever. In the Bailey off Grafton Street, there amid the low light on the fine mahogany and brass, he would drink with his friends, and as somebody ordered still another round, Aidan almost got more drunk on the imagining of what lay ahead than on the stout itself. His friends recreated favorite episodes of *Dallas*, assuring each other that it wouldn't be long before Aidan owned a spread like Southfork, and it became a common gag for one of them to start humming the show's theme song whenever a grinning Aidan approached the gang of them again on his way back from a trip to the jacks. Somebody always seemed to be saying something along the lines of how he himself wouldn't mind "putting it to that little blond one" on the TV show, and the others agreed that they would *wholeheartedly* drink to that.

The crew at the Bailey now included Norman Cleary. He was closer to Aidan's brother's age, a few years older than Aidan, and he had grown up a couple of streets over in another one of those Kimmage row houses leased from the Corporation. In truth, when Aidan started frequenting the Bailey, he was surprised to find Norman there, and it couldn't be denied that the Bailey, with its writers and theater people, was a rather pretentious spot for even university types to drink at, let alone a garage mechanic like Norman. On the other hand, while Aidan hadn't seen much of Norman Cleary since Aidan was still in the aforementioned short pants, there was now something distinctive about the muscularly handsome Norman of the very black hair and the very fair skin and the very, and near startling, green eyes. There was also something about his master of ceremonies smoothness that made him far more fit for the posh Bailey, when you thought of it, than any of the brainy university engineering grads in Aidan's set. Norman was soon very much a regular in drinking with Aidan and his friends, and on Aidan's final evening in Dublin (he was to fly out the following night at three a.m., and he would spend the whole of the next day with his father), Norman led the toast to Aidan's good health and safe voyage. This was over at McDaid's, not far from the Bailey and more intimate. Norman spoke well in the toast, showing a poise and seriousness that, frankly, surprised Aidan. It was easy to see how Norman had dated a truly ravishing West German girl from UCD a couple of years earlier, while most of the legion of undergrads who pursued her failed to get anywhere, and it was easy to see how, as Aidan's brother had assured him, Norman was possibly the only male "on the whole bloody island, the North included," who didn't have to voyage to Amsterdam to finally surrender his virginity.

Everybody complimented Norman on the eloquence of his toast.

"He's a good man, a genius, this Aidan," Norman said, "and he deserves the best."

He looked right at Aidan with his green eyes, sincere. Aidan nodded.

"Thanks," Aidan said seriously, moved by the praise.

Then Norman changed the mood, laughed.

"Not that I'd let you go over there and have all that sweet Texas bum to yourself, mind you."

At which point, Norman opened the flap of his tweed sport jacket, slipped his hand into the inside pocket, and pulled out what he had "just happened to pick up" at the American Embassy consular section in Ballsbridge that afternoon; he showed them all his green Irish passport, complete with a temporary visa in back for the U.S., his destination being Austin, Texas, to be exact.

Norman had been telling himself for all too long that he should be doing something more with his life than wrestling with a spanner in a grimy garage, he explained to them at McDaid's that night, and with Aidan going off to Texas, that had given him a destination, he said, a plan at last and something to follow through on.

"You won't be alone there," he told Aidan, looking directly at him again, serious again, "you'll have a mate, you will."

Aidan had to admit that during the first few months in the States—living by himself without real friends, set up in a cramped one-room motel apartment with a grumbling window air conditioner off Interstate 35 in Austin—he looked forward to Norman eventually arriving. And, at first, when Norman did show and suggested they split the rent on that motel apartment ("One of us can sleep on the mattress, one on the spring—this kip would be a palace back in Kimmage"), Aidan didn't mind sharing (Norman, in his two months in the motel, never contributed an American dime to the rent), and it was good indeed to have Norman's cheery company, to ease Aidan's loneliness.

Aidan worked hard that first year. He realized that with this job he could solidly establish himself in the electronics industry, and his diligence translated to two quick promotions with the company in his second year in Austin. In the third, the man who had originally hired him, Dick Evans, started to take an obvious proprietary interest in Aidan's success. Dick Evans said the main offices in Chicago had approved the plan that he had mentioned to Aidan over dinner at Dick Evans's home in suburban West Lake Hills the month before.

▮ ▮ ▮

"This is all new," Dick Evans said. He was tanned, had a neatly styled haircut and an even-toned voice. "Why I want you for it is because we have to put our best foot forward and not come out of this with egg on our face. I know you won't disappoint me. I've always known that, since I first saw your resume."

Aidan couldn't help it, but sometimes he couldn't do anything but picture, actually envision in detail, the ridiculous clichés that filled Dick Evans's upbeat American speech—Aidan saw a foot in a polished Gucci loafer inching, well, just a bit forward, and he saw a smear of bright orange yolk on each of their shaved faces—though, naturally, Aidan did listen; he was, and always had been, appreciative of Dick Evans's support of him. Aidan was being tapped for a new joint venture between the School of Business at the University of Texas and several major businesses and banks in the city, a program called "The Executive MBA." It would allow him to keep working four days a week for the company while attending classes for two years, with concentrated instruction on Fridays and Saturdays.

Aidan recognized this as more than a lucky break, in fact. Admittedly, it was tough to cram in a full-time job with the classes there at the thoroughly impressive University of Texas campus with its lavish Spanish architecture and seemingly miles of terraced gardens, fountains, and wide pedestrian malls; yet the classes themselves, in marketing and macro-economics and the rest, were pretty easy compared to those he had to go through to earn that engineering BS back at University College Dublin. Aidan did well.

And Aidan started dating, learning about American women. But he didn't consider any of the relationships to be much more than passing. For a while he saw a young woman, prettily gap-toothed and pleasant, who worked in the company payroll offices as an assistant. Then it seemed as if one fellow engineer or another was always offering to fix him up with a friend of a girlfriend or wife, and so for a stretch there was a succession of different women. On a business trip for the company to Phoenix, he met a woman his age on the Air West flight; she was sitting by the window and he by the aisle, and with what at first seemed like miles of distance between them, the rust-red middle seat very empty, she struck him as entirely unapproachable—she looked so coolly blond, so faraway. Aidan flipped down the tray in front of him to do some work, and he noticed that she herself did the same, arranging some computer-printed spreadsheets:

"It never stops," she said, smiling.

"I suppose you're right about that," he said, "and it looks like you've got a bigger stack of it than me."

She laughed.

She worked for a medical insurance company that covered cities in the southwest and Florida, the "New America," she told him. They chatted for most of the short flight. They shared a cab from the airport into the city, and when he suggested dinner together, she said that she knew just the place for real interior-Mexico cuisine, after which she spent the night with him at the hotel room his company had booked for him downtown. He soon realized that her coolly blond image that had made her look so pristine and unapproachable on the plane, was more or less only that—an image and the way she carefully, maybe laboriously, put herself together, with the lightened hair, an awful lot of pancake, and what turned out to be contact lenses tinting her naturally brownish, even dull, eyes a vivid turquoise. The sex with her that first night, and on subsequent nights when she visited him in Austin or he saw her in Phoenix, her base, was in a word "wild." Nevertheless, Aidan suspected that it, too, was somewhat programmed, and she must have acquired most of her tips on "how to turn your man on" from women's magazines, which seemed to constitute her sole reading, never a book of any kind. She often talked about her body as the "menu" she was offering him for the evening, and she would take off her clothes after their preliminary energetic kissing and say in a singsong, standing naked before him, even modeling with various poses, some slow gymnastic contorting thrown in: "And, what would you like on the menu tonight, sir?" Who knows, Aidan might have been half addicted to it, until he eventually started fabricating excuses to cancel their rendezvous in either Austin or Phoenix, reminding her that with his MBA study intensifying he just didn't have all that much time for a long-distance affair.

Perhaps as an antidote, he next dated a literature graduate student he had met in the Cactus Café snack bar in the student union. She was an intelligent, serious young woman from a top-notch school in the East, Brown University, and she was working on a dissertation involving some rather complicated literary critical theory that looked more opaque than nuclear physics, or that was the way Aidan joked with her about it. She was red-headed and snub-nosed, pudgily buxom, and he appreciated how she didn't wear makeup, how she was always comfortable in her graduate student jeans and a loose

T-shirt or plain blouse; he even liked how she took an adamant pride in scoffing at everything materialistic, putt-putting around town in her ancient white Ford Escort that a local mechanic managed to keep running well. In fact, Aidan greatly enjoyed her friends, all quite bright and dedicated to their study, though he could find somewhat tiring their endlessly gossiping about the important research their own professors were or were not doing. Aidan wondered if he himself was on the right track with this so-called executive MBA, which seemed far removed from the mathematics that originally interested, and also challenged, him when younger. (He wondered if he might get a Ph.D. himself, change tack completely and try to become a professor. He also wondered if what he took to be that original love of math when young was only his pursuing it because he knew it was practical, would lead into engineering and land him a job, and he had to admit that if he could study *anything,* do the considerable work required for a Ph.D., he would like to delve into history or political science, the kind of thing that was always discouraged back in Ireland because such study seldom led to employment.) The sexual side of his dating the grad student wasn't very comfortable, he realized. She seemed to avoid acting affectionate around him when in the company of other female literature grad students, too conscious of what they would think in seeing her as a fawning woman. And after a party or their being together with his own friends from work, at a music nightclub or bar, she sometimes carried a coldness back to the bedroom, with loud argument on a couple of nights and her complaining of the overfrequency of their lovemaking. The relationship, like that with the young woman from Phoenix, didn't work out.

Of course, Aidan knew that most likely he never would veer from his current career path, and he knew, as well, that he continued to be entirely appreciative of this opportunity for study and Dick Evans's unwavering confidence and interest in him. Dick Evans even monitored Aidan's grades.

"You're making me proud"—Dick Evans smiled in approval when he said that at lunch one day—"damn proud."

It was while Aidan was studying for the MBA that he again began seeing more of Norman Cleary there in Austin. Which came, Aidan knew, after Aidan had for a time made an effort to avoid him.

Aidan had come to dismiss Norman's compliments—his repeatedly saying that Aidan was a genius and also saying that he, Norman, had been watching Aidan from afar, admiring how brilliant he was, ever since childhood in Kimmage—yes, Aidan decided that such talk was just part of Norman's con, right from the start. Norman had been broke when back in Dublin, and Aidan was now convinced that as soon as Norman heard that somebody from the neighborhood was heading to America, he made it a point to attach himself to him, even use his, Aidan's, name on his visa application as a sponsor, somebody with gainful employment in the States who could financially vouch for him. And it wasn't simply that Norman had freeloaded at that ridiculously cramped motel apartment next to the noisy freeway for a full two months, until Aidan managed to solve the problem only by moving to a new place of his own, and it wasn't simply that Aidan had lent Norman close to two thousand dollars in those first years, none of it repaid.

▮ ▮ ▮

It was something more than that—it was, well, *Norman.*

▮ ▮ ▮

Aidan might have been naive, and he knew he might also have been a hopeless product of his old-fashioned Catholic-school upbringing. Nevertheless, he had to admit that he was put off when drinking with Norman one Saturday night during the time they were both still holed up in the motel apartment (Aidan, as usual, paying for the Budweisers at the bar), true, Aidan was put off when Norman casually told him that he had gotten a girl pregnant back in Dublin not long before leaving; Norman laughed about it, said with a wink, "I never fancied myself the marrying kind." And Aidan hadn't pictured Norman as that either, but in Austin Norman eventually did, in fact, get married, and Aidan, considering himself wiser after Norman's mooching, understandably had suspicions about what was going on.

She must have been a dozen years older than Norman. She was divorced with two kids, living in a neat tract house in one of the good North Austin neighborhoods and teaching elementary school. Slim and polite, she was certainly attractive at her age, and right after the marriage Aidan was with the pair of them for a picnic one Sunday in the big and lushly verdant expanse of Austin's Zilker Park. Her two little kids ran around in the sunshine; Norman assured Aidan, as his new wife listened, that the marriage itself was all done in a whirlwind and something like that could happen when two people were so much in love. Norman then said he had to apologize to Aidan for there not having been a larger formal ceremony, to which he would surely have invited Aidan. The wife—noticeably reserved, in a tasteful blue smock with Mexican embroidery—appeared content to sit on the blanket spread on the grass and simply listen to Norman some more, gazing at him a little dreamily, Aidan told himself. Needless to say, Aidan had the strong feeling that the marriage was only Norman's way of assuring that the immigration service didn't keep bothering him about temporary visas. Still, Aidan tried to make himself believe that it might actually work, it might be something more than a ploy to acquire unchallengeable legal status. Because, if nothing else, at least during that day in the park Norman looked quite happy, and having a family seemed to bring out some equilibrium in him; also, it was better than the madness of Norman *before* marriage, when he had been becoming close to a joke in Texas, as he tried so hard to act so much like an American, one dispatched straight from Central Casting at that. (When Aidan went back to Dublin for a two-week vacation after his second year, he didn't tell anybody about the money he had foolishly given to Norman, but, rather, he kept his brother and friends heartily laughing with a description of decidedly handsome Norman in sandals, a pastel polo shirt, plaid Bermuda shorts, and Ray Ban aviator sunglasses, driving around town in a 1960s maroon Ford convertible that he had managed to put a payment down on with money he made on his latest job as a cable-line installer; the kicker of the story was that when Norman bought the creaking, mile-long crate it had been a hardtop—Norman, with his own garage experience, borrowed some blow-torch equipment from a pal and completely removed said steel hardtop, to assure he had the mandatory American convertible, *per-*

manently topless.) To repeat, Aidan wanted to believe the best, give Norman the benefit of the doubt concerning his marriage, but whenever Aidan did run into Norman around the city, it seemed, Norman was never with his wife; he was always with a different girl, always without his ring.

Aidan in time found himself definitely trying to avoid Norman—for nearly three years—though he couldn't help but have to deal with him now and then, which meant the expected minor disasters. There was too often the scenario of Aidan introducing Norman to whomever he was with, a friend from work maybe, and then the inevitable report later of Norman hitting on that somebody—if it were a man, for money, or if a woman, for dating that would just lead to Norman taking full selfish advantage, only looking for some recreation outside his marriage. Then there came two specific and very painful incidents.

Having not seen Norman in Austin for months, Aidan one evening took him up on an invitation to hear Norman and his band play at a local pub that was bringing in entertainment every night for a full week before St. Patrick's Day. On a whim, Norman had organized some friends for what he referred to as a "traditional Irish bunch"; the friends were musicians who could function reasonably well with guitar, penny-whistle, and drums, and Norman appointed himself lead singer for the group, called (Norman said it took him a month to concoct a perfect name) the Bogside Rover Boys. He had business cards advertising the band—buff and printed in kelly green, with a shamrock in one corner—made up to hand out to anybody who might be interested in having music for a private party or such. Norman didn't really consider them professionals ready for regular bar entertainment, he was honest about that, and he confided to Aidan that if the band had any useful professional application, it was for his meeting more people around town, therefore increasing his standing with—and spreading good will on behalf of—the cable TV company he worked for. He had an overseer's job there now; Aidan had heard that Norman rose fast in the company, especially after Norman apparently continued to work and fill in on extra shifts during a strike organized by fellow installers. Gone, it should be added, was Norman's former comic American guise, and all that Aidan could conclude was that Norman must have seen better advantage in becoming the Genuine Irishman, one sure enough of himself in that role that he didn't mind being part of something as ludicrous as this corny Irish band. But Aidan did have to give him credit for his singing, and he soon conceded that Norman's voice was very good—most impressively strong and clear on the tear-jerking standard of "The Ballad of Kevin Barry." During that one night Aidan heard them, when the band performed as part of the week-long St. Patrick's Day fest, there was free Guinness from the bar's owner for Norman and the band, as well as for the contingent of other Irish who gathered with them at a table in the place. It was packed, the smoke thick and wafting marbleized yellow, which reminded Aidan, nicely so, of pubs in Dublin, even if the watery "American Guinness" was nothing like the real thing back home. The trouble began when a skinny kid, who was at the university on a track scholarship from somewhere in the west of Ireland, possibly Mayo, turned noisy in his drunkenness, happily enjoying himself in the full celebration of a holiday that was, in truth, more or less simply a tourist event in Ireland. The kid got quite loud in his excitement, and, taking a break from playing and now sitting at the table with Aidan and the others, a stern Norman barked at the kid:

"Quiet, will ye. This is no place to be embarrassing our people."

The kid, with a boy's acne and droopy eyes, suddenly looked crushed, and sitting there beside the kid, Aidan wasn't about to let Norman bully him; after all, the kid was *only* a kid.

"Easy, Norman," Aidan told Norman outright; he was serious.

"Easy, my arse," Norman gruffly dismissed Aidan, turning back to the kid. "Behave yourself, and never forget who you are, who you represent."

"For fuck's sake, Norman," Aidan said, inadvertently slipping into his own full Kimmage brogue, "what are you trying to turn this into, the fucking Saga of the Irish in America?"

At which point Aidan slammed down his half-finished pint glass. Obviously upset, rattled, he shook his head, walked out.

Aidan didn't expect to hear from Norman, who called him just two weeks later, surprisingly, with no mention of the exchange, but to ask Aidan a favor. Norman wanted to know if, by chance, Aidan had a copy of his University College Dublin diploma with him; to which Aidan answered, without thinking, that he did, or he was quite certain it was with some other papers he had somewhere, anyway. Norman then talked a good deal about how he himself now had an opportunity he might never have again, and all that Aidan had to do was to say no if he didn't relish the idea. However, Norman assured Aidan that if he agreed, it would be very easy. Norman said he was being seriously considered for a job managing a restaurant owned by a national chain that was opening one of its upscale places in Austin, and Norman said he knew it was time for him to move on from the cable company and get experience in a field where he might apply his real strengths. He said he was always aware that he had a unique knack for dealing with people, the pure power of his personality, and he was destined for something like the service industry, in this case the restaurant trade; learning the business now as a manager would give him the experience he needed, so he could open a restaurant of his own someday. Aidan listened as Norman kept on speaking in his measured tones about how he would understand if Aidan didn't want to do it, and Norman laid on the usual flattery, about how he honestly did admire Aidan, and if Aidan hadn't set the course for him, he himself would never had mustered the spunk to leave everything behind at home and come to America. That done, Norman moved to the heart of the matter, began stating directly what he needed, explaining that he had a friend in a photocopy shop who could handle the details, find the right kind of paper and the rest. It would merely entail preparing an exact duplicate of Aidan's diploma, then doctoring it a little to affix his own name. Norman emphasized:

"Why these bollocks need a diploma for somebody managing a restaurant, who the hell knows, Aidan, but I have this chance now, a chance that might never pass my way again."

And this was the second painful incident, coming not long after the first, with the kid at the bar. Norman's mistake in his petition,

Aidan later thought, was that with Norman indulging in so much prefacing, his usual supposedly sincere talk laced with accolades about Aidan, Norman had given Aidan time to think, to organize himself and be firm. Aidan also figured that Norman phoning him only weeks after the run-in at the bar was understandable: Norman probably felt that he was the one who had been in the right then, convinced that Aidan knew that he, Aidan, had behaved badly, making a spectacle of himself by storming out of the place, which might mean that Aidan would feel apologetic and softened, ready for this current proposal. But Aidan was well beyond falling for Norman's maneuvering, including the repeated claim of Norman having observed and admired Aidan since they had been scruffy kids in those Kimmage streets. Aidan suspected that there might not really be a job Norman was pursuing at the moment (even though Norman was specific about it, claimed it was the Ristorante Mezzaluna in a new shopping complex up by the stylish Aboretum, most likely more hot air), and Aidan wouldn't have been surprised if Norman just wanted a forged diploma for whatever future use he might make of it.

"I can't do that, Norman," Aidan told him flatly on the phone. "I really can't. It's totally out of the question."

He didn't hear from Norman for a very long stretch after that.

But when Aidan was suffering through a low period again, when none of his relationships with the women he continued to meet seemed to lead to anything and when he began questioning again the whole course of his own career, it was Norman to whom he expressed his concerns.

And Norman listened, let him pour it out as an old friend.

▮ ▮ ▮

They were both older.

Aidan had long since finished the MBA, with honors, Dick Evans throwing a graduation party for him at his large home in West Lake Hills. Norman was divorced and currently in real estate sales, which definitely were booming, now that more electronics companies were moving from California to Austin in the 1990s. Aidan and Norman had gotten into the pattern of having a once-a-week meal together, if only for old times' sake and to talk of friends and family in Dublin. They could now even joke about things, like the crazy way that Norman had slowly and smilingly produced the passport with the visa as lifted from his tweed sport jacket back in McDaid's on Harry Street, and the episode about the diploma, too.

"I must have been out of my mind," Norman laughed

"Yeah, you must have been, completely daft and then some," Aidan laughed. "The pure *cheek* of it."

There seemed to have emerged an easy honesty between them.

Aidan confessed to Norman how he still questioned his own career, and how he had had such little luck in finding the right woman. And he could tell that Norman understood, was concerned. And Norman often talked about the sadness of his own divorce, and, as Norman said, so what if the marriage had given him the permanent legal immigration status that he might have been seeking all along? He admitted he was ashamed about how he had acted toward Elizabeth, the woman wearing—Aidan remembered this, pictured it clearly—the embroidered blue Mexican smock that afternoon when Aidan had met her in sunny Zilker Park, looking absolutely happy, pleased to be with handsome Norman; Norman said he missed the two children of hers, who had become almost like his own. But Norman added that Elizabeth was indeed older, a dozen years was a big difference, and Aidan had to understand that situation; she was too old for him, really, and if he had hurt her with his string of affairs, he hadn't really meant to. Aidan listened, did understand, and Aidan confessed to him how goddamn lonely he himself was sometimes. They continued with the weekly dinners. Then one morning at a managerial planning meeting for the company, the kind of session that now included Aidan, too, Dick Evans called Aidan aside, asked if he had a moment to talk about something. They were in a corridor.

"Well, I did recommend him," Dick Evans said, "figuring he was a friend of yours from way back, and a fellow countryman, I suppose. I just thought I'd let you know."

Aidan reddened, trying to appear relaxed about it.

"He's kind of a character, Dick. I can tell you that," Aidan said. "I guess it was my own fault. I still see him now and then, and I must have been talking too much about you, about all you've done for me."

"Now let's not get started on that," Dick Evans said, smiling.

"Believe me, I never told him to contact you, or use your name."

Dick Evans was a man so fair, reasonable, and essentially wholehearted in his belief in Aidan, that he did go as far as vouch for a—could he be described any other way?—*snake* like Norman Cleary. It seemed that Norman was switching from one real estate firm to another, this latest one an outfit that hoped to cash in even more on the sale of pricey housing to high-tech people, maybe some from Aidan's own electronics company, and apparently Norman had put down Dick Evans's name as a reference to get the job. Norman had never so much as met Dick Evans, yet Dick Evans's recommendation came on his casual knowledge of Norman's association with Aidan. Aidan was furious. He phoned Norman that night.

"Jaysus, Aidan," Norman nonchalantly defended himself, "how the hell did I even know one of them would call your big-shot friend Evans. Nobody ever follows through with those references, they just want names. I knew it would be good to have somebody from your company on my list, seeing that professionals and execs of that sort will be the target clientele for the houses we sell."

Aidan, his head already filled with the envisioning of potential swindles that Norman might perpetrate on any future sales he landed by using Dick Evans's good name, told Norman that he had *finally* had it with him, this was the *last* time that he was going to let himself be used or suckered by him.

"You're a fucking chancer, Cleary," Aidan told him.

"Will you listen to yourself, Aidan, getting worked up about nothing. It was just a reference. You talked about him, so I used his name. I got the job. It all worked out fine."

Norman simply wasn't bothered by Aidan's anger—whatsoever.

"Relax, OK?" he said to Aidan.

"This is the *very last* time, Cleary, I can tell you that!"

Aidan told him to please never call him again.

■ ■ ■

Through two Irish brothers, doctors who had emigrated to Austin, Aidan met the woman he would eventually marry.

It was an arranged pairing, in a way. The brothers had hired the younger sister of their best friend from medical school back in Dublin to come over to the States and work for them as a receptionist, with secret hopes that she would prove right for Aidan; they had gotten to know him through the Irish community in Austin, and they were convinced the two would be perfect for each other. Her name was Brigid Anne. She was twenty-two, had taught Montessori school classes in Dublin's Dartry suburb, and had a certain life in her, an energy, as well as a sweetness that Aidan had not found in any of the women he dated in America. She was also entirely beautiful. Almost as tall as Aidan, she walked with perfect posture, a slim body athletically lithe; her cheekbones were high, her eyes a near colorless blue, and her nose strong and long, but not in any flawed way—the features were maybe those of a classical Roman statue (the ancient Romans had once colonized Ireland, hadn't they?) or those of a born stage actress who had the facial definition needed for projecting well in a theater. She had a habit of reaching up with both hands to fluff her cascading hair, push it back from her temples; it wasn't any affectation or to call attention to the glossy, truly full mane of it, but somehow it just spoke an alluring in-betweenness of age, a woman with a girl's long hair that she didn't quite know what to do with, the gesture almost saying each time she did it: "I know, I should cut this hair, but I hate to think that by doing so it will mean that at last I have to grow up." Aidan knew that he was enamored with her from the start, and as he tried to impress her by taking her to some of the most expensive restaurants in the city—often the one in the lavish Driskill Hotel downtown, frequented by high-rolling lobbyists and the state legislators they were wooing, where a bottle of vintage red wine alone was an easy sixty or seventy-five dollars—yes, while he made the effort to impress her at the Driskill and elsewhere, she would sit there, very beautiful and sometimes maybe turning quiet, finally telling him softly but rather chidingly in her wonderful Dublin intonation when she took a look at the bill, before Aidan could slip his wallet from his blazer pocket for a credit card to pay with:

"Aidan Conroy, you might be minding all that money you earn a bit better than this."

Perfect.

She talked about her work at the Montessori school as if she had cared very much about those little kids, she even talked about the patients who came into the office of the two doctor brothers she currently worked for—orthopedic MD's—as if she cared very much about those grumpy people, their ailments becoming her own concern. It took Aidan some time to win her, and while if it were up to him he would have married her a week after their first date, she said that she needed more time, wanted to be certain that he was certain. Which he respected. They were married back in Dublin, right before the company assigned Aidan (at last sure of the importance of his career, also sure of having found the love of his life) to a solid executive position in the Chicago home offices.

He acquired full dual citizenship. He would always be Irish but was now certainly an American, too.

▮ ▮ ▮

It snowed so much in Chicago.

And it happened during a particularly blizzard-blurred winter, when Aidan was always barely managing to get out of plowed O'Hare one day and then back into it the next, making another quick overnight trip for the company; he traveled more on his job lately. He went to the Austin offices on this trip, and with his meetings and business for the company completed there and before flying home, he had lunch with one of the doctor brothers for whom Brigid Anne had worked. It was balmy enough to dine outside on the restaurant's terrace there in the honey sunshine of Austin in winter, the palmettos all around them rattling their sharp spears in the welcome warm breeze. The doctor, Joe Nugent, listened to Aidan fill him in on all the news of Brigid Anne and the three children, two boys and a girl now, up in Chicago, and when they were enjoying a coffee afterward, Joe Nugent added as an aside:

"And I was sorry to hear about your friend Norman Cleary, the accident."

"Norman?" Aidan asked. "An accident?"

Apparently, Norman had been killed in a mishap on Lake Travis outside of Austin the fall before. Norman had been in an overpowered cigarette boat. Joe Nugent said cigarette boats shouldn't even be allowed on the lake for reasons of their noise alone (the echoing racket of one of them shattering the glass in the picture window of a waterside home of a radiologist Joe Nugent knew), and there was the sheer speed of such boats in that blue expanse surrounded by dry cactus hills being quite dangerous: Joe Nugent said Lake Travis could look very large until you tried to negotiate a simple turn at fifty or sixty miles an hour in a cigarette boat—at which point the lake didn't prove to be that big at all. Of course, Aidan knew of Norman's success, how he had used the money he made during the real estate boom to finance first a single film shot in Austin, as a chance investment, before going into movie-making as his full-time occupation. Before long, Norman had negotiated a deal with Sony to expand his operation. He became a major financial backer for films shot locally (which meant a "producer," as Aidan understood it); he had emerged as somebody who had the reputation of being wise enough to capitalize on letting the creative decisions be made by those recruited from the pool of exceptional young talent available at the University of Texas's renowned graduate film school, and wise enough, too, to know that the major West Coast companies were keenly interested in on-location shooting and production in Texas, a state free of the usual entertainment-industry labor unions. Aidan knew all about Norman's success, and Aidan's own brother had sent him a long profile piece on Norman that appeared in a Dublin magazine detailing it, but Aidan certainly hadn't heard word of his death. Joe Nugent explained there had been extensive coverage in the Austin paper, also on the TV stations. It seemed that Norman had been out for the afternoon with a bunch of people from the so-called industry in that luxurious cigarette boat of his, which, to

Aidan, sounded thoroughly in character with Norman's grand Texas lifestyle as described in the magazine piece. Joe Nugent said there had been a lack of rain that fall, and the cigarette boat hit a sand shoal usually deeper in the water; the boat flipped like a tossed matchbox, everybody else thrown free to the cushiony wet, except for Norman at the wheel. Norman was killed instantly, having suffered a massive head injury, Joe Nugent was quite sure. The news came too fast for Aidan to properly respond then, but subsequently, all through the long winter, Aidan found himself thinking more and more of Norman.

Sometimes Aidan felt poorly because of his falling out with Norman, and he rehashed their arguments. And sometimes he felt poorly because the truth of the matter was possibly much larger than that. Aidan saw the events in a chain, thinking how, as it turned out, Norman would never have ended up in Austin to be killed by a thirty-eight-foot, half-million-dollar cigarette boat flipping over if Aidan *hadn't* decided to emigrate to Texas, if because of that Norman *hadn't* embarked on the plan to follow Aidan there, and . . . and . . . but Aidan caught himself, he knew that such reasoning was a far-fetched reading of the whole thing, and he shouldn't affix any blame whatsoever on himself for what had happened, that's for sure.

But he did harbor some dark, perhaps strange other thoughts concerning Norman's death, and worst was how Aidan couldn't help but occasionally take real satisfaction in the fact that he had won at last, so to speak, and now Norman Cleary would *never* be able to take advantage of him again—Aidan somehow felt finally liberated, free from something that had plagued him for a very long time in his life.

▮ ▮ ▮

Sipping a scotch late one night after his children had been put to bed, in the dark and relaxing on the big naugahyde sofa there in the glassed-in back porch converted to a den, Aidan sat alone and watched the snow falling outside, the clusters of birches in the spacious backyard of the house in suburban Winnetka snakily white themselves, almost ghostly. He sipped, and for some reason, he was just staring at the snow, so heavy that it seemed there was before his eyes one of those celluloid rolls they used to employ in the movies to mimic snow; it kept coming, very steadily, very hypnotically. Then for a few minutes it was as if he wasn't sitting there in the shadowed blue darkness at all, the amber scotch in hand, but he was walking home from school again as a child in Kimmage, coming upon—in the late afternoon and amid the budding of Dublin in early spring, the sky a cloudless blue—the scene of the older boys playing soccer, what he often drifted into picturing lately; that moment had become sort of his own little prayer, as it represented a true happiness that once seemed forever lost to Aidan, but that he had more than found again with Brigid Anne and in the contentment of his current family life. *The sound of the ball echoing with each solid kick, and the George Harrison song, his riffing guitar on "My Sweet Lord"—how perfect it was, how fine!* Aidan sipped the scotch, smokily aromatic, and he told himself that it almost wasn't right, not at all fair, in a way, for him or anybody else to be this happy. (Only a couple of years later would his drinking get very bad, the Irishman's curse, Aidan would admit to himself; and only later, in the course of their arguing about the drinking, the constant fighting about a lot of things, would Brigid Anne confess that she had known Norman Cleary when she first got to Austin—it seemed that she had met Norman in a trendy Sixth Street club, she was there with some other girls, and how could anybody *not* be attracted to him, she said, with those deep-green eyes and that strong build of his, the way with words he had; she admitted she had slept with him that very night, which was prior to her being introduced to Aidan and their eventually dating seriously.) Aidan now looked out the windows there on the glassed-in porch of his fine home some more, the snow right out of the old Joyce short story, Aidan told himself, and he thought how everything had turned out well indeed.

He was happy.

▮ ▮ ▮

"I'm *so* goddamn happy," Aidan said aloud and grateful, pretty drunk.

ADDITIONAL NOTES CONCERNING THE ELEVATOR IN THE DICTATOR'S PALACE

It is on the second floor.

Or, more exactly, the elevator is stopped and left forever open like that for display on the second floor of the palace.

The palace itself is in Catete in Rio de Janeiro, today but an everyday neighborhood and far from fashionable.

The palace is a faded pink, block-shaped building, three stories, with ornate white trim and many long windows; it was built in the mid-nineteenth century by a Brazilian coffee-growing magnate of German descent. The facade of the building, showing its set of big carved wood doors for the entrance, is almost flush with Rua do Catete, there in the neighborhood's main commercial pocket. The area has some colonial buildings and more nineteenth-century buildings, pastel masonry, with apartments upstairs and all manner of open-fronted enterprises lower down—shabby lunch counters, cluttered shops for anything from stationery to kitchen appliances, and who knows how many *botecos,* or bars; the *botecos* are of the sort where the flimsy plastic tables and chairs provided by the major *cerveja* companies—royal blue for Antarctica, canary yellow for Skol—are constantly arranged and rearranged on the sidewalk out front by attentive waiters and where the tall brown bottles always come served in insulating sleeves, rather grimy foam plastic, also provided by the beer companies.

The street has four lanes and is one-way. At the intersection where the palace is, on the corner with Rua Silveira Martins, the taxis coming down busy Rua do Catete, packs of them, float to

stops, jockey for position in the lanes at the traffic signal—then, when the light changes, they move off again in a collective swooshing acceleration. The sidewalks in Catete are lumpy, uneven black-and-white mosaic tiles like just about all the sidewalks in Rio, something tracing back to the sidewalks in Lisbon, apparently; street boys sleep in nooks here and there, shirtless and shoeless in the heat and dreaming whatever street boys do dream amid all the graffiti—graffiti itself being an entity that sometimes seems to define Rio. There is also a fine public park behind the palace, once the palace's private gardens, shady with flowering fruit trees and mop-headed palms and many massive ancient banyan trees showing sturdy trunks of thick, vine-like growth entwining upward, like the fingers of some fairy-tale giant. There is an ornamental duck pond in the park (*"I get so scared sometimes," you said to me*), and there is a decidedly formal garage building, six doors in front and its faded pink hue matching that of the palace; there, the big Cadillacs of the dictator were once housed, and reportedly it is where his police, under the direction of his brutal, hated brother, swerved in at all hours of the dark tropical night in their own unmarked sedans, transporting another suspect sitting beaten and cuffed in the rear seat, to be brought through secret passages to the adjoining old residences, which back up to the park and face the Rua Ferreira Viana. Those residences had been commandeered and the buildings converted into interrogation rooms and holding cells, as all the promise of the dictator's first years in power in the 1930s, a man of the people, indeed, metamorphosed into the growing paranoia of his last years in power, the early 1950s, when he did put that brother in charge of the police; his closest advisers, many of the generals, told him that appointing the brother was a large mistake.

The sea is not far away, beyond the far end of the park and across the very busy oceanside freeway that winds along Flamengo Beach. Flamengo Beach is too polluted for swimming now despite its long, wide sweep of handsome white sands (*"I mean, I get so scared about everything, Jack, I really do," you said to me, whispery*); the beach, maybe a couple of miles all told, and the shimmering blue water of Guanabara Bay that it faces are tucked in by the kind of jagged green mountains that just sprout up everywhere in Rio, as common, surely, as those dreams upon dreams fueled by the broken street boys sleeping.

The palace, now called the Museum of the Republic, hasn't been regularly used as a palace since the death of the dictator, on the morning of August 24, 1954. The dictator committed suicide in his bedroom on the third floor after he was informed that the military was on its way from the central barracks and coming to the palace, to demand his resignation; he was over seventy, and in a botched attempt to have a journalist assassinated outside of the journalist's apartment in Copacabana—a journalist who had ignored censorship and had been altogether too daring in his loud criticism of the regime—yes, during that attempt an Air Force officer who was with the journalist had been accidentally shot and killed, and the military and most everybody else simply could not accept that. There was rioting in downtown Rio and rallies for the opposition in the city's main square, Praça XV; there were charges that it was the dictator's son who ordered the murder, then charges that it was the dictator's manipulative adult daughter, to whom he had often turned over routine affairs of state as he got older, who ordered the murder. However, as it turned out it was not a family member but one of his own inner circle who did so—the dictator had nothing whatsoever to do with it. In another of those odd facets of Brazil that marks its complicated history and maybe more complicated national character, it was the sole black member of the inner circle, head of the elite Palace Guard and a man who had worked his way up from poverty, who personally ordered the killing, totally on his own; historians inevitably point out that he was somebody who the poor in the *favelas*—those hillside slums that continue to grow, continue to threaten to swallow and finally devour the entire city whole some day—often cited as one of their own and good evidence of the dictator being, therefore, one of their own because he had entrusted the man, a *preto* with humble beginnings, with such a high office.

The truth of the matter is, the dictator wasn't a thug.

He was from a prominent land-owning family in the handsome southernmost region of the country, Rio Grande do Sul, toward Argentina. He had distinguished himself at the prestigious military academy there as a young man, then studied law; he spoke French fluently. Of course, he had seized power by force in 1930, and he had subsequently dissolved the legislature in 1937, proclaiming his so-called Estado Novo regime, the New State, and himself the supreme head of it, a dictator, but he had also raised wages for workers and built schools and many agricultural facilities throughout the country. Even when finally ousted, after elections were reinstituted following World War II, he quietly retreated to the south for a few years and then managed to come out of his exile like a hailed returning Napoleon, summoned to leadership by his network of political cronies who had stayed on in the capital, never disbanding; managing to play along with the people's current need for this ritual of an electoral process, he became a legitimate candidate and won the vote, installed himself in the Presidential Palace once more. And once more he was exactly what he had always been, the democratic process of elections restored or not—the dictator.

Of course, the palace had no elevator at the time of original construction. The elevator was added to the building several years after this coffee magnate's mansion was converted to the Presidential Palace in 1897. The palace served as such until 1960, the year the capital of the nation was moved from Rio de Janeiro to perhaps that strangest of all strange dreams, a completely new major world city of miles and miles of daringly futuristic architecture and looping freeways leading nowhere there on the windswept high plains of the far interior, Brasilia. Or, more exactly, the Presidential Palace was at least officially designated as the residence until 1960, because after 1954 and the suicide no head of state spent all that much time at the palace (*what did you say that afternoon? what did you say to me after we each went our separate way there in the museum, as we always did when in a museum? and I, who had been wandering the rooms on my own, I found you standing in front of the elevator, no*

longer used and today a display in itself, and silently staring at it, looking so lovely, with your auburn hair loose and wearing simple white slacks and a simple white blouse, the rope-soled canvas espadrilles, blue, that you thought would be good for walking now that we had both realized that this trip to Brazil and the week at the beach there in Ipanema wasn't working, as we finally admitted that none of that was helping any of it—we couldn't get away from what we had to get away from back home just by resorting to geography, just by taking ourselves several thousand miles from home on a jet hissing on and on in the night through so much darkness, another continent altogether—and I suppose that morning we agreed at the hotel, exhausted with talking any more about any of it at that point, realizing that it was getting us nowhere, we wearily agreed that if in Rio we should at least see some of the city other than the beach and its tourists out there in Ipanema, there was downtown Rio, its wide boulevards and many monuments, there was the Opera House, and there was the infamous Presidential Palace in Catete, and how did you put it when I came up behind you in the empty museum? you were standing there, half lost in thought, I suppose, still staring at the elevator, your voice whispery as you turned to face me, your very rare gray eyes looking right at me and suddenly more lovely than ever, but more fragile and vulnerable than ever, too, as I felt worse than ever about what I had done, asking myself yet again how I could ever have done what I had done—you said to me: "I get so scared sometimes. I mean, I get so scared about everything, Jack, I really do"), and, in truth, the Presidential Palace was seldom the full-time residence for any head of state after 1954; plans for it to become a museum were announced in 1960. The elevator, which is left open that way for the display, on the second floor, was built by the American company Otis.

The Presidential Palace, a place usually quite empty even as the museum that it is today, has on the first floor several very new galleries; they are darkened, windowless rooms of black walls and modern track lighting, with artifacts and photographs and framed copies of old newspapers, all documenting events in the history of the Republic.

Also on the first floor, in back and overlooking the well-groomed gardens, there is the long room called the Ministerial Hall, which was used as an operations headquarters during World War II. It was here that the dictator gathered his ministers and top brass from the various branches of the military around the huge table for reports and decisions, and set out in front of the twelve high-backed chairs now are old green leather portfolios, stamped with the official escutcheon of the nation in gold. At this table Brazil formally declared war on Germany and Italy in 1942, though that came about only after much early sympathy with, and even frank admiration of, the fascistic Axis cause, as elsewhere on the continent; perhaps, in essence, the declaration was merely a gesture to ensure the dictator continuing approval from the United States, including the substantial military aid that did result.

A marble staircase, milkily white and flanked by smooth, thick marble railings, is carpeted in red and leads up to the second floor. It is a large, wide staircase that conjures up words like "grand" or "ceremonial," and the rooms on the second floor have kept the names given to them by the original inhabitant, the coffee magnate who built the place, once one of the wealthiest men in the country, probably in all of South America as well. They are laid out around the periphery of the main staircase.

There is the Noble Hall, running the full length of the front of the building, with a gilt-trimmed embossed ceiling, glistening chandeliers, and long pleated drapes, also a true expanse of polished wood floor in a herringbone pattern; it was a room for balls and the formal receptions honoring diplomats and heads of state.

There is the Blue Hall, also called the French Hall, where that is the color of the motif for the wallpaper and furniture and intricately patterned carpets, Louis XIV and XV, apparently.

There is the Yellow Hall, also called the Venetian Hall, and the decor works on a motif of that color in its various shadings and gradations, thoroughly Italianate.

There is the Chapel, which itself is a single room, but with the drapes drawn a rather dim one, dust motes suspended in the shafts of sunlight that do peek through the uneven meeting of the drapes here and there; there is dark-wood furniture and a small, carved dark-wood altar up front, though the furniture is arranged in clusters, more or less like that in a parlor rather than as in what it is, a chapel—apparently, in large country estates of the day in Brazil there was always a separate chapel building on the premises for family worship, yet here, in the city, that had to be incorporated into the mansion proper.

There is the Moorish Hall, an exercise in considerable arabesque detailing for all the embellished trappings and, in a way, a good reflection of the fascination with things whimsily exotic, the categorically Oriental, of that nineteenth century.

There is the Banquet Hall, located directly above the Ministerial Hall below, in the rear and again overlooking the lush gardens, where the hibiscus seem to perpetually blossom their full fleshy scarlet, the oleanders show their repeated punctuating stars of bursting bright white; each place at this table is set with fine china and silverware, and along the walls are glass-doored cabinets, ceiling-high, with more of the antique china, more silver place settings and at least a half-dozen polished tea services.

It probably is true that even on days when the museum does have more people—when it isn't as empty as on a weekday afternoon in the heat, maybe on a Sunday when there is no admission charge—most of those who visit then probably go directly to the third floor and the bedroom that has been kept exactly as the dictator left it; actually, it could be that few visitors even as much as

linger amongst all that very faded opulence of the several named rooms on the second floor. If a wide marble staircase leads to the second floor, there is but a narrow angular set of steps, yet again white marble, leading to that top, third floor, so cramped, in fact, that if there might be heard somebody coming down the steps, then somebody going up the steps would most likely wait before ascending, just to avoid having to squeeze by. At the head of the stairs is a uniformed guard like all the uniformed guards, female, who maybe politely nods, and then there is the bedroom itself, the only room open to visitors on the third floor, which formerly must have been devoted entirely to living quarters. It is very large but uncluttered, unlike the formal named rooms below, with plain pale-green walls devoid of any pictures, a dark hardwood floor, gold drapes for the long windows; the furniture—the double bed, the several sideboards and chests with mirrors, the two night tables—are of a design, vaguely Art Deco and tortoiseshell-grain veneer, that must have been considered very fashionable in about 1930, when the dictator and his wife did first occupy the premises. The spread on the bed is dark-blue satin; there is a small bedside lamp with an amber shade on each of the night tables, and attached to each lamp is a frayed electric cord operated by an old-fashioned click switch on the cord. In the somewhat stark expanse of it all, or emptiness, there is a newer chaise-longue recliner upholstered in olive faux leather; there is a single, round tortoiseshell-veneer table exactly in the middle of the room's rectangle with two wing-back chairs upholstered in the same functional olive faux leather, and set on the table is a black bakelite telephone from the period, bulky and rotary-dialed.

In the far rear corner is a showcase. In the showcase, displayed flattened-out for viewing, is a man's silk pajama shirt, seeming very old. It is gray-and-white striped, with a torn hole the size of a small coin right at the embroidered monogram on the single breast pocket, where one's heart would be, and the puncture is edged with dried brown blood. Also in the showcase, placed beside the pajama shirt on the black velvet, is a revolver, nickel-plated and the handle pearl, and beside that is one lead slug; dull gray, pitted as if by corrosion, the slug really isn't in the shape of a bullet, but now more like the lump of a pebble, lopsided, even amorphous. There is a photograph copy of a small page with the handwritten note that the dictator left, the text of it firmly, albeit melodramatically, proclaiming to the nation what he personally saw as his selflessness and utter patriotism right to the end.

There is also a certainly dated bathroom, quite large, high-ceilinged and with two more of the long upright windows; the room is essentially aging white tile for the floor and walls, and aging white porcelain for the sink and the bidet and the toilet and the bathtub on legs, the old chrome fixtures lusterless and the finish worn through to the yellowish brass in spots.

On one of the sideboards in the bedroom, next to the door to the bathroom, is a clock in a casing of frilled gold, the only object distinctly decorative in the room; beside the clock is a standard office-style prop-up calendar on a brown plastic base, a pad with one page for each day, and, true to the event of the suicide, the page left displayed shows the large numeral "24" in bold red and below that the day of the week, "Sexta-feira," and the month, "Agosto," both in bold black. Actually, the room's pale-green walls aren't completely bare because there is one oil painting, above this sideboard, and it is a portrait of the dictator.

He must have posed for it later in life. He is wearing a formal black cutaway, the green-and-yellow silk sash that indicates his position as head of state making for a diagonal across the vertical row of pearl studs of the starched, high-collar shirt and bearing several medals. Looking at the painting, it is easy to discern that he wasn't a very big man in stature—or, there's something about how he appears to be purposefully jutting out his chest, cock-of-the-roost fashion, that betrays the truth that he had to assert himself, he wasn't imposing. His eyes are dark, his nose thin and somewhat beak-like, his receding gray hair combed back straight from his forehead for this semi-profile pose. In a way, he does look in this portrait rather thuggish, and granted he did come from an old, established land-owning family, granted he was very well educated and did speak and read French fluently, having a fresh supply of history books in that language delivered to him from Paris monthly, other anecdotes in the biographies indicate another side of him.

On Sunday evenings he would sometimes leave the palace, with his wife and a single bodyguard, to walk to the garage in the gardens in back and get behind the wheel of a Cadillac, not one of the armored official limousines, always chauffeur driven, but the powder-blue soft-top convertible he kept for his personal use; wearing casual clothes, he would drive the Cadillac—slowly, ostentatiously—the few blocks along wide Rua do Catete to the other end of the Catete neighborhood, still very elegant then and not run-down like today, and go to one of the three movie theaters on the Largo do Machado, the central square there. Or, to be more specific, he would never fail to go to a film in such a theater whenever there was a new American Western playing on what must have been the sort of huge screen common in that period, the sound track blaring loud with guns whistlingly ricocheting and overdramatic stagecoach-chase music in that large darkness surrounding the shadowy audience; he often spoke of how much he enjoyed a good Western.

And in the journals he kept regularly, the jotted notes of his daily activities, he expresses in one entry several lines of remorse about having to have his police beat up, bloodily, the son of a prominent architect that morning, the young man being a student who was arrested and suspected of expressing Communist sympathies at the university in Rio; then in the next several lines summarizing the rest of his day's activity, he casually notes how pleasant a time he had later that evening attending a lawn party for a *churrasco*—barbecue—at the lovely home of society friends of his wife's family in the definitely very exclusive Gávea district.

In the palace, if there is the narrow set of steps that leads up to and then down again from the bedroom of the dictator, it only makes sense that beside those stairs, functionally positioned, is where the elevator would be installed, doors left open now, as said, for the display back on the second floor.

The exact year the elevator was added to the palace was 1906.

It was ordered from that American company Otis, as also said; the manufacturer is announced on a bronze plaque affixed to its rear wall, right next to a routine square white card in a small frame providing information—in a black cursive script and entered on the printed lines there—concerning the capacity, in the number of persons the apparatus could accommodate as well as the weight limit in kilos. The elevator is not very big; it is, very much so, a residential elevator.

Seeing that the varnished mahogany doors are now left open like that for the display, a swaybacked gold velvet cord across the entrance ensures looking but not entering by those who visit the museum. And how the elevator is outfitted is in keeping with such a setting as this, a Presidential Palace. It has two gilt-framed mirrors within, one on the right side and one on the left side. The carpet for the little square of the floor is the same rich-red broadloom as that on the marble steps of the building's main staircase (*and there was a clock ticking somewhere, not the one upstairs in the bedroom, of course, but the sound of a clock ticking steadily, hollowly, perhaps the sound coming through the open doorway to the room beside the elevator, there on the second floor, coming from the so-called Banquet Hall, where the long windows overlooking the park in back that had once been the palace's gardens were open to what was such a hot and very humid afternoon, and outside dark clouds had been amassing behind Pão de Açúcar, the boomerang rise of the landmark mountain at the end of the sweep of Flamengo Beach just beyond the streets of Catete, which meant a tropical downpour was about to move in from the sea, and the uniformed female museum guards came from the other rooms, the Blue Hall and the Yellow Hall and the Moorish Hall, they came to gather at the row of open windows in the Banquet Hall to chat some and watch the soaking torrent once it began, and the downpour surely interrupted the dreams of the street boys out on the Rua do Catete sleeping in those nooks, huddled, perpetually hungry, and the rain surely scattered the men drinking at the tables on the sidewalk in front of the many* botecos *there,* *they maybe picked up their large bottles of beer and their glasses for a few moments and stood under a dripping awning themselves with the waiters, who would laugh about the rain, they would all watch it intensify, louder and harder, then diminish before long, stop, and the waiters, in their own sort of practiced dream scenario, what they perhaps performed in their own somnambulistic imaginings at home night after night, the waiters eventually would stroll out to the plastic chairs and tables on the sidewalk when the sun came out in earnest again, to carefully wipe away the wet with their bar towels so the men drinking could sit down again—Rio smelled rich and heady, like sweet mud, in the warm sunshine after such rain, the sky stretched so large and blue it seemed solid, near impenetrable above the soaked, steep green-jungled wall of mountains rising up right behind Catete there away from the sea, Catete being a wonderful pocket of the city, really, the statue of Christ the Redeemer with arms perpetually outstretched atop the highest mountain, the peak called Corcovado, clearly visible now*), the walls in the elevator have a pattern running in a wide band around the middle, showing embossed white grape bunches and bunting against the light blue of the elevator's walls; the motif of it resembles, even as large as it is, that of Wedgwood china.

The fixture for the single lamp built into the elevator's ceiling is brass, a wire mesh covering the half sphere of it, and the controls for operating the elevator are on a panel inside the open doors of the elevator. They are on the right-hand side, if the operator were facing the doors.

There is a small dial to indicate the floor number. There are two cast-brass levers, flat, tapered slabs to be gripped at the thick end, one a large lever and the other smaller. There is a brass wheel, for the operator to spin it like a bank-vault's wheel and engage the safety-latching mechanism.

Also, all the brass in the elevator is polished. It is polished very bright, gleaming, in fact.

THE MANHATTAN LUNCH: TWO VERSIONS

I. Magazine Girls

For about a month after Hennessey was outright fired by the brokerage house, waiting to get what was sure to be the indictment from the federal court, he simply didn't go out very much.

Most of the time Hennessey stayed in his spacious apartment on West Fifty-fifth, and he made sandwiches for nearly all his meals, occasionally heading to one of the many reasonably priced restaurants on Ninth Avenue in the evening. On Ninth Avenue he would first walk some. He would maybe go to a place called El Deportivo that was Puerto Rican, nothing fancy, where along with the stewed *guisada* they gave you a choice of white or yellow rice and black or red beans (he always went for the yellow and black combination); or there was the Galaxy Café, where, never taking one of the booths or the tables in back, Hennessey would sit at the diner-style counter just staring at the framed photographs of supposed entertainment celebrities there on the wall above the shelves of pies and cakes under glass (he wondered if anybody else his age, thirty-five, even remembered anymore shaved-headed Telly Savalas shown with his name scrawled prominently in one corner of the studio-lit shot). But when Hennessey found himself paying at the Galaxy's cash register one evening and being told that because he had arrived before six he qualified for what they advertised with a window placard as the "Early Birdies' Special," he became self-conscious—after that, despite the decent meals there, he started avoiding the Galaxy altogether, if truth be known. Of course, he avoided news on the Internet and especially in the newspapers. *The Wall Street Journal*'s extensive coverage of the alleged financial scandal was painful to face, and much worse would be to pick up the floppy tabloid slab of the *Post* and possibly see (this happened once) his own name prominently mentioned in yet another piece about the "outrageous swindle" and it being a good example of the current "rampant greed," or that's what it was as far as the noisy *Post* was concerned.

He had played hockey in prep school (his father, a state-office clerical worker in Massachusetts, moonlighted weekends as a salesman in the appliance department of Sears to help pay the bills to send him to ritzy Milton Academy; his kind mother, so concerned that Hennessey do well in everything in life, always encouraged him even when his grades weren't all that good), true, he had played school hockey, though Hennessey certainly hadn't been of the caliber to play college-level, at Division III Bowdoin or anywhere else. Still, he liked hockey, and it got so that his evenings took on a pattern of watching all the televised Rangers games that winter, with the home ones broadcast from the Garden less than a couple of dozen blocks away. On some evenings he watched the pregame show and thought he might take a cab or even walk at a good clip down to the Garden to buy a twenty-five-buck ticket from one of the guys in hooded sweatshirts perpetually peddling them outside; there was always an available seat, scalpers' surplus, when it was somebody of little consequence like the Phoenix or Vancouver team in town, but he never quite mustered the resolve for that.

He slept a lot, screened calls to make sure that it wouldn't be somebody from his family or whatever who might be offering more advice or condolences, neither of which Hennessey really needed. But one night at about nine he looked at the caller-ID to see that it was Tom Bettencourt, an old pal from Bowdoin. Tom was somebody Hennessey had spent a lot of time with when they'd both first found themselves in New York after graduation, before Tom's marriage and his kids, and Hennessey did answer the ring, glad to hear Tom's sort of dry but laughing voice again. Automatically, Hennessey went through his side of the story on what had happened, though Tom really didn't seem to want to hear too much about that, which was refreshing. Then Hennessey asked Tom about his wife and kids, probably perfunctorily and part of the set protocol carried out by a bachelor when dealing with an old friend now married. Tom himself didn't seem to want to dwell on that either, and they just laughed some about guys they knew or girls they dated at Bowdoin or nearby Bates College, even the wonder of "Lobster Night" every other Sunday; with Bowdoin being right there in Brunswick, Maine—and, so, a ready supply of lobsters from the docks only miles away—a Bowdoin guy working his way through a bona fide pile of the red carcasses on a Sunday-night plate oddly became a routine event.

"We got tired of lobster, can you imagine it?" Tom laughed.

"I can imagine it, all right," Hennessey said. "I used to have recurring nightmares about all those shells to be cracked, like it was so much endless work I had to do."

Which was how they both simply started agreeing that they surely should get together, it had been too long since they had. That also led to Hennessey learning that Tom Bettencourt wasn't working at the *New York Observer* anymore, but had moved to the staff of *Vanity Fair*; he was doing the same kind of editorial work he had done at the *Observer*, which involved some article-assigning but mostly copyediting. Tom suggested that with the building for Condé Nast located so close to where Hennessey lived—it being right off Times Square, a new skyscraper with the distinctive rounded-off edge to just one corner of its facade at Forty-second Street—they should have the lunch at the Condé Nast commissary. Tom assured Hennessey the scene there was worth seeing, and though it was only a cafeteria, this was an exceptionally classy one and designed by the famous postmodern architect, a guy who had done major museum buildings and such throughout the world but whose name Hennessey didn't recognize; plus, as Tom added:

"It can be a real trip, the scene there, because it serves all the magazines the company owns, us and *The New Yorker* and the rest. And if we're real lucky we'll see some of the models from *Vogue*, who come to the building for meetings to discuss shoots, I guess, even come for the actual studio shoots somewhere in the building. And I'm talking supermodels, man—certified Grade A and then some, if you know what I mean."

Hennessey laughed, and while he was still fully aware that Tom had indeed brushed aside any mention whatsoever from Hennessey about his current problems, Hennessey knew that he, Hennessey, was *very* comfortable with, and therefore appreciative of, that brushing aside, if only done out of politeness on Tom's part—or perhaps because of the fact that their friendship had nothing to do with Hennessey's current serious problems, really.

Nevertheless, Hennessey nearly backed out of the lunch at the last minute. He rehearsed a couple of excuses to make, because on Monday of the week when they were supposed to meet on Thursday, Hennessey had gone to Lower Manhattan to talk with his lawyers again, a session that hadn't gone well at all. But on Thursday—an overcast midday with that distinct smell of possible snow in the cold February air—he walked on Fifty-fifth over to Broadway and headed into Times Square, past the theaters and to the sleek skyscraper—bone-white stone and tinted glass—that housed the Condé Nast operations. He had to go through surprisingly extensive security, and the guy in the blue blazer standing at one of the upright reception desks—there were several, like an airport-counter operation—called up to Tom at the *Vanity Fair* offices and then issued Hennessey a pass with his name on it, printed out right there, the guy instructing Hennessey to keep ahold of it and directing him to the particular elevator in the long row of them that served the floor he needed. Hennessey folded the sheet, tucked it in his toggle coat's side pocket.

Tom Bettencourt wore slacks, an open-collar striped dress shirt, and chocolate suede desert boots, no suit jacket; his tuft of red hair was still as wild as ever, but now, somewhat moon-faced, Tom looked decidedly heavier, more of the father that he was, maybe, since the last time Hennessey had seen him (Tom had two young kids, both boys). As it turned out, they didn't head right to the commissary, but went on an impromptu tour of the offices, which admittedly Hennessey found interesting, not quite what he had expected. Actually, the place was rather empty, quiet, with a sequence of white-walled rooms uniformly carpeted in tasteful dark blue, the furniture just black steel desks and chrome-and-black-leather chairs; Tom explained that the editor in charge now—the guy who had brought Tom with him to the magazine from the *Observer* when the editor came to take over here—was a minimalist at heart and had the whole place redone that way. There was one very interesting room where mock-ups for the individual pages of the upcoming issue—entire articles and advertising layout—were lined up in sequence on lit electronic panels around the white walls, strung like boxcars, and then there was Tom's own small office. It was white-walled like all the rest, and Tom, obviously proud, showed Hennessey a literary journal that came out of some Midwestern university in which he had recently published a short story. With his wise-guy laugh, Tom informed Hennessey that he still hoped to finish a novel and publish it, doing something significant with real literature, rather than—he loopingly waved his hand while sitting there in his chair and leaning back from the bare black-steel desk, as if to take in the whole operation of *Vanity Fair*—yes, rather than what was around him: "All this yuppie horseshit of slick magazine writing, the glitz and high-class gossip that *Vanity Fair* is really all about, you know."

At which point Tom got up and said it was time to eat, the two of them taking an elevator down several floors to the commissary. Tom nodded hello to a few people they passed in the offices on the way out, also exchanged talk with somebody in the elevator.

The commissary was as thoroughly dramatic as promised, a true expanse with some smaller private rooms off the main concourse and easily a couple of hundred people eating at the tables arranged in clusters, restaurant style. The colors were bright, all oranges and blues, and the undulating free-form panels of the dividing walls suggested giant futuristic bird wings almost flapping along beneath the glowing inset lights up top that looked like night stars against the high ceiling's solid black background. Yet the more impressive show was probably not in the design within by the famous architect (who in this assignment, Hennessey told himself, appeared to be straining for effect) but there at the table Tom selected for its view. The skyscraper's side was glass here, and outside, seemingly close enough to touch, was the panorama of Bryant Park behind the ornate rise of the Public Library—the wispy, winter-bare trees of the park, also its paved terraces and walkways and its many benches; everything in the winter day was rendered a mesmerizing underwater hue due to the tinting of the huge glass sheets that formed the sweep of the building's facade at this level relatively lower down, four or five floors above the street. They talked about how good the food was, just cream soup and pita sandwiches for both of them, but *quite* good, they talked more about what they had read about Bowdoin lately in the alumni magazine, so much new construction there and also Bowdoin's unlikely genuine track star, a sprinter somehow recruited from Jamaica, an acknowledged hotbed for sprinters, somebody who had nearly made it, believe or not, to the summer Olympics for his country the year before; they talked of a lot of small things, and Hennessey had to admit that for the first time in who knows how long he was feeling something close to relaxed.

All of which is to say, that made what happened all the more strange when it did happen. Because when there was an actual nudge from Tom's desert boot under the table to signal Hennessey that about to enter were two of the sort of models he had mentioned on the phone, "magazine girls" and definitely from *Vogue,* Hennessey did look that way, watched the pair of models come from a smaller dining room off the main concourse and make their way to the front doors, having finished whatever meal of probably a simple salad and iced tea that they had merely poked away at.

Both were tall, classically so at maybe five-ten, and the one with ash-blond hair, mile-high cheekbones, and the mandatory pout, she wore just casual jeans and a sweater; the other, with a glossy black pageboy cut so straight in bangs that it could have been done using a steel rule to guide the scissors, such full lips, she was dressed equally casually, loose corduroy slacks in her case with a sweater—both wore pristine running shoes, most likely taking a break from a shoot. They were undeniably and entirely lovely, bordering on ethereal, with that calculated rhythmic strut that fashion models never really abandon, whether it be entering a bar in the Hamptons in the summer—as Hennessey had come to learn from his own carefree seaside summers renting a fine beach house there with bachelor pals—or now simply leaving a cafeteria—shoulders alternatingly swaying, perfect posture and the long, long legs seemingly a couple of paces ahead of them, almost as if each of the girls were leaning back to hold an imaginary pooch tugging her along on a leash. Yes, Hennessey looked at them as he sat at the table, the clutter of dishes from the meal in front of him, he looked at the girls—and he simply started crying, full-fledged, hunch-shouldered sobbing, pretty loud.

Tom at first must have thought Hennessey was joking around, and then—as Hennessey didn't let up and people at other tables nearby were, in fact, looking their way—Tom seemed to just want to be the hell out of there. Hennessey, still crying, mumbled something about how absolutely *beautiful* they were, and Tom, speaking low and with a touch of detectable anger—as more people at other tables were definitely looking at them now, it was embarrassing—Tom finally said to Hennessey at the table, "What the fuck is the matter with you, man?"

Everything was quite awkward as Hennessey, composed again, and Tom parted ten minutes later, uneasily shaking hands down in the lobby.

The next week Hennessey tried calling Tom Bettencourt a couple of times, leaving messages both at his office and at home, but Tom didn't phone back. And by the following week Hennessey was busy and he had no time for something like calls to Tom Bettencourt right then, with the indictment about to come down at last. Or perhaps Hennessey convinced himself that Tom Bettencourt, who aspired to publishing short stories in literary journals of the flimsily bound variety that he had shown Hennessey in the office—journals of no consequence that surely nobody really read, in all likelihood—wasn't worth dealing with, would never amount to much in life.

Truth of the matter was that Hennessey suddenly was *extremely* busy.

His head lawyer told Hennessey that he, the lawyer, would need to meet with him personally several times more that week before the upcoming two sessions for Hennessey with the prosecuting lawyers and investigators, one staff of them from the state attorney general's office and then the other with the federal Securities and Exchange Commission, the latter pushing for considerable prison time.

II. Falling into Paintings

Hope's life at seventy-eight had its understandable routine. There was time with her one daughter Anne, living up in Larchmont, and the two grandchildren, also Hope's abundant reading and the so-called appreciation courses she took, sponsored by Columbia.

Which is how it happened.

Actually, the worst thing about it all was the coverage that started turning up everywhere, the attention compounding and lasting for a full few days. First on the local New York news and then, apparently, on various news websites, a compact version of what happened provided by a wire service.

At her age Hope didn't know what to think of attention like that.

■ ■ ■

She wasn't what her adult daughter Anne or anybody else would consider very media savvy, not by any means. And for Hope, more than simply fainting that way during the lecture for her seniors art appreciation course there in the Metropolitan Museum of Art and hitting the painting's sheened canvas, which ripped badly in the course of the collapse, yes, more than that was the certainly odd adventure of being rushed by a wailing yellow-and-blue ambulance van right down Fifth Avenue. They sped beside the Park with its trees leafless in winter, then swerved across town on maybe Fifty-seventh—and this she distinctly remembered—the two muscular EMS attendants in their dark-blue jumpsuits occasionally looking down at her and smiling as she lay stretched out under a blanket, both, comically, with identical trimmed mustaches; one was talking to the other about where they were heading on this particular run, St. Clare's near Times Square, which they apparently had nicknamed the "junkie hospital." She was out of the emergency room by seven that evening, all tests proving she was fine, in truth quite fit for a woman of seventy-eight years old, the peachy-cheeked young intern told her. Her daughter Anne showed up from the suburbs in Anne's husband's Saab wagon to drive her back to her apartment on the Upper East Side, in what used to be commonly known as Yorkville. Anne wanted to stay for the night, but Hope assured her there was nothing wrong, even tried to make a joke out of the whole thing by saying she had no idea why those attendants called St. Clare's the junkie hospital, demeaning it that way, seeing that to her everybody there had seemed professional, attentive, and efficient, especially the boyish intern who, when asked, told Hope in detail all about how his own parents in New Jersey had sacrificed a lot to send him through Albert Einstein for medical school.

▪ ▪ ▪

The phone started ringing that evening, when a cousin in Connecticut had first seen the short TV squib of the story showing the museum gallery and the large Delacroix canvas, which, as Hope had already been assured by everybody at the hospital, could be repaired easily enough, despite the vertical rip being quite long; then later that evening there was Ray Finelli, the Columbia grad student conducting the class for her group, yes, cheery Ray telling her the same; then another call from Anne who was obviously excited, it now appeared, that her mother had become the object of such celebrity. Anne called again in the morning after she heard the story about the torn painting and what had happened to her mother being given mention on the NPR morning news, which Hope liked to listen to but was intentionally avoiding when she did get up and begin to prepare her coffee and juice and toast at her usual seven o'clock.

Hope had no caller-ID on her one phone, in the living room, but there was a cheap and basic answering machine that Anne had bought for her at Duane Reade a dozen years ago and that Hope often switched off even when she had no specific problem to deal with and before this happened, wanting to protect her time to read; Anne had wanted to buy her a cell phone, but Hope didn't like the idea of it—too many interruptions when you maybe were, in fact, somewhere trying to relax and read a book. And after a second call came from Anne that morning and then three other calls from various people in the art appreciation class for seniors sponsored by Columbia—Gladys Revotskie and Mary Torrey and Julia Heyman—Hope grew tired of having to explain the situation again, telling yet somebody else how she had been assured the damage could be repaired—which had seemed foremost in her own mind while at the hospital, not any question of her health—and also telling whoever was calling how the young intern at St. Clare's said it must have happened because she had skipped lunch that day. The intern decided the culprit was simple blood-sugar level and it could happen to anybody, even somebody his age. She had told him, when asked, that she had eaten some rye crisp, cottage cheese, and a slice of Plumrose ham for lunch at about eleven before she met with her group in the lobby of the Met that afternoon, which was, actually, her normal meal at midday; nevertheless, the cheery young intern, thinking that it was much less than she usually ate, immediately concluded almost with an "Aha!" that she had picked the wrong day to do what he saw as "skip lunch." Hope herself knew it had had nothing to do with blood-sugar level.

But in a way, not talking on the phone and not being occupied with some conversation was probably worse, because it gave her too much time to think about the incident, let the slow, emphatically full-color reel of it—after all, this was *Delacroix*—play itself out again on what could have been the big screen of her imagination. Everything had started off normally enough: Hope noticing the usual few yellow school buses parked out front of the Met in the gray of the February day, Hope walking up the long rise of steps and, at the doors, past those glass canisters filled with the little metal entry tabs that they tell you to deposit for recycling on your way out, Hope at the coat room checking her winter coat with her gloves and knit hat carefully pushed into the pocket, keeping her red handbag in which she had a small pad and pens in case she wanted to take notes, and then Hope meeting the bunch of others from the appreciation class at the far end of the massive lobby by the bookstore. Grinning Ray Finelli in his graduate student's black jeans and black turtleneck herded them together as if he were a conscientious grade school teacher, Ray laughing, always pleasant, amid all those voices of the many museum-goers echoing around the big white pillars and along the lobby's high, gracefully arched walls; it was something Hope always liked, the bustle and palpable excitement of a museum lobby—the *anticipation* of what's to come. The lecture from Ray that day was on the nineteenth-century painting in France that had laid the groundwork for the two great movements that eventually marked, as he explained, the latter part of that century—Impressionism and Symbolism. And while they did find themselves in a gallery with dark-green walls showing a half-dozen Corots and Millets, smallish and more or less uniformly murky, the mishap happened when the bunch of them were standing there and listening to Ray talk right in front of the huge and decidedly vivid Delacroix canvas. It was the scene of a sultan and his warriors, in turbans and robes and with the horses' jeweled, gleaming harnesses and saddles flashing as brightly as the Moors' scimitars themselves, preparing perhaps for battle in front of the golden walls of a kasbah fortress; the Moroccan sky was so big and so blue above it all that just to look at it was enough to make you dizzy on its own, near overwhelming in its richness and also its trueness—the essence of something that you really couldn't name, or probably well beyond naming, which made it that much more, yes, true and rich and, undeniably, an *essence*. Ray Finelli was still talking, the dozen or so of them were listening attentively, Hope was staring at that blue sky—and the next thing Hope knew everybody was gathered and looking down at her as she lay there tangled like a dropped puppet on the honey parquet floor and against the dark-green wall, finally opening her eyes, blinking. She would later decide that it must have been her elbow that hit the thin, taut canvas and caused the damage on the way down.

Actually, thinking too much about it, she did turn on the answering machine again in hopes that somebody *would* call, and at four, when Anne's twin daughters were home from junior high, they took turns on the phone, wanting to make sure themselves that she, "Gram," was all right. Like their mother, they apparently were a bit excited, too; they said they had told the other kids at school about it, urging them to "check it out" on the Web.

▮ ▮ ▮

The third day was little different, more calls, including two from reporters. Now that she thought of it, Hope was surprised the reporters hadn't contacted her earlier; one was from a large New York all-news radio station and one from a weekly newspaper in Brooklyn that Hope admittedly had never heard of. Both reporters sounded young and with both she was polite, avoiding making any more comment, and no sooner did she finish with the second call than she answered another ring, Ray Finelli phoning again. He reassured her not to worry, saying once more it was amazing what restorers could do with canvas damage nowadays and emphasizing that the Met, of course, had "humongous insurance" for this kind of thing, not to worry in the least; however, he said that at some point she might have to file a more complete report with the museum people—he would keep her informed. But by the fourth day the phone had quieted at last, and when it did ring late in the morning she listened to the prerecorded greeting that came with the answering machine say with its packaged, game-show-announcer's voice, even-toned, "We are not home now" and the rest of it (Anne had explained to Hope even before the museum incident that, for security, it wasn't advisable to give as much as your first name or any sort of personal greeting message on a machine); there followed a message with a male's voice, a little raspy and older-sounding, first saying he hoped he had the right number, and then identifying himself as Dan Sorensen, somebody who, as he said, he hoped that she remembered after so many years. She looked at the little green light on the black machine flashing rhythmically while the message was being taken, and she picked up the receiver before he was finished:

"Dan?"

"Hope?"

And they began talking, as naturally as that. She hadn't heard from Dan Sorensen for who knows how long, it amazingly being close to a full sixty years, they eventually decided with some extended calculation, as they laughed and talked about so many things, Dan explaining that he had seen the news squib and simply looked up her number in the phone book. There was so much to be covered, so much to be talked about, though once the family material got filled in—Hope telling how her husband Edward had died ten years earlier, her one daughter Anne and Anne's husband the investment banker had two wonderful girls, twins, living in Westchester, and

Dan talking of having survived two wives, no children, admitting that probably his work as a civil engineer when younger, with considerable travel to Europe and South America for that work, never let him think about starting a family until it was too late to do so—yes, once all that was out of the way, even the explanation of how Dan himself lived not far from her and on the Upper West Side, had lived there for years after his retirement, everything did return to talk of when they had been boyfriend and girlfriend during their last year in high school. Or, high school for Dan, anyway, and the girls Catholic day school on the Upper East Side for Hope—what they used to call an "exclusive" school and run by the Order of the Sacred Heart nuns, originally French.

"You know," Dan now said, "I knew when you first told me back then that you had decided to go to that even ritzier women's college, a place with that same order of swank nuns up there in the suburbs, your Manhattanville College, my days were numbered, all right, that it was only a matter of months or even days before you would meet some guy from some place like Harvard." But then he seemed to question himself on that, an automatic addendum: "And it was Harvard for your husband Edward?"

"He went to Yale, actually."

"I guess I always thought it was Harvard."

"No, both of Edward's degrees, for college and then law school, were from Yale."

"What's the difference, way out of my league in either case," Dan laughed, and Hope did, too.

They ended up talking for well over an hour, while neither of them seemed to notice the time, and there was more laughing, more remembering, Hope sitting there in her apartment's living room and somehow not sitting there whatsoever, just picturing places that came up in the conversation, like a slow slide show, just picturing people and especially picturing Dan—square-jawed and handsome when they had been together when young, his thick chestnut hair carefully parted on one side the way boys did groom their hair back then and the large blue eyes that, true, often made him look perfectly startled, perhaps with life itself; sunburnt Dan in khakis and canvas shoes and a crewneck sweater, a refreshingly cool summer evening after a fine day at the beach for the two of them out on Long Island in Hope's precise picturing now—and soon, on the phone, they were agreeing to meet for lunch the next week, that somehow happening without Hope even noticing it, she later told herself.

And all the following weekend Hope also told herself that thinking about Dan now, plus once or twice mentioning him and the upcoming lunch to her daughter Anne, she seemed to forget altogether what had happened in the museum on the gray afternoon less than a full week before. It would be good to see Dan again, which is what Hope kept telling herself that weekend, wondering what Dan looked like today, wondering what he would think she looked like today, wondering about just about everything concerning Dan and probably excited, though she wouldn't openly admit that. It went on throughout Saturday and Sunday, right until Monday—when Dan did call again; he was laughing, despite what he had to tell her, sounding boyish and the voice no longer strange or raspy, as it had been when she had first heard it unidentified on the earlier call and he had begun to leave his message. Dan explained now that he would have to ask for "the old Yankees-game rain check" on the lunch, and the doctor he had seen that very morning wanted him to book into the hospital immediately, Mount Sinai, for some tests.

"One thing I forgot to mention when we talked the other day, Hopey"—she wondered when somebody had last called her Hopey? her mother, her own three sisters? all now dead—"I've had a lot of problems with my ticker these last few years, they rope me in for these tests all the time. So, a rain check it will be, OK, Hopey?"

"Yes," Hope said, rather softly, saying repeatedly that she surely hoped the tests worked out OK.

▮ ▮ ▮

Dan Sorensen died during heart surgery at Mount Sinai that Thursday. Hope went to the funeral services at the Catholic church on Columbus Avenue the following Monday, attended by only a dozen people, mostly retired elderly colleagues who had known him from work. But she didn't go up to the burial at Woodlawn in the Bronx, even though the kind, polite Hispanic priest had offered to let her come with him in his car, saying he could drop her off at her apartment on the way back; she admitted to the young priest that she was quite tired, and he said he understood.

As sorrowful as it had been, she was appreciative that she had at least talked to Dan before he passed away, and she was appreciative that they had shared for at least that hour of phone conversation the memories of other times. And by that spring, April and then May, Hope was back to her routine of reading and spending time with her grandchildren, with the confused episode of her moment of celebrity entirely behind her, that day when she had fallen into the canvas; Hope was looking forward to receiving the printed schedule from Columbia of appreciation courses for seniors for the coming academic year, thinking she might sign up in one for literature this time.

In other words, Hope's life returned, very much so, to its normal routine, except for the strangest part of it all, the dreams she kept having night after night, it seemed, in which she was always falling into—sometimes tumbling into and sometimes leaning into and sometimes full-fledged being swept along for a collision with the canvas about to tear—Hope falling into so many paintings of so many artists she did know because their work was unquestionably famous—falling into Monet's feathery pastels and those giant water lilies, and falling into Whistler's obliquely named "Symphonies" and "Nocturnes," and, almost humorously, it seemed, falling into Grant Wood's stony-faced Iowa farmer and his spinster daughter, pitchfork held upright like a lance, several Mondrians and Picassos, too—and also falling into paintings she had never known or never heard of, with such a variety of frames encasing them, all of which Hope seemed to remember from the dreams, distinctly, those frames, some frilled gold and elaborate, some brushed stainless steel and starkly minimal, and who could calculate just how *many* paintings all told—and Hope perpetually falling.

In the morning Hope, having her coffee and juice and toast, would try to recall which paintings they were, what exactly it was she had fallen into this time, if, in fact, she had had another dream like that the night before.

On the other hand, maybe Hope didn't think of any of such dreaming whatsoever (*had she actually once fallen into that big, vivid Delacroix canvas of swashbuckling Moorish warriors atop their fine steeds that winter day at the Met? did anybody ever actually fall into a painting as she had, literally, and had there been the odd few days of celebrity for Hope that February before, then the whole, even more odd business of the call out of the blue from Dan Sorensen after all these years? had that happened? or had that been a dream, too? she wasn't so sure anymore*), no, maybe she didn't think of any of it any longer, and it was merely a matter of Hope knowing more than ever now what she had already come to quietly accept.

▮ ▮ ▮

Because it was true—Hope was getting *close*.

TELL ME ABOUT NERVAL

. . . and there was that one winter afternoon, after I left the hotel on Montmartre, because sometimes after I would see the other boy, the French boy Alex from the university and the bleak graffiti-splattered classroom building on Rue Censier, then everything would seem more strange than ever, sometimes I wouldn't go right back to the apartment on Rue Broca, I mean I couldn't go back there right then and just talk and try to act naturally around Billy, and it was the same for me that afternoon after I was together with the French boy up on Montmartre, and I suppose a better way of putting it would be that I really couldn't face Billy, I couldn't face him just yet after having spent the afternoon with Alex in another one of those one-star hotels where we did go in the afternoon . . .

▮ ▮ ▮

. . . and Alex would laugh, handsome Alex, lanky and his oaky blond hair needing a cut, the old sheepskin coat with its brown suede worn shiny and his black jeans, the long, long red-and-yellow scarf wrapped two or three times around his neck the way that only a French boy would dare to wear a scarf like that, I told him it was "very baroque" and he just smiled, dimples showing, he knew how handsome he was, and sometimes he would almost stand back and watch to see if I, an American girl, was maybe, well, shocked by the place where we would go for the few hours, the latest hotel he had discovered that was cheaper than the last, shabbier, and to tell the truth the hotels usually weren't even one-stars, and he would smile some more and laugh, this boy Alex, he would say that one-stars were getting way beyond his means, and, in fact, what I learned is that there is a kind of hotel graded below one-stars, old hotels that can't even get any rating of stars, and inevitably attached to the facade of such a hotel there's only the standard ancient plaque of a sort of polished black stone with gold lettering promising "Tout Confort," meaning all the amenities, the very premise of that suitably ironic, I never meant to hurt Billy, I know I can still say that I loved only Billy during all that time we were in Paris together, living there in the apartment on Rue Broca, and of course I was excited only a year before back in the snowy dream of Ithaca and when Billy got word from the departmental chairman that he was awarded the grant for the research year, when he was told it was approved and so we would be going to Paris for Billy to finish work on the dissertation for which he already had a book contract, with a university press, it seemed like everything was ahead of us, I mean not just eventual marriage and a life always together but, "Can you believe it, Paree!" which is what my sister Madison sighed when I told her, she was a year ahead of me in college and I roomed with her, and I can admit that before going I pictured just about every cliché of our living in Paris, sometimes I saw myself riding a wobbly black-fendered bicycle down a Paris side street, the cobbles lumpily purple, with a freshly aromatic baguette balanced across the tastefully weathered wicker basket in front, sometimes I saw myself actually sitting with a book and looking suitably and even existentially bored at one of those little round tables with a faux-marble top and a frilly cast-iron stem in the clutter of a café *terrasse,* probably under the green awning of Deux-Magots or the cream-colored awning of Café de Flore, I had never been to Paris, I had never been anywhere, really, I had only seen pictures and movies, and even in Ithaca I always felt more like a townie than a student because I had come there from Saratoga Springs, from one place in the low mountains of upstate New York for me and my sister and then to another place in the low mountains of upstate New York, I had never been anywhere at all, and Billy had been my grad-student TA for the one French literature survey course I took, which I didn't even do well in, it fulfilled a humanities distribution requirement I had during sophomore year, so how could I expect to think in anything but clichés, and that particular afternoon with Alex it wasn't much different, it was an afternoon in late February and Alex undressed me at the hotel up on Montmartre, he would always do that, undress me slowly himself, he was a French boy, he really was, and Cornell was letting me transfer credits from the confused attempt at a university with the classy name and called Sorbonne Nouvelle there in Paris to cover what remained of my course work at home, I was a senior, and if being away from campus meant having to wait until the hot, cicada-buzzing summer in Ithaca to graduate, what did a few months matter, I could finally get everything done then with a couple of required-to-graduate courses, two semesters of each course crammed into one summer session, more distribution requirements for my degree, a class in government and a class in geology, or I saw the basic geology as being the easiest way out of the undergraduate science-distribution requirement, at Cornell it attracted all the oafish hockey players, "Rocks for Jocks" is what they called the course, and before we left, even then when we got our visas and we made our many plans, back in Ithaca, Billy would tell me about Nerval, what seems so long ago, but it wasn't all that long ago, and I don't know why it was Nerval I always wanted to hear about, always wanted to know so much more about, I suppose, and with Billy doing his study of the French Symbolists it could have been any of the other poets, and it could have been Baudelaire, or maybe Verlaine or Rimbaud or Mallarmé, all of them who came after Baudelaire and who were *really* the Symbolists, the way I understood it, or the way Billy explained it to me, all of them who maybe learned everything they knew from Nerval who had come along even before Baudelaire in what amounted to that spookily dark and therefore wonderfully mysterious nineteenth century of French literature, and I was just a bonehead sociology major, why, I had been in a sorority for my first couple of years simply because at Cornell my sister saw that as a large accomplishment in itself, especially the fact that we were in the same sorority my mother had been in at Cornell, all over-the-top mock Tudor and color-bursting maples in fall, all over-the-top mock Tudor and equally color-bursting lilacs and forsythia in spring, my sister Madison who probably would have been a Home Ec major as my mother had been if they still had a major called that, Madison clung to tradition, it was all foolishness, the keg parties at fraternities were foolishness, the big dances where a date should definitely be a member of one of the best fraternities were foolishness, and when I met Billy everything suddenly was different, and even if he was finishing his Ph.D., Billy my TA for that French class, he was only a few years older, and with Billy I realized how much I had missed, he was quiet and even shy, he *knew things,* which is what I tried to tell Madison but Madison didn't understand at first, or I don't think she understood any of it, she couldn't figure out why I was even with him, until she realized that my being with Billy would mean my getting to live for a year in Paris, then she was giddily envious, Madison was like that, she talked about the wonderful clothes I could buy in Paris, the fashionable restaurants I could go to, her fantasies of Paris maybe more skewed than mine, and for me just the fact that Billy had come from New York City to Cornell seemed important, so brainy that he had graduated from CCNY at twenty the way brainy kids only in New York City somehow do, and that seemed to speak a whole other world to me, one of books and ideas, and when we had our first dates he was very kind to me, we would go to a movie and then have cheese-gunky pizza afterward and he would tell me it was amazing how I noticed things, I would look at the softly falling rain making repeated fan-shaped swirls on the streets, finding it beautiful as we walked along under his umbrella after the movie, let's say, and he would say he loved how I noticed things, and even when I tried to make his interests my interests, when I, too, wanted to learn about the Symbolist poets that he studied so hard, he gave me a book that he told me would be a good introduction, a paperback reprint of an old book written around 1900 or something, Billy said it was definitely as good as anything ever written since then when it came to the Symbolist poets in France, it was the book that introduced all of England and even T. S. Eliot to the Symbolists, Billy said, Billy adding that T. S. Eliot was an energetic imitator who stole from the Symbolists, Eliot proudly admitted it, Billy said, and to be honest I didn't get too far in the book, the writing seemed old-fashioned and slow to me, but I kept thinking about the cover of the paperback Billy had bought at a used bookstore on the Commons in downtown Ithaca, the book was called *The Symbolist Movement in Literature* by a man named Arthur Symons, and this particular edition was one that had been reissued long ago in the 1960s and given a new introduction then, with a cover trying to be hip, and I checked inside the cover for the reprint date, 1967, but it was that cover itself that I really kept looking at, I still think of that cover even today and it brings back all the sadness, what eventually happened to Billy, and the cover was beautiful even if it was hokey, *really* sixties-ish, all right, it said at the bottom of the cover that originally the book cost only ninety-five cents, I couldn't believe that any book *ever* cost just ninety-five cents new, the paperback itself was *so* old, and the cover had a black background, and up top there was the title in bright white letters and then the author's name in bright orange letters, both against that black, which was the black of night, I suppose, and below that there was a drawing that filled most of the cover against all the surrounding black, and it showed the opened palms of a person's hands, sort of cupping a beautiful butterfly, the markings on its spread wings bright orange and bright white and very bright turquoise blue, as if the hands had found what the person had been searching for at last, there was the *it,* there was the *secret* to everything, and once Billy caught me just sitting at his desk in his room in Ithaca, a room with so many stacked books from the library that it smelled of musty paper and Uris Library, dull, pulpy, but sweetly so and nice, I was staring at the cover, and I almost had to snap out of it, the kind of trance the cover left me in and simply the idea of it, I maybe whispered low, more to myself than to him, "The cover is very beautiful," and he looked at me sitting at his desk with the book, Billy with his glasses, steel-rimmed and the lenses round, like two quarters shining, Billy's mussed brown hair always seeming as if he had just woken up even if he hadn't just woken up, and he said again how he loved how I noticed things, and he even chided himself aloud for being so caught up in what he said he was always caught up in, words and words and more words, he told me that he had never so much as looked twice at that cover, and then he said it was, in fact, true, and this was what his Symbolists were all about, a search for the *it* of everything, the *secret* hidden in the black darkness of night that could suddenly somehow be there like a butterfly in your own cupped-open palms, entirely as if in a dream, and right then Billy leaned over and gently kissed the top of my head as I sat there at the desk, he said that not only was I beautiful but the way I noticed things was the most beautiful thing of all, Billy was like that, kind to me, and to be honest I didn't want to read that book or any other of the stacks and stacks of books Billy had, it was better when Billy would tell me himself about all those poets, and, as I said, the more he told me about Gérard de Nerval the more I wanted it to be only the story of Nerval that he told me, and Billy said that early on in his research he had made the major mistake of overlooking Nerval, Billy told me how earlier, when he hadn't read enough Nerval and had just heard scattered facts about the writer, he categorized him as just another effete aristocratic French madman dabbling in poetry, until he learned more about him, his life and his work, the "de Nerval" part of his name wasn't aristocratic but merely something he had concocted to replace his real surname, part of the sadness of his early life, Billy said, because Nerval's father, a field doctor with the army in the Napoleonic Wars, had brought his young wife with him on the campaign, the woman setting off to accompany the father only months after Gérard was born and the child handed over to the care of relatives back in France after she died of fever in a camp somewhere on the front in Poland, Gérard was raised by an uncle in the Valois region of northern France, and Gérard simply made up the name with the "de Nerval" in it to represent some anchoring in his life, to say where he was from, and actually he was quite modest, and when he did drop out of medical school in Paris, Nerval an only son constantly disappointing his stern father the doctor, yes, when he did start publishing his dreamlike poems and stories and plays and accounts of travel in very dreamlike faraway places, like Cairo, a white city in maybe 1850 shimmering under the Orient's sun, or Istanbul, a city of spired mosques at the time and rising even more dreamlike under the stars and moon of the Orient's inky night sky, he often signed his pieces with only his given name, "Gérard," entirely modest, shy, soft-voiced, not all that big in stature and prematurely balding, falling hopelessly in love with actresses whose presence there before him in costume frills and heavy makeup under the glow of the bright gas stage lamps made them ethereal for him, entirely otherworldly, women he idolized from afar and was hesitant even to try to meet, Billy told me that you could read all the biographies in the world about Nerval and never find anything bad anybody had to say about him personally, and often I would ask Billy to tell me about Nerval again, I think I just liked hearing the words spoken like that by Billy when we studied together in the Greek coffee shop near campus in Ithaca or in the dark of his room after making love, and, true, Nerval was institutionalized on and off throughout his short life, considered mad by some, and, true, he did end his life by hanging himself in an alley one cold January Parisian night when he didn't even have the money for a room in a cheap lodging house, but that wasn't what Nerval was really about, Billy said, and for Nerval it was all a matter of what the title announced in Nerval's most important work, the novella called *Le Rêve et la Vie,* dream and life, one maybe the other, no difference whatsoever, and when I asked Billy to tell me about the lobster again, because I liked the way Billy told that story, Billy said that it really wasn't true, or in all likelihood it wasn't true, it was just part of the Nerval madman legend, but I told Billy I didn't care, I wanted to hear it again, how Nerval in black top hat and black frock coat, his clothes admittedly frayed, could be seen around the Palais-Royal colonnade arches right in the center of old Paris and across from the Louvre, walking a pet lobster on the leash of a gold ribbon, Nerval apparently calmly answering anybody who asked, telling them in his soft, smiling way, that he had always liked lobsters better than dogs, and lobsters didn't bark and frighten everybody, lobsters knew the true mysteries of the sea, the messages of the Ocean Floor itself, gentle Nerval explained, mysteries that were maybe like the beautiful butterfly held in cupped palms, I knew, and the French boy, Alex, that afternoon we met again after classes, he suggested that we take the blue-sparking Métro to a hotel up on Montmartre, I told him I wasn't sure and . . .

■ ■ ■

. . . and we were standing there in front of the coffee machines in the foyer of the classroom building, where it seemed that most everything that went on in that building, the classes upstairs, almost didn't matter, the lobby was more important, everybody congregating there in that lobby amid all the half-euro coffee machines, everybody even smoking there and not caring how signs everywhere said there was no smoking allowed in the building, green rubber tile and bright yellow-and-green walls in a giant free-form patterning that somebody must have thought at one time was modern and very daring in the run-down reinforced-concrete block that was the classroom building off Rue Censier, not far from the domed Panthéon, and Alex told me I had to go with him, I had to be with him that afternoon, it was a perfect winter day to be on Montmartre, he looked so handsome, but he always looked so handsome, and I had my book pack over my shoulder, and I was standing there with a sugar-syrupy espresso just bought from one of the machines, it was in a tiny translucent white plastic cup and I had to balance it, keep it from spilling, I couldn't push him away even if I wanted to, and there were all the other students standing around, the pretty French girls in their jeans and tight sweaters cursing about professors, the guttural-voiced boys with them doing the same, everybody shoving in and out of the big doors splattered with more broadsides pasted over the older peeling broadsides, shabby the way that everything associated with education in France seemed shabby, the buildings anyway, the windows in that big foyer fogged up with steam from so many people there and because it was cold and damp outside in the gray afternoon of trees with coathanger-bare black limbs, the rich smell of exhaust sooty in the air, Paris in February, everybody buying those little cups of espresso that truly were wonderful, coffee out of a thumping machine that was probably better than any coffee in a coffee shop you might get back home, strong, good, and it was as if Alex liked how he had me cornered, I was in a nook away from the crowd about to sip my coffee and he found me standing there, where he knew I would be waiting for him after class, he was tall, his oaky blond hair touched what could have been the ruff of that red-and-yellow scarf he always wore, wrapped in loose loops around his neck and the tails of it cavalierly dangling, he had a movie star's firm jaw, he had dimples, and with me still attempting to balance the little coffee cup that way, he started nuzzling his face around my neck, kissing me, whispering to me about what he told me was my beautiful hair, whispering to me about what he said were my beautiful breasts and what he called, above all and specifically, my "very, very beautiful bum," because that was the word he used, a British word, really, and whenever with me he wanted to speak only English, we didn't speak French together, and if I was back at Cornell or any other school in America, surely, something like his fondling me would have meant a scene, but in Paris it was no scene and nobody else so much as glanced our way, and in one class I took, the professor, wanting to get the class started, would repeatedly have to call out to a girl to please come in from where we could all see her vigorously making out with her boyfriend in the hallway and take a seat so that he, the professor, could begin his lecture, and in another seminar where we all sat around some marred light-wood tables arranged in sort of a *U*, one gruff, curly-topped boy, decidedly Belmondo-ish, announced to everybody at the start of class one day, shaking his head in consternation, that he simply had to move and take another seat, because too many of the smiling girls sitting across from him were wearing short skirts that particular day and he would only be looking under the table and at, well, those short, short miniskirts and *beyond,* and he wouldn't be able to concentrate on the class discussion at all, the dowdy female prof nodding in agreement and fully understanding his point, she calmly told him it might be a good idea indeed to move, and it was something that if it had happened back in the States would have gotten the boy tossed out of the room, immediately, sent directly to some stern assistant dean of students and then referred to rehabilitative campus counseling on so-called gender relations or something, but the French were so relaxed about sex, why, even the huge and utterly stark white-tiled lavatories smelling of their disinfectant in the building were entirely unisex, and I now told Alex I should get back to the apartment on Rue Broca and work on an assignment for my History of Central and West Africa class, and he continued to nuzzle and whisper who knows what around my neck, lifting my hair to do so now, his breath tickling, warm, letting his other hand firmly continue to explore the shape of what he continued to call my "bum," kneading one side of me there and then the other in my jeans, it was hot in that foyer, literally steamy, there were giant fan-blowing heaters overhead and the windows were thoroughly fogged up, I couldn't do anything, really, I was laughing low and girlishly, saying to him, "Come on" or "Quit it," he called me *chérie,* maybe the only French word he used right then, he continued nuzzling and pawing, I was trying not to spill the full cup of espresso, still holding the thing with both hands, he had me where he wanted me, and I liked it, and then we were, in fact, outside in the gray day together, we were in the Métro car heading up to Montmartre, because Billy would be logging his long hours of archival research in the new national library complex for the whole afternoon, the library all shining steel and tinted glass, futuristic, the François Mitterrand complex right beside the wide green river in the Thirteenth Arrondissement, Billy carefully transcribing his notes to his silver laptop, hours upon hours of poring over old letters and manuscripts in the huge reading room, more tinted-glass windows and more clinical gleaming stainless steel, he wouldn't be back at the apartment until after seven, and he wouldn't even have to know that I hadn't been in the apartment all afternoon studying, or maybe studying at one of the everyday cafés with their out-of-date video games and authentically inattentive waiters at the tiny asphalt traffic circle at the Place de la Contrescarpe not far from Rue Broca, and the Métro line up to Montmartre was one of the old ones, the tracks narrow or something so they had to use the older and smaller cars on it or something, and the car was almost antique, glossily buff-colored, the bench seats facing each other were actually trimmed with varnished real wood, the latches for the wheezing automatic doors that opened at every empty stop then in midafternoon were old-fashioned and chrome, like two *S*'s with knobs on the curlicues of them, I was trying to lose myself in details, it wasn't a matter then of a butterfly spreading its beautiful half-dreamt wings slowly in your cupped palms and revealing the ultimate secret at last, it wasn't a matter of sweet little Gérard de Nerval, half broken but more than half saintly, too, in his threadbare frock coat and top hat walking his pet lobster as it happily crawled along, and I suppose I was trying to lose myself in details in order to forget everything else, as I did open my eyes once in a while to look around and then closed my eyes again, continuing to return Alex's hard kisses with all the energy I could now, the train's wheels ground loud with the sound of metal agonizing on metal, slow on all the curves on that line up to Montmartre, the electrical connection sparked blue in the tunnels, like lightning but silent lightning in a dream in this swallowing blackness, very far away from everything else that had been the first twenty-one years of my life, my sister Madison and her worrying about who was paired with who for sorority-fraternity dances, my own predictable kidhood there in Saratoga Springs, where even if our father was a doctor, a GP, we lived pretty simply and like everybody else in our neighborhood of winding tree-lined streets, everything picture-perfect, American, my mother the former Home Ec major taught Madison and me how to bake, how to make clothes from rattling tissue-paper patterns and carefully piece together the cut cloth at the musically humming and aptly named Singer sewing machine, Madison and I were *hopelessly American* kids, yes, my mother the homemaker, my father the kind, level-headed doctor who cared so much about his patients, why, my parents were so suburban that they even bought station wagons, *Volvos*, Madison and I had been nowhere, we knew nothing, really, and Cornell with its imposing gray-stone buildings and the Clock Tower's chimes melodically announcing the hours and the start of classes as students hurried across the criss-crossing, argyled walks didn't even feel like anywhere anymore, because I was *here,* and the car was almost empty, we pretty much had it to ourselves, so it didn't matter *whatsoever* if we smooched and smooched and crazily smooched like that, he tasted fresh, his teeth clicked against mine, he was hungry for me, I was even more hungry for him, if that was possible, I almost didn't want to hear him ever talk again, because when he did talk it would only be about American television shows that he thought were "cool," American rap singers or American rock bands that he thought were "cool," stupid things, really, and for a minute or so I looked up, once when the doors opened as somebody stepped out at the stop and then the eerie flügelhorn sighed its long, lingering note and nobody got on at that empty stop, because most of the people in the car had already gotten off well before, maybe at Châtelet-Les Halles, the doors did thump shut, I did see what I really hadn't paid much attention to before, the little decal on the window of one of the doors with a circle and inside the circle the outline of a Scottie dog with a diagonal red line drawn across it, no-dogs-allowed, though below that symbol, I knew, it gave the hours that dogs were, in fact, allowed to ride on the trains, like now in the empty midafternoon, and the strangest thing was that just when I looked at that decal, I also looked around the car while Alex began biting softly at my neck, he had one arm around me and the other hand was slowly moving, touching, moving some more, eventually to my jeans there at the lap, where I knew he could already feel what was surely my dampness, he said "Nice," and I saw sitting at the far end of the car an old woman, alone, and very neat and proper, with rouge and powder and gray hair in a perfect perm, sitting very upright and wearing a good winter coat, beige, maybe cashmere, and a matching tam, and she had a little wicker basket on her lap with a dog looking out from within it, a black poodle with iodine eyes, a tiny pink tongue, and I got a little dizzy to wonder if I really was seeing her, or if I just imagined her because I had seen the decal on the door about dogs, the hours they were allowed to ride, maybe nothing was real, after all, and Alex's hand was *there* again, his beautiful fingers were moving *there* again, I said the only thing I could say, "Mmmmmmm," or at least something like that, I was short of breath and dizzy, because, true, maybe I wasn't where I was, Billy always said I noticed things, but maybe I noticed too many things, or maybe I noticed nothing at all, because when you think of it maybe there is nothing at all to really notice, and once Alex and I got to the Montmartre station we walked with arms around each other, staggeringly, up that crazy corkscrew staircase that's like a staircase in a lighthouse, maybe, a staircase that does sort of rescue you from the otherworld of the Métro, there underground in the darkness where the electricity sparks blue, where the metal wheels grind so loudly, and the hill of Montmartre itself was surely far above that, and we tried to keep climbing the stairs with his arm around my waist, with my arm around his waist, Alex pulling me close to him, our book packs making it all the more awkward, we laughed and our laughter echoed in the empty cement chamber of the cavernous cylinder for the staircase, a staircase that seemed as if it would never end, up and up and up, until you could first see a bit of milky light and then were almost delivered into the daytime once again, the tiny traffic square with more winter-bare trees, the cafés glowing buttery in the dim air that smelled as if it might snow, an ammonia-clear something in the air, and big, vagrant gold leaves fallen from the plane trees lay stuck to the very black damp pavement here and there, almost a dance-step pattern for us to staggeringly follow through the side streets of Montmartre, which does feel like its own separate village, maybe not like Paris at all, maybe not like anywhere at all, Billy said I noticed things, Billy and I had been engaged since the summer before, and Alex kept tugging me closer like that, and I asked him if the hotel he was taking me to on the Rue des Trois-Frères was "Tout Confort," and it was just a question, but when I said that, it did something to him, he had sleepy sea-blue eyes, lashes too big for a boy, he had dimples, he had such an oaky, thick mane of hair, repeatedly pushed back from his forehead with a casual shove of his hand, Alex square-jawed and lankily tall, he could have been a movie star or a rock star the way he looked and he knew it, and he stopped me there, asked me to say it again, and I asked him "What?" and he said I should repeat what I had just said, he was smiling, pleased, and at first I just did so more or less as an interrogative, my cheeks maybe puffed out and my lips probably pouting to get the three little bursts of the syllables in what I hoped was authentically emphatic French pronunciation, "Tout Confort?" I asked, and with that he kissed me firmly, once on the lips, he asked me to say it again, "Tout Confort," which I did, and he did it again, he kissed me hard again, as I stood there just looking back at him, he told me I was "cute" when I said that, he seemed to like the fact he knew the word "cute," he told me it made him crazy to hear me say that, and I said it again as we entered the ramshackle Hôtel des Trois-Frères' lobby, passing, yes, the old gold-on-black plaque out front announcing "Tout Confort," and at the hotel desk the balding stoop-shouldered man in a gray cardigan was certainly used to renting rooms for the afternoon, he took the bills Alex tugged from the pocket of his jeans, and we climbed the stairs laughing, arms linking us again, to go down the dim corridor with its brown linoleum to find Chambre 46 behind its door that had been painted maroon so many times that the glossy surface of it was ripply, and inside there was the yellow wallpaper, flower-print and stained in splotches, and there was the ancient bidet on wheels and hooked up to a flexible accordionized pipe, its chrome tarnished to green, and there was the tiny chipped oval of the sink and the marred tortoiseshell-veneer furniture, the smell of everything minty from the little bars of blue soap set out on the wobbly glass tray above the sink, and he was starting to undress me already, pulling at my jacket, and I pushed him back, I told him to wait, and I went over to close the drapes for the one big French window that looked out to the grim courtyard's well inside the building, I looked long enough to see that outside other paint-peeling window sashes were hung plastic supermarket bags surely with meat and fruit and milk and whatever else needed to be kept cool in them, the impromptu refrigerators of the ghostly people who actually must have lived alone in the cramped rooms of a place like the Hôtel des Trois-Frères, I walked back to him, he unbuttoned my winter jacket, a dark-blue wool sailor-coat thing, then started on my blouse, I stood facing him, I said to him softly "Tout Confort" just because I knew he liked it, he still had on his own ratty sheepskin coat and the red-and-yellow scarf remained around his neck like a flowing serpent, *baroque,* he unbuttoned my blouse, pushed away my bra, too, he started kissing my body, I ran my hands through his thick hair as I stood there, his tongue was wet on my breasts, warm and very wet, "Tout Confort," I said again, my eyes closed, listening to the silver steam-heat radiator jangling a huffy staccato as he continued, as he lowered himself down, moved his head lower and lower, the room was very warm, his hands were moving over me as I just stood there, I was almost a statue he was sculpting with the life of his breath itself, as he started fiddling with the single button and then the zipper of my worn Levi's, then his fingers were on my ridiculous scant lavender panties, he was nibbling, he was a French boy, not all that bright but he was a beautiful, beautiful French boy, his name was Alex, and . . .

▮ ▮ ▮

. . . and later, back at the square with the frilled green Art Nouveau subway station, more golden leaves splattered on the damp black pavement in the streetlight, I left him there, I would take a train during the early evening rush hour back to the Left Bank and Rue Broca, he said he was going to just walk over to the other side of Montmartre, down the hill beyond the now glowing white dome of Sacré-Coeur, the stars already big and looking so close in the black winter sky that had at last cleared, it was colder, he said he had some friends from the university who lived in the Nineteenth there, out by the hissing Périphérique freeway, we kissed, parted, and I went back down the corkscrew staircase and again far, far below Montmartre alone, everything almost a photograph in reverse development of our walking up those steps earlier, except that I was, yes, alone, and somehow I couldn't just go directly back to Billy now, I needed time, and for some reason and with nothing much to think about, with no direction whatsoever, there in the station I was lost, and before I even got on a train that would weave its way through more of the darkened tunnels again, I found myself thinking of Gérard de Nerval, and if nothing else that gave me a destination, I looked at the Métro map under glass downstairs in the station, I stared at the jigsaw puzzle of its faded colors and the glass itself clouded over with scratches and graffiti, and I put my finger to the red dot indicating the Palais-Royal stop, and in the car packed during rush hour now, I rode as the doors repeatedly wheezed open and shut to shuffle the crowd this way and that, in and out, the car smelled of maybe vacuum cleaner innards, half electricity and half merely dust, which is the smell of the Métro, and you have to understand that at that point I didn't know a lot of things, and the things I didn't know were things like how I would soon learn beyond any doubt from the other girls in my classes, those French girls who smoked and cursed, who seemed to know everything while I an American girl knew nothing, I learned that Alex was what could be called a cad, was even legendary in that role, he preyed on American girls in exchange programs and he bragged to his buddies who played on his rugby team with him how he did so, conquered such girls one by one then eventually lost interest, as he later did with me, it was a game for him, he singled out any American girl almost as soon as she walked into that lobby of the classroom building off Rue Censier, and with all the bohemian airs he laid claim to, his seeming to bask in his knowing about those cheap hotels that always looked as if they were right out of some old black-and-white French *film-noir* movie with subtitles, yes, despite those bohemian airs, it turned out that actually he had grown up in ultra-genteel Neuilly in a sprawling posh apartment overlooking the Bois de Boulogne with parents who were both prominent well-to-do lawyers involved in national politics, and, of course, I had no way of knowing then that the lies I told Billy after being with Alex and the lies that I was sure I could remedy in time wouldn't, in fact, ever be a matter of being remedied in time, and within a few months Billy and I were back in leafy Ithaca again, several thousand miles away from Paris, or maybe a couple of *universes* away, everything metamorphosing as if in a dream, or that's how it felt, I took that course in geology called Rocks for Jocks, the professor had everybody in the course buy a special geologist's hammer with a red handle and a pick-like shining steel head and there were day trips by bus to stone outcrops along Cayuga Lake in the sunshine of buzzing bees and hovering dragonflies, Ithaca, we were supposed to be gathering rock samples for study, but really we were just enjoying being outside like that, I took a course in general political science, nothing more than a glorified junior high school civics class in the government department, where in this case the bored professor himself suggested we forget about the bulky overpriced textbook and simply read a few newspapers online for homework and then discuss in class the next day whatever we had read about current events, summer school was like that, with the lecture hall windows wide open and the buildings-and-grounds guys somnambulistically riding their snoring lawnmowers in circles and endless circles in the brilliant, chlorophyll-charged sunshine of July and August, Ithaca, and I was the one who discovered the hard lump on Billy's neck that September, right below his ear on the right side, I felt it in an embrace, he didn't want to have it checked at first, though maybe he already *knew,* and he said at first that it was nothing and he didn't have time to go over to the university health services, he was so busy with his research, and Billy often said he couldn't believe how lucky that an incorrigible bookworm like him had been to have found somebody like me, he told me I was rarer than rare, he said he sometimes felt that he himself was no better than one of his French Symbolists, Rimbaud or Mallarmé or Verlaine, even gentle Gérard de Nerval, dreaming everything that seemed to pass for a life, no sense of what made up real life, Billy said he sometimes thought he was dreaming me, and I always told myself that I would tell him about Alex, how stupid I had been, how selfish I had been, I told my sister Madison about Alex and she of course wanted to hear all the details, giggling, she said I should *never* tell Billy, she reminded me that Billy and I were *engaged,* "He's your fiancé, for gosh sakes!" but I was going to tell Billy maybe by the end of the summer, I planned to do it, I rehearsed it all, but then there was the lump, and the cheery lying doctors in their neat white lab coats, all of them wearing horn-rimmed glasses, every one of them, or so it sometimes seemed, the doctors talked of remission and told Billy one thing as the treatment began, hopeful, but the blood-count tests and Billy's body just wasting away told another story altogether, and in a way Billy was already gone, so what would my telling him or anybody else anything amount to, except to say how in that darkness of an early evening in Paris I did get out at the Palais-Royal Métro stop, and there were the guys dressed in baggy red jackets and red baseball caps handing out the free evening papers that were big in Paris then, only sports news and gossipy celebrity news, plenty of ads, there was the very strong smell of the cold and there was the long arched colonnade of the Palais-Royal sort of golden in the evening lamplight, the slabs of purplish paving stones, small shops lit along the colonnade, people walking this way and that now that the work day was done and all of them bundled against the evening's cold, and I knew that it was here, at this very spot, that Nerval strolled nonchalantly with his little lobster, he had it on a ribbon for a leash, I walked past the Palais-Royal courtyard with the black-and-white-striped columns sprouting at different stubby heights dotting the entirety of its perfectly square expanse, some attempt at postmodern art that looked goofy indeed now that it was no longer very new, I mean it seemed to be trying altogether too hard to be daring and offbeat and, well, so postmodern, I could tell people were looking at me, they knew all about me, I could tell that even then, and I still couldn't go directly back to face Billy, I walked, but the very strangest thing of all was that even then I knew, realized beyond any doubt, that maybe for the rest of my life I would only want to be as young as I was then in Paris, and somehow Billy didn't matter, even Billy's illness wouldn't matter to me, I already sensed that probably for the rest of my life I would only want to be twenty-one years old and have a French boy slowly undressing me again in a shabby hotel room high atop Montmartre, a room with its floor of more brown linoleum, its walls with stained yellow flower-print wallpaper, the entire place aromatic with the miniature minty bars of soap, a swaybacked bed with a faded and thin nubbed beige spread, a bidet on wobbly casters that could be rolled under the sink, and maybe, in the end, it was simple, it was just to be so *alive* like that, and maybe there were no secrets of the sea that Gérard de Nerval's lobster had heard whisperings of, maybe there were none of the wonders of shopping and the restaurants in Paris that my sister Madison had naively imagined, maybe there was just a girl like me knowing that, yes, nothing in her life would ever again be quite like having that handsome French boy named Alex ask her to say "Tout Confort" again, the girl pouting the pronunciation, as he would kiss her hard on her lips in approval each time she said it, "Tout confort, tout confort, tout confort," and I finally headed back to the Palais-Royal Métro station to take a train back to Rue Broca, because it was getting late, Billy would certainly be wondering where I was, he probably had already walked over to the

Place de la Contrescarpe to see if I was at one of the cafés facing the little traffic circle with its always dry fountain, there where I often studied, and a clock was sounding the hour of seven exactly, probably from some church or the shadowy but very golden Palais-Royal itself, because how had Nerval put it, expressing it perfectly in that title of the work that was without question his most important work, as Billy had assured me, or as Billy now dead had assured me, *Le Rêve et la Vie,* dream and life, which could just as easily be life and dream, and I think I do know now all about Nerval, nobody but nobody will ever have to tell me again, and in the Métro station I slid my plastic student Carte Orange through the machine, I pushed my way past the thumping spring-loaded turnstile, and . . .

OH, SUCH PLAYWRIGHTS!

. . . the scarcely existing present—
which after all is our only possession.

—Arthur Symons

I. Kaleb's Play

After the bicycle accident, Kaleb's wife Lourdes María told friends that Kaleb hadn't been sleeping well.

"He had a good deal of trouble sleeping," she remembered, "it wasn't like him."

She said she simply attributed it to the fact he was so caught up in what he was working on—excited, even dreaming about the play during those uneasy nights—that maybe he wasn't as totally aware as he should have been on the bicycle that day. The accident happened when he was no more than fifteen minutes uptown from SoHo on the blue ten-speed, heading to the small but very respected repertory theater on West Fifty-fifth, almost clear over to Eleventh Avenue.

Kaleb had first stopped at the photocopy shop to pick up the three unbound copies of the script of his new play. The teenage girl working there, smiling, gave him the cardboard box containing the copies with a handful of big butterfly clips, and Kaleb smiled back, thanking the girl. He shoved the clips into his small red nylon backpack, zipped it up, slipped the pack's straps over his shoulders; with the box under one arm, he walked outside to where he had locked the bicycle against a street sign. It was the play that was never staged but came to be known—among friends and those in the group of actors and playwrights associated with the repertory theater—as "Kaleb's Play." For years it was called that.

It didn't matter that at thirty-five, then in 1982, Kaleb was a hardworking young playwright of considerable note, had already seen three of his plays produced, including one that enjoyed a well-received, if not especially long, Broadway run with name actors. Actually, all that did seem to matter was how on that beautiful afternoon in late October—the air cool enough for you to feel it in your nostrils if you inhaled deep, cutting wonderfully sharp and refreshing, and the big trees in Madison Square Park across from the photocopy shop igniting in their best scarlets and golds, back when Madison Square Park itself was still a bit seedy, no shortage of junkies on the walkway benches even in daytime—yes, what mattered was that this particular play being delivered to the theater was a new work, one he was apparently *very* excited about.

Kaleb unlocked the bicycle. He used bungee cords to securely attach the box of unbound copies onto the chrome rear carrier of the blue ten-speed (he had bought the bicycle at the Sears on Massachusetts Avenue in Cambridge maybe a week after he'd arrived at Harvard as a scholarship boy from Ohio, it was that old), tucked in his wool scarf at the neck of the old leather bomber jacket he wore with worn Levi's and a knit watch cap (once a high school quarterback, he was athletically handsome at five-ten or so with a square jaw and a sweep of mahogany hair, his good looks earning him the small parts in TV soaps that kept him financially afloat when younger and just starting out in New York, before marrying Lourdes María—her wealthy father was a major figure in the Mexico City movie industry, so after the marriage there was enough money that Kaleb didn't need to hustle for acting jobs), and he pushed off on the bicycle. Eventually working his way to the West Side, he pedaled beside the moving traffic on Sixth Avenue as he headed uptown. At West Fifty-fifth and Sixth, he cut over, stopping and straddling the bike with his Nike running shoes toed to the pavement at the red lights at Seventh Avenue and next at Broadway, then resuming the pedaling, maybe thinking about his upcoming meeting with the resident director of the theater group, David Hextall, to give David this new script. He shifted into higher gears and built up some speed again as West Fifty-fifth became less commercial and more just stately old apartment buildings with entry awnings out front and the surely bored uniformed doormen that Kaleb could see staring out—somewhat ghostly, in a nice way—from behind so many big glass doors. Kaleb watched the red turn to green ahead of him as he cruised toward the intersection with Ninth, on the far corner of which there was at the time the rather funky red-brick A & P, where at any hour of the day you probably could spot as many recognizable actors and actresses (doing their routine grocery shopping) as anywhere else in the city.

The cab was a battered canary-yellow Crown Vic, and without question the driver was accelerating in running the traffic signal that had just turned on Ninth Avenue—he must have been doing an even fifty. When the wailing ambulance arrived from Roosevelt Hospital only a few blocks away, the last thing anybody was thinking about—either the sidewalk bystanders stunned at what they had witnessed or the efficient EMS workers—were the scattered sheets of the three copies of the play, let loose from the gray cardboard box that all but detonated in the impact. The four lanes of Ninth Avenue were covered with the strewn white pages, first drifting like piled snow and eventually scattering more in the slight breeze of the afternoon and then that from the swooshing traffic there on one-way Ninth once it was fully reopened again; the reporting police simply tossed what was left of the old blue Sears ten-speed, as tangled as a nail puzzle, into the trunk of one of their cruisers.

All of which is to say, it might have been different if a copy of the play had actually been recovered from the scene. Or different if Kaleb's beautiful, quietly elegant wife Lourdes María, the young woman from what could justifiably be called the true Mexican elite, had found a carbon of the typescript amid the clutter on his desk in their spacious loft apartment in SoHo, or even a handwritten draft of the work. After the funeral and all the following year, Lourdes María looked and looked very carefully throughout the apartment, searching closets and drawers, also going through Kaleb's many worn spiral-bound notebooks left stacked on his desk, but nothing concerning the new play was written on those aqua-lined pages either. The director David Hextall from the repertory theater often asked her about it, and while she said she knew that Kaleb had been entirely satisfied with the play, convinced he had definitely produced something important, she couldn't recall him ever talking about its subject, though she added that he seldom talked to her of the content of any new work while he was writing it. Those other playwrights and actors who had known Kaleb asked her about it, too. Why, even a critic with an overdone British accent from *New York Magazine,* who was doing a round-up article on the best of the current crop of promising new playwrights and who admitted to Lourdes María that when starting the article he hadn't been aware of what had happened to Kaleb, he phoned her to ask her about it, saying:

"I'm intrigued—or even more than that, I'm *super* intrigued, if you get my drift."

People mentioned it to other people, and before long the work was referred to by the appellation it did come to acquire, "Kaleb's Play," the one he had been in the process of delivering by bicycle when he was killed. From there it only compounded.

People—more playwrights and actors, other critics—talked of its quality, how wonderful it had been (while, of course, nobody had ever seen or read it, nobody knew its *actual* title); they claimed that if it had been produced it would certainly have proven to be the pinnacle of Kaleb's achievement, even of his life, cut altogether short by the accident. When the small and respected theater near Eleventh Avenue folded some years later due to a financial downturn, David Hextall (not only director but also founder of the theater, suffering personal problems of his own, including a statutory rape charge involving a teenage actress from the High School of Music and Art who he'd cast in a production) said that in looking back he knew that everything would have been different if they had had a major work to save their theater somewhere along the line, a genuine artistic *and* financial hit, such as "Kaleb's Play."

Yes, that's how it continued to be known as the years went by, if, after too many of those years, Kaleb himself was ever remembered at all; there was never any mention of his other work, just Kaleb's Play.

Though many years later, when the two children were both off to college and Lourdes María was at last remarrying and vacating the SoHo apartment, she did, in fact, find what she believed to be an early typescript of a few scenes transcribed from a dozen accompanying loose-leaf pages of what was Kaleb's athletically rough yet clearly legible handwriting in dark pencil; they were in a corrugated box of his belongings she had previously overlooked. When she read in the play the entire scene of the bicycle accident written out very carefully—*everything just the way she herself often dreamed of it after the accident, right down to the girl smiling in the photocopy shop near Madison Square Park that brilliant autumn day and handing Kaleb the three copies, right down to the Yellow Cab coming out of nowhere and running the light at the intersection, the pages of the play blowing away forever, scattering farther and farther in the empty, moonlit darkness of Ninth Avenue that night long after the squad cars had left, even the fact that in the play she saw how the main character based on Kaleb, depicted accurately therein, admitted to himself that he had been very restlessly excited with his own dreams during uneasy sleep in the months while writing it*—true, when she read that scene, she knew then that the only thing to do was to dispose of the whole box, put it in the big green alleyway dumpster along with whatever else she was emptying out of the apartment in SoHo and move on at last with her own life.

After all, a play was only a play, fragile unreality, but life was life.

Remarried to a well-known Hollywood producer significantly older, a longtime business friend of her father, Lourdes María in time relocated with him to Los Angeles, living in a sprawling home with fine vistas high up in Westwood's Holmby Hills. She appreciated the ongoing California sunshine and also the feel of downtown L.A. itself, especially the South Broadway district of crumbling old movie theaters and department stores, all thoroughly Latino now. Sometimes she drove her sleek, long-snouted beige BMW coupe from Holmby Hills to downtown—the tinted windows rolled up, the air conditioner softly whispering its coolness—to just ease up and down South Broadway in the afternoon, slowly circle around the blocks of the streets between it and palm-studded Pershing Square, too, that reminded her of so much of Mexico City, a place—she told herself yet again—where she had once been completely happy as a girl growing up there, well before the loss of her gifted, handsome young husband Kaleb and the considerable sadness that came to define her life.

2. "Brothers in Outrage"

It wasn't that Bill Connaught O'Connor didn't know about the son he had by the woman who lived in Pennsylvania.

Apparently, she had worked as a nurse there for all those years while raising him on her own. The son was the result of a one-night encounter after a rock show in New York City. That was back when Bill had part-time employment in the sixties as sort of a resident stage roadie setting up shows at the old Slate's Rock Emporium music venue in the East Village; he supported himself that way while trying to get somebody to notice the plays he ceaselessly wrote in a walk-up cubbyhole a block away from Slate's, before his prominence as a playwright. To be honest, when it came to this son it was probably more a matter of Bill simply managing to repress the fact that the boy existed, as he had repressed a lot of things in life, no doubt—all the money he'd made on his plays and then lost (plenty of booze and drugs, close to a rock-and-roll lifestyle) and the three wives in the course of as many brief marriages who he'd had and then lost (which maybe went with the territory of the lifestyle). A couple of times he had sent checks to the woman in Pennsylvania—when he did have substantial money steadily coming in, years before—but she herself surely had long ago given up on hearing anything further from him.

He was a big man in physical stature, wide-shouldered and grizzly-bearded. Once a true late-1960s artistic rebel yet very successful in the playwriting world, Bill had come across as a supremely self-confident force to be reckoned with back then, an undeniable presence wherever he appeared; he still wore the bib-front overalls and flannel shirts and Kangol caps (backwards like a beret) he'd always liked, for perhaps a don't-give-a-damn image that matched his sheer size. And lately Bill sometimes tried to tell himself that maybe nothing had changed since those old days, though, in actuality, everything had changed—Bill Connaught O'Connor barely got by now.

He was past fifty, his health wasn't that good. In addition to the recurrent bouts of serious depression, he had already undergone a joint operation on one knee and the other was heading that way, which could happen to such a big man carrying that kind of weight; he moved slow and somewhat uneasily, his gait like that of a pro-football ex-lineman who had seen far too many tough games. If it weren't for his having gotten an apartment in Manhattan Plaza—subsidized housing for people working in the performing arts, between Forty-second and Forty-third on Ninth—he might have been in very large trouble merely to provide for himself a place to live. The impressive high-rise of bright orange brick and abundant glass had first been developed as potential luxury housing in the early seventies, and it seemed it couldn't miss, being so close to midtown. But at the time, nobody in the category of the well-to-do was willing to live in what was still very much the old, rough Hell's Kitchen neighborhood; the developer had to get HUD and the city to bail him out with a quickly cobbled-together scheme of designating the building subsidized housing like that, locked into the setup probably forever, even as the area gradually became rather gentrified.

Right before his son, now a student at Brooklyn College, did show up in his life that one day smack in the heart of frozen February, there had been a painful exchange for Bill in the building. And it was something that for Bill just about confirmed how bad everything had gotten, how far he had fallen in the full twenty or more years since he had been one of Joseph Papp's darlings for productions at Lincoln Center, its Forum Stage, and then Papp's own Public Theater, no shortage of easy, extremely lucrative Hollywood script-writing work coming Bill's way in those days, too. A guy named Ira, who lived several doors down from him in the high-rise and worked as a Broadway stagehand, longing to write plays himself in middle age, mentioned his avocation to Bill, and Bill started giving him informal instruction gratis, going over Ira's manuscripts with him in Bill's small efficiency apartment a couple of afternoons a week. In other words, Bill spent considerable time with the guy, which got Bill's mind off the truth that nobody seemed to want the plays he himself kept writing, his supposed agent not even returning his calls. For hours Bill worked with skinny, whiny-voiced Ira in his jeans and droopy turtlenecks, and if nothing else it reminded Bill of the satisfaction he'd experienced when he had taken brief teaching gigs at Yale Drama School early on. (There was his seminar called "Brothers in Outrage" on the avant-garde playwrights who had influenced him when first starting out—from Beckett to Ionesco to LeRoi Jones—that he taught as a semester-long invited visitor for two years running at Yale Drama, commuting by train one afternoon a week from the city, and the class became notorious in theater circles.) Yes, working with Ira was satisfying, even if, admittedly, the guy was a sad sack who didn't appear to have much real talent, would be better off sticking to his union stagehand work and appreciating how by doing so he at least qualified for an apartment in Manhattan Plaza, with such decent rent for that location in the city.

Truth of the matter was that Bill was *totally* broke, the electric bills unpaid, his phone about to be disconnected. The restaurants and most of his regular bars along Ninth Avenue, where he'd cadged drinks and meals on nonexistent credit lately, had pretty much eighty-sixed him en masse, raucous Bill inevitably causing a scene whenever he started drinking too much scotch on ice late at night, getting really loud. Having ended a long session of going over Ira's play at the end of the winter day, Bill asked Ira—as Ira was leaving Bill's apartment, standing at the door—if Ira might go down to the small supermarket on Forty-third and buy him a couple of boxes of wheat flakes and a bunch of bananas and a gallon jug of milk, the kind of low-budget sustenance Bill had been more or less surviving on for the past month.

Ira stood there, holding out his bony hand palm up, saying:

"Twenty bucks should cover it, Bill."

It was all Bill could do to keep himself from flying into a rage, slugging the scrawny bastard right then and there, Bill getting a little short of breath as he pictured Ira's fragile skull, absurd black square-framed glasses and all, imploding like a crushed paper lantern in the thrust of Bill's anvil of a fist—but Bill didn't slug him; he just tried to keep his voice calm and low, saying raspily, "Fuck off, Ira, OK? Just fuck off, man, and don't bother me anymore, OK?"

The whole exchange kept haunting Bill. It became a stinging indication of how his time was worth nothing anymore, not even the price of cereal. And this was *Bill Connaught O'Connor,* once a young lion indeed, showing up at opening performances in a limousine dispatched for him and with two gorgeous hookers in the back seat sniffing coke with him simply because he knew that an appearance flanked by hookers would shake people up, true, *Bill Connaught O'Connor,* once somebody who had often been newsworthy and seen his name in the gossip columns of the *Post* or the *Daily News* after he performed another one of his absolutely wild stunts in a Theater District restaurant. (Drinking alone, sitting at the bar in one restaurant, he'd once overheard a certified yuppie at a nearby table with a bunch of other yuppies all fresh from a show, men and women, say something stupid about Eugene O'Neill, and Bill just got up—grizzly-bearded, lineman-big, wearing the backwards Kangol cap and bib-fronts and a tattered camouflage jacket that strained to cover the bulk of his broad chest—and approached the table; saying nothing, Bill lifted the guy's plate of pasta calamari and dumped it over the head of this stockbroker or whoever he was, then casually walked back to his bar stool to quietly resume where he'd left off drinking—the incident got good play in the *Post*.) In short, Bill Connaught O'Connor, who had been a theater celebrity and then some, was now having to admit to the fact that recently the tenants' association at Manhattan Plaza had voted—charitably and unanimously—to adjust the monthly rent he paid to below the minimum. Rent was based on a flat percentage of yearly income, and as to the touchy question of income, Bill didn't have much beyond the unreliable trickle of royalties from the occasional small-time stagings of his early plays, always somewhere in the sticks now, plus the infrequent tiny residual checks from having had bit parts in movies—some old friends in the business knew of his plight and a few times they'd found for him a little something acting in films being shot in the city.

Concerning the son, a phone call came first. The kid was named Rory, and on the phone—tentative in the beginning, obviously frightened—he said who he was, before long not nervous at all once

Bill assured him that he, Bill, figured Rory would call him at some point, Bill repeatedly telling Rory to just, "Relax, man." Within a few weeks of their first meeting that winter, the two of them were spending a lot of time together. Hell, did Rory ever look like Bill when Bill had been young and growing up back in Providence: the shag of sandy hair, the clear Irish skin, the general bulk of him, Rory wide-shouldered and even loping along—nobody would have questioned he was Bill's son, that's for sure. And wouldn't you know it, the son wanted to emulate Bill and was studying theater and film there at Brooklyn College. For a while the two of them could be seen around Manhattan Plaza together, moving up and down Ninth Avenue, too, an older, decidedly scruffy hipster, Bill, with a younger college-age hipster in a pea coat and jeans, Rory. Around that time, a reasonably good theater in Seattle revived one of Bill's early plays and there was at least *some* money coming in again.

It would have been obvious, in fact, to anybody who dealt with the pair of them—such as a fellow playwright, Jim Lombardi, who Bill introduced his son to while passing through the Manhattan Plaza lobby one day—that the kid was in absolute awe of his father, still a major artist in his eyes. They usually tried a bar or two along Ninth Avenue in the evening—Bill had been eighty-sixed at the upscale West Bank located on the street level of Manhattan Plaza, where theater people (working actors and playwrights) did drink, if not eat, alongside the "yuppies" (always Bill's blanket categorization) who frequented its restaurant, but Bill was still welcome at comfortably funky Rudy's on Ninth, with its free hot dogs grilling behind the bar, two-buck cans of Pabst, and red vinyl-upholstered booths sloppily repaired with duct tape—and after a few hours in the bars they often ended up at a new coffee shop next to St. Clare's Hospital. A small place, it was run by two young guys who had formerly been in a local band; one of their fathers, a rich attorney wanting to give his only offspring a hopefully stable livelihood, was now bankrolling this coffee-shop idea. Bill and his son usually joined the bunch of guys Bill's son's age who hung out there with the young owners, all of them intently listening as Bill held court. A loud, definitely animated Bill told them hilarious stories of his rock-and-roll adventures, rubbing elbows with musicians in legendary bands while working at Slate's Rock Emporium before he was discovered by Joseph Papp of the dark suits and mysterious dark sunglasses, Bill becoming one of the famous impresario's first protégés, and he told them about the craziness of working big-money scriptwriting stints out in Hollywood and once even spending the night with Tuesday Weld. In the otherwise empty place, the wiry red-headed kid with a goatee—a former bass guitarist and now the coffee shop's co-owner, still wearing a white apron from his work manning the espresso machine behind the counter, though there was no coffee for these nightly bull sessions, just a good supply of red-and-white Budweiser tallboys bought at a Ninth Avenue bodega for all to consume—the kid talked about how he had recently seen the old film *Play It As It Lays* starring Tuesday Weld; he noted how convincing she was in her leading role—beautiful, eerily soft-spoken, haunting—and not the ditzy blonde that she had usually been stereotyped as earlier in her career.

"Man, and this guy *slept* with Tuesday Weld," he said.

"Who didn't?" Bill pronounced in his deep, authoritative voice, a bushy eyebrow slowly raised.

Everybody around the table laughed, Bill's son Rory beaming, again obviously so proud of his father, a hero for him. And it went on like that right into the spring that year—the two of them more like a couple of buddies than anything else, even doing drugs together now and then in Bill's cluttered efficiency in Manhattan Plaza—until one night, it seems, they were alone, and the talk got more serious than usual. They were in that dim bar called Rudy's on Ninth Avenue, not in the coffee shop where the young guys would laugh so much at Bill's tales and maybe ask Bill yet another time to bellowingly give his one-line philosophy about what the good life essentially boiled down to—"Co-co and limos and plenty of wild young women, boys!"—all of them roaring; this conversation now, as Bill and his son sat alone and side by side on the red-topped bar stools in Rudy's, had turned very serious. There was soft talk from Bill about the many things he had messed up on in life, softer talk from his son about how lonely he had been as a kid, how it hadn't been easy on his mother either, working sometimes double shifts as an RN in the hospital in Scranton and trying to raise him on her own. When Bill asked him if he'd ever thought about him in all those years, wondered about his father, Rory in the pea coat—his complexion milkily white, the longish sandy hair touching the coat's collar, a young guy nearly as big as Bill—suddenly seemed but a scared little boy, admitting somewhat hesitantly, his voice uneven, close to breaking:

"I had no idea who you were, but I dreamed of you, oh, how much I *dreamed* of you, all the time, not even knowing who you were."

Bill just looked at him.

"I dreamed and dreamed of you each night," Rory said. "In the dreams I seemed to be talking to you, kind of whispery, you know, telling you everything about what happened to me that day."

Bill didn't know what to say—it hit him like a full, hard punch to the gut.

So, it possibly might have been that night at the bar, Rudy's, that changed the whole thing. By the end of the spring Rory had his college final papers and exams to think about, the two seeing each other less, Bill going into another one of the bouts of depression and guilt. Despite all his bravado—the old and loud assertion of himself as the wild playwright, uncompromising and always calling his own shots, as he had once been—this dark, leaden depression did plague him on and off throughout his adult life, and now it returned with debilitating force. Never mind meeting up with his newly discovered son, he seldom answered the phone or even left the building anymore.

There was very heavy drinking, by himself in his apartment, complete with raving about the stupidity of past directors and producers that could be heard in neighboring apartments, the occasional loud thump of Bill collapsing to the floor in another blackout, too, and then there was a return to dabbling with the heroin that he'd thought was well behind him in life; he ended up in Bellevue for a month. However, going there might have been more of a plan he agreed to ahead of time, calculated, Bill sort of invoking a psychiatric out, to dodge the situation in which he owed over a year of back rent to Manhattan Plaza; the tenants' association had become less understanding and now threatened to bring him to court for the entire unpaid amount. He moved to a state-run halfway house in a small town somewhere on the Hudson after that, and word got back to New York that even beyond not mentioning much about his son Rory to anybody anymore, Bill Connaught O'Connor questioned if, in fact, he was actually Rory's father, the object of those many heartbreaking dreams that Rory said he'd had about him when a kid.

People claimed that Bill Connaught O'Connor—medicated now, almost lifelessly docile, diagnosed by one physician as perhaps clinically bipolar—sometimes went as far as rejecting the whole idea that he had ever been involved in theater, and in more lucid moments he might make a sinisterly dark joke to somebody who visited him at the halfway house about how he should have chosen something saner by definition than pursuing the life of a playwright, maybe he should have been a junior high school principal in Providence like his own totally square father—though people also said that they weren't so sure he was *entirely* joking about that.

3. A Reading in the High-rise above Tenth Avenue

By about seven-thirty that warm late-June evening in 2007, they were deep into the reading of the second act of the play. It was a full-length three-act that Jim had been working on for over a year now.

The two actors sat at the table in the dining/living room in playwright Jim Lombardi's modest place in Manhattan Plaza, high up on the fifteenth floor. And in the course of the actors reading, Jim walked slowly around the room, script in hand, the red-bound cover rolled back; he interrupted them once in a while after the delivery of a line, for the three of them to talk about that line for a bit, decide if it did or didn't work.

Also in the course of it, Jim would have been dishonest if he didn't admit that there was something rather inherently sad (hopeless? even heartbreaking?) about the three of them working so hard every Thursday evening these past several weeks, reading and reworking Jim's play together—a play that in all likelihood (rock-hard probability?) would never find a backer for production. Thick gray hair combed straight back, a slight paunch, tinted glasses, wearing a dated, loose-tailed Hawaiian sport shirt of big blue parrots on a yellow background along with the baggy cargo shorts and comfortable Wallabies—that was Jim Lombardi, his plays the subject of at least a dozen long articles over the years by U.S. academics as well as French and German theater scholars there in the faded journals in the bookcase behind the table, though the work never having found much success commercially. Jim's wife was a classically trained singer who now taught privately, and Jim had managed to stay solvent with a job in the so-called Literature Department of Pratt's downtown-Manhattan satellite campus. The job sounded ritzy, the art school being as renowned as it was, but for Jim it basically meant five sections of "bonehead" freshman English and sophomore lit, both required for the budding painters, sculptors, and animators who had scant, if any, interest in writing and literature; it paid terribly, by the course, and at his age and into his sixties, there was no security whatsoever in the position, Jim hired on a year-to-year basis.

At one point, when they were close to finishing up for the evening, the actress Lydia Ellstrom, reading the female part, asked Jim to listen to a particular line delivered two different ways. She said she wanted input on the intonation, and while Jim wasn't sure he noticed any real marked difference, the actor Neddy Burt, across the dining table from Lydia and reading the male part, proceeded to discuss it with a full analysis bordering on benevolent exegesis.

"I honestly think," Neddy said, going on and on, well along in his commentary, "what needs to be established here is how she would respond to such a close friend of her husband telling her something outrageous like that—angered but subtly curious about it, too."

"Sort of curiouser and curiouser," Lydia said, apparently amused by Neddy's thoroughness; she smiled, winked at Jim.

She had been a beauty, a tall Minnesota blonde, Nordic, though as Jim remembered one director years ago saying, "Forget Minnesota, and there's something purely Texas about her that I love, hearty and brash, no matter where the hell she's from." She was in her fifties now, caught up in raising her son by her marriage to a Wall Street lawyer who still would repeatedly and proudly tell the story of how he had pursued and won her when—never having been introduced to Lydia but hopelessly smitten—he went to something like fifteen consecutive performances of a play she'd once been in with a lengthy Broadway run, the guy eventually stoking up the courage to approach her after a show. At the table, her own copy of the script before her, pencil in hand, she wore casual pink Capri slacks, navy-blue canvas slip-ons, and a white sleeveless summer blouse; with her sculpted cheekbones and that definitely Nordic overbite, she was still striking as all hell, granting she rarely got much work anymore. Neddy Burt was lanky and hollow-eyed, his hair buzz-cut probably in deference to his thinning pate; he wore a scholar's round tortoise-shell glasses that tended to slip down his nose, his forefinger always coaxing them up. Neddy exuded a certain sensitivity and vulnerability, the wasting-away ethereal poet type. That might have been due to the fact that with Neddy originally from Wales and having managed to camouflage well his accent in over thirty years of New York acting, enough of a tinge of that accent still leaked through to make him seem slightly out of date and Old Worldish—or it might have simply been due to the fact that after his wife had died of breast cancer five years ago, Neddy did seem perpetually and understandably sad. He wore old jeans and a gray pocket T-shirt, everything rumpled and somehow very much an actor's off-stage attire. He could go six months or more lately without as much as a small role on or off Broadway, let alone anything in the Shakespeare that he was known for when younger, and he had confessed to Jim earlier—when he'd first shown up, much too early and well before Lydia—that this would mark the first July and August since he honestly could remember that he didn't have a regular summer-stock gig somewhere; an offer from a Vermont theater where he'd worked before had fallen through at the last minute. They talked about the line in the play some more, the three of them bouncing ideas back and forth, and then the two actors continued reading their parts.

A half-hour later, Lydia looked at the oversize clear-plastic watch she wore, campy, and said that she'd better get moving, take the subway back downtown to pick up her son after his karate class; her husband couldn't do it today, he was working late, she explained. Neddy, who surely had no place to go, made more or less a show out of noisily gathering up the script and some notes of his own he had been taking, probably so that he, too, would look busy. At the door to the apartment, Jim thanked them for coming. They all agreed they had made very good progress in polishing Jim's play and that they would meet again the next Thursday at six, to continue on with the third and final act, which they hadn't gone through yet.

Lydia and Neddy left, Jim shut the door.

Jim's wife wouldn't be back from giving a voice lesson for an hour or so, and in the apartment in Manhattan Plaza, the subsidized housing for those in the performing arts (both Jim and his wife qualified for residence, had lived there since they were married, a second time for each of them), Jim experienced a rush of loneliness, as followed by a feeling of pure futility, or maybe utter hopelessness—or *something*. He remembered that he would have to teach two sections of freshman comp at the Pratt summer school because he needed the money, and there were bills piling up for his aging mother in the nursing home in Queens; Jim was also helping out one of his grown daughters by his first marriage, who was having her own financial problems. Jim had grown up in working-class Queens, his father a bakery company's home-delivery man, and Jim had always been crazy about writing plays, first at CCNY as a commuter student and then at Carnegie Mellon School of Drama—a place as good as Yale Drama at the time, possibly better—for an MFA. His work, produced off-Broadway and winning several awards, certainly brought the notice of academics for a while, who sometimes named him as one of only a half-dozen American playwrights doing anything *genuinely* serious—which most likely had been his downfall. Being pigeonholed as the acknowledged darling of academics, including those snooty French and German ones, meant that lately most producers saw his work as good but perhaps too artistically high-brow.

Jim walked over to the sliding glass doors that opened onto the balcony, cluttered with a couple of lawn chairs and a seldom used charcoal grill. Stepping outside to the little space, high up in Manhattan Plaza's back facade, above Tenth Avenue there on the West Side, he stood at the concrete parapet in the rather ridiculous Hawaiian-print shirt and looked down to the blue Hudson and then the rise of the New Jersey Palisades topped with repeated puffs of such feathery green trees across the way. The enlarged disc of the sun, deep orange, lay so low in the early evening's humid haze that the air itself had taken on—particle by individual glowing particle, it seemed—a peach-hued texture; horns far below blew discordantly, but being distant like that the noise was soft and somehow entirely pleasant. Actually, even this high up, there was the good smell of the city in the heat of the tag end of a summer day, a vague, metallically dull aroma of asphalt and exhaust, tough to describe but always so wonderful maybe because it does *define* New York. Having left one of the piers that were now in use again around Fiftieth Street, a massive cruise ship—bright white and its cabins stacked high, the behemoth like an ancient floating city in itself—was setting out for some surely far-off destination, dreamlike, gliding very slowly along, as Jim Lombardi just stared at it, took in the whole scene so far below.

He thought about things.

He thought about how goddamn much he'd always outright *loved* the theater, how just seeing a play was different from reading a short story or a novel or a poem—it was always in the way characters hauntingly came *alive* right before an audience's eyes in that darkness of a stage, more than dreamlike, and even a film didn't have that essential magic: a film wasn't conjured-up flesh and blood, it wasn't human breath. And he thought, and knew, that just as much as he loved the theater, those two actors with him this evening outright *loved* the theater, too—it had all of them going through this pantomime of activity as they had been doing these Thursday evenings, to probably convince themselves they remained in the thick of things, were still involved.

Jim knew that when his wife Sarah arrived she would ask him how the reading went, smiling understandingly, and Jim found himself thinking about his wife, and also thinking some more of Lydia and Neddy, both of whom had acted in a couple of his earlier plays. Then he found himself thinking of, picturing clearly—this is where it got strange—a certain snowy evening who knows how long before. What triggered it was how, during the reading at the dining table, Lydia had asked about the playwright Bill Connaught O'Connor, wondering if Jim would ever hear how Bill was doing now that he was so long out of Manhattan Plaza and still in a medical facility somewhere upstate, as a friend had recently told her. And the mention of Bill Connaught O'Connor now reminded Jim of that night of a snowstorm in probably January many years ago. It was when Jim had just happened to run into his friend Bill—a fine, dazzlingly iconoclastic young playwright in those days—at the bar of the rundown old steakhouse where theater types always used to hang out, Tommy Shay's on Seventh Avenue, an establishment later leveled in the name of redevelopment. Jim sat down at the bar beside Bill, the two of them drinking together, both soon excited, talking about their new work under way. And before long they were joined by the handsome guy Kaleb Townes—he had died while only in his thirties, Jim remembered, it was a bicycle accident or something, with Kaleb a bona fide Harvard grad who was all the rage just then after a successful Broadway production and who had married the lovely, very wealthy Mexican woman—yes, Kaleb had shown up there that night, too, now that Jim pictured the scene. And with Kaleb pulling up a bar stool, there was the trio of young theater pals and they talked and talked, exchanging ideas about technique and also the great plays in dramatic history they admired and had learned from, all thoroughly excited about what they themselves were writing and what lay ahead of them in the theater—*Oh, such playwrights we were back then!* Jim now told himself. It was wild, all right, and old and wily white-haired Tommy Shay, the owner, didn't want to interrupt it, telling them—the only customers remaining at three a.m.—to leave a list of anything they drank beside the cash register at the bar and they could pay the next time they came in, because his bartender had left and his cooks had cleaned the kitchen and he personally was calling it a day. He said they could talk forever if they wanted to, to eternity, but he, for one, was going home to get some well-deserved sleep. Tommy Shay instructed them to switch off all the lights when leaving and exit through the back alleyway door that would latch and lock automatically. Or, that must have been what happened, Jim now thought, because Tommy Shay never gave them a key or anything—or did he, possibly telling one of them to return it the next time he came in? Repeatedly getting beers for themselves from the cooler behind the bar, they stayed there till dawn, for hours and with more spirited talking, no idea of the time. They finally closed up the place, and then—the morning sunshine blindingly bright on Manhattan's fresh, newly fallen snow, their breath making clouds of steam in the cold air—they walked the several blocks to the chrome-sided Market Diner down by the West Side Highway, where they slid into a booth and enjoyed a big breakfast together of bacon and eggs and plenty of strong, hot coffee, still talking and talking and talking some more.

Man, that had been nice, Jim thought.

He shook his head.

He stepped back into the apartment, rolled shut the big screen panel of the sliding door. He looked at the red-bound copy of his play on the table, there beside the salt and pepper shakers, and pulled out a chair at the table, sat down. He opened the script and looked at that one line Lydia and Neddy had discussed at length—because, upon more consideration now, Jim thought he saw what Lydia, and then Neddy in his detailed analysis, had been getting at, and Jim thought he knew what was needed to, well, *fix* it.

And leaning over with pencil in hand and striking out a couple of words, penciling in others, he realized he definitely knew how to fix it. He penciled in more words, struck out some of those, then penciled in several other words. He read over what he had written, changed some of the wording yet again.

He nodded, put the pencil down on the table, satisfied; he reread the line as revised, twice and then three times—yes, it now looked exactly right.

Or maybe it was more than that, because Jim Lombardi, there at the dining table with its flimsy place mats and the plastic salt and pepper shakers, was suddenly convinced that he might really be onto something with this play, and it could be—why not? because he felt *good* about this one—the *best* thing he'd ever done, a play that *any* producer in New York would be crazy to turn down.

TUNIS AND TIME

I.

Layton found himself working on a second week in the city. Everything was supposed to be routine in Tunis, just asking a few questions of an informant named Khaled Khemir. Layton was set up comfortably enough in a white wedding-cake rise of an old hotel on Avenue de Paris, the Majestic.

It was a run-down place but with at least airs of former opulence. The cavernous lobby, all red and white marble, had a sweeping staircase and elaborate chandeliers; there was a splattering of old clock faces on the wall behind the desk giving the hour in various major cities around the world (he kept noticing those clocks, and how it seemed that the one for New York had been replaced recently with a newer one for Karachi, perhaps understandable in an Arab-world country in such an uneasy moment like this internationally). The manager was a handsome guy in his late thirties, muscular and mustached, his hair in a styled shag. Always wearing a tailored French suit, he had once played for the revered Espérance Sportive soccer club there in Tunis, his celebrity status landing him this easy job now.

Layton liked talking soccer with him, and the manager seemed to have no problem with Layton being an American.

▪ ▪ ▪

Layton probably didn't need any formal cover in Tunis. Nevertheless, his informal one, in case anybody got nosy, was a line about being an academic researching an article on Flaubert and his time out at the ruins of nearby Carthage, which had resulted in the historical novel *Salammbô*. It wasn't the first occasion that Layton had resorted to the fact that he had been a French literature major in what felt like some other lifetime indeed back at Harvard. In truth, not much of the literature stuck with Layton, and often alone in a hotel room somewhere, a ceiling fan chugging, he seemed to recall nothing substantial from any of those novels very clearly, or anything, maybe, beyond the stuff that people who hadn't even read the books most likely had heard of: the famous black hearse-like carriage rocking away with Madame Bovary and her young law-clerk lover coupling as it rambled around the cobbled streets of Rouen, or even the famous centipede crawling up the famous bare white wall in the modern plantation house, seemingly the main action in Robbe-Grillet's static slim volume. True, little of that came back to him, yet what did often unexpectedly and repeatedly return was a memory of the construction of the odd covers themselves of the Livre de Poche editions. He remembered 1968 or 1969 and leaving his rooms in Winthrop House on the river, to head over to the Square and the Coop Textbooks on a side street. And what he also definitely remembered was how those imported paperbacks for his French lit courses were coated in clear cellophane, which somehow wasn't made for the New England climate, the coating soon yellowing and cracking, peeling free completely before long. That always represented some essential flaw to Layton, and in the lavender rain and heading back to red-brick Winthrop House on the grassy banks of that Charles—yes, back then rain *could* be beautifully lavender in Cambridge, a guy like Layton *could* once be young and also hopeful that he would be lucky in life, everything would turn out OK and good things were ahead of him—Layton almost asked himself before he cracked the spine of another new Livre de Poche, "How long before this one falls apart?"

Layton knew, though, he had to be careful of thinking of things like that, especially careful of thinking too much when by yourself in a hotel room in a very hot country, a place like Tunis, let's say.

As for the two blond girls from Montpellier, nearly a matching set and half Layton's age or less, Layton had noticed them around the downtown even before he got mixed up with them. Actually, how couldn't you notice them? Any tourists that there were in Tunisia seemed to stay at the resort towns beyond the city and out on the coast, a sleek bus occasionally herding a pack of them in for a morning shopping trip to buy the overpriced souvenir junk (cheaply plated hookahs, tiny stuffed camels, etc.) in the Medina, but little more than that was seen of their presence. And the usual tourists certainly weren't two svelte five-foot-nine girls wearing platform heels, designer jeans, and halter tops, tanned and made up like dolls there under an umbrella at one of the big cafés along Avenue Bourguiba, runway model material—though Layton would eventually learn that they were more than broke, that they had jumped a hotel bill up in ritzy Sidi Bou Said and had originally left France without so much as bothering to book a return ticket back to Montpellier simply because they were sure some playboy in a white yacht (OK, maybe two playboys, in their own nutty daydreaming) would eventually ferry them home, in *real* style.

The girls at an outdoor café—one of them in oversize sunglasses pushing her long fingers in a raking shove through the spill of blond hair, then the other in oversize sunglasses taking that almost as a cue, as if to say in her whispery French, near baby talk, "Wow, it's been a while since I pushed my hand through my beautifully lustrous spill of long blond hair that dusts my fine bare and tanned shoulders," and doing the same.

They were like that, Véronique and Jeanne-Isabelle.

II.

"You shouldn't have come anywhere near the embassy," Cunningham from CIA said.

"It was at night, my first one here," Layton said, "or the evening, anyway. I like to get a feel for a place, if you know what I mean. See where everything is. I just left the hotel and strolled around some. I could have been anybody walking in that well-to-do neighborhood there."

"Nobody saw you?"

Layton and Cunningham were having a late lunch in a modest enough place on Rue du Caire, good couscous. Layton knew that CIA saw FBI as yokels. And this Cunningham with his front of a job in the embassy's consular section was no different; he surely didn't take to the idea that Layton was supposedly needed at the moment, and surely for Cunningham—lanky, bespectacled, and self-satisfied at forty or so—an FBI yokel could only mess things up. Layton continued with the couscous, and he had to hand it to Cunningham concerning the meal: at a few dinars, the heap of the tomato-sauced stuff with its squash and peppers and carrots and potatoes, a tender central chunk of lamb topping the semolina, was maybe proving to be exactly what Cunningham had promised, "Just try it and you tell me, if it isn't the best fucking couscous of your life." But cuisine wasn't the issue at hand there in the cubbyhole, where at the few tables the other men eating sat facing the window and the afternoon glare outside, schoolroom style. Cunningham asked Layton again:

"Nobody saw you?"

"Relax, will you. I walked. I passed that big, sort of Art Deco old synagogue on Avenue de la Liberté that looks like a fortress, all the cops and armored Land Cruisers or whatever around it. Then I got into your embassy neighborhood, upscale and tasteful, where I must say I was surprised to see so little security, except for the concrete barriers in front. The whole operation was closed down for the day. What did I see? I saw the locked glass door to the consular section and a lit waiting room, empty. I saw a sign saying that visiting the consular section was a no-charge deal, and if anybody tried to charge anybody else waiting in line for preferred service or anything else, that it should be reported. A sign like that is a new one on me, and that's exactly what I saw, all I saw. And I doubt anybody saw me."

"Don't worry about the security. It's totally unseen."

"What's the deal on the synagogue?"

"There's still a Jewish community here, a small token one that's getting smaller. The police presence outside is just a token, too, trying to put on a good face to show outsiders that Tunisia isn't to be lumped with the rest of the Arab world."

"Which, of course, it is."

"Of course."

Cunningham appeared to be softening, also appeared to appreciate how it was obvious that Layton was enjoying the couscous.

"Good, isn't it?" Cunningham said.

"Best fucking couscous of my life," Layton told him.

▮ ▮ ▮

That a supposedly retired agent from the Bureau was on assignment in Tunisia was an anomaly, to put it mildly. That Layton had even signed up with the FBI after law school was probably more of an anomaly, bordering on freak occurrence, to put it frankly.

Layton went to law school, UVA, after Harvard. He studied law maybe only because he felt that he owed his uncle who had raised him for all the man's kindness over the years—the bachelor uncle, a judge, so much wanted to see Layton a lawyer. Layton hated the drudgery of tort and contract courses. And to make matters worse, it was the 1960s, that time of evening news clips constantly showing more frightened American kids in camouflage uniforms being spilled out of teetering helicopters and onto the yellow rice paddies in Vietnam; Layton knew he would get heat from his local draft board in Rhode Island once his law school deferment expired. Layton decided to beat the government at its own game, and he joined the FBI to dodge the draft, if that made any sense. Assigned to D.C., he married a girl who was a secretary for a congressman, they had a son, but the marriage didn't work out. In fact, nothing was working out for Layton for a while; the snub-nosed girl with red hair who was so pretty and was so much fun as they relaxed on weekends with other couples at barbecues and suburban cocktail parties out in leafy Fairfax, his young wife, well, somehow her prettily snub-nosed, red-headed innate cheeriness wasn't a good mix with the darkness of Layton soon questioning most everything—the meaningless job, the dead end of claustrophobic family life. After a complicated divorce, Layton didn't buck the transfer from Washington to Detroit; he needed a change.

Layton was among the first agents assigned full-time to the Arab community there, and seeing that the bulk of the community was essentially Christian then—Lebanese, Syrian—his fluent French was his credential, a language they often shared. His work wasn't so much a matter of any terrorism, but just dealing with normal crime (often rings for the pilfering from warehouse loading docks of expensive color TVs or a few crates of Cutty Sark, what qualified as a federal offense because it involved interstate trucking). When monitoring of foreign students became a priority during the 1980s and more agents were transferred to those squads, Layton welcomed the reassignment to Boston, a better city than Detroit and one he knew well. After all, New England was home for him, granting it was very different now—his elderly uncle had died, even Layton's second-rate prep school on the North Shore was long gone, the staid fieldstone buildings in a setting of sprawling green playing fields close to the sea now converted into, wouldn't you know it, condos. Layton lived in a small Beacon Hill apartment with a lot of windows, which didn't make it seem so small. He dated an attractive gray-eyed stewardess for the old TWA for a long while, then a divorced art gallery owner for a longer while. Admittedly, Layton didn't relish putting in time with her at another opening amid the usual empty small talk and the cheap white wine and tasteless canapés lifted off a silver tray. He also didn't like to hear the woman, Marion, wheeling and dealing in the sale of canvases on the phone, because, as Layton soon learned, the peddling of art wasn't all that different from the peddling of storm windows, even life insurance to the over-fifties crew. However, he did savor how she had a gift for spotting work by younger artists who might be the real thing, and merely to hear her say something in her raspy, authentically Vassar voice like, "Does anybody know how successful nineteenth-century American painters were at getting at the very *essence* of black, Heade especially, does anybody have *any* real idea?"—something like that was enough to convince Layton she was rare, much better company than the attractive TWA stewardess or the several younger, so-called professionals he met in the Newbury Street dating bars, the quintessentially empty chatter of that scene. But he didn't marry Marion, and they went their separate ways.

There were a couple of somewhat major cases for Layton. One had been in his very first year of service in Washington when he got assigned to a Weatherman bombing squad. The other came through his contacts in Boston; Layton managed to gather solid information after Arab terrorists blew out of the sky a Pan Am jet over the small town in Scotland that gave the disaster its name. But outside of that, there wasn't much to distinguish Layton's career with the Bureau. Early on, his superiors had obviously identified him with the play-it-safe foot-draggers, even if he was from Harvard and not the usual type of reliable Catholic-college boy Hoover always had such belief in for his corps; true, while Layton didn't entirely fit the profile, nobody differentiated him from the common terminally lazy variety of agent, Catholic college or otherwise, just dreaming of retirement and finally paying off a mortgage in some platted neighborhood in a dull suburb like Fairfax. Layton admitted the Bureau had wasted his life, or his professional life, anyway; he often thought he would have liked to have gotten a Ph.D., or done just about anything other than put up with as many years as he did of endless Bureau paperwork and office politics. The set retirement age for agents was fifty-seven, but he never made it anywhere close to that. Layton took a cut in pension early when his grown son, who Layton hardly knew (his ex-wife had remarried), talked him into investing in the son's own business; it was an internet start-up, a foolish scheme, something to do with selling rock-and-roll trivia to keyboard-clicking, credit-card-wielding fans online. Layton went along with it, invested heavily, probably because he felt guilty that he hadn't been around to raise his son; Layton saw in him a certain vacant lostness that made Layton want to believe that the bragging kid might turn things around, end up making a success of such a farfetched enterprise in a new media field, another budding go-getter of a Ted Turner, possibly. Increasingly more money was borrowed against Layton's pension, Layton fell into deep debt, and by the time the Bureau approached him to come out of retirement and do some part-time work—a contractor of sorts, what they referred to as an "asset"—he had no choice but to sign on. The fact of the matter was that after September 11, Layton was suddenly very much in demand, one of the few veteran agents with any substantial time in Arab domestic surveillance; plus, his having handled a Weatherman bombing case and then the Lockerbie bombing case made his dossier more noticeable. He still had his contacts and informants, a list built up through considerable work and despite the legendary FBI stinginess. (While the high-rolling CIA might set up ski lodges and yachts to lure sources, it wasn't like that for the FBI; more than once at the Boston FBI office Layton had put in for a voucher to bring an informant to a good restaurant—a Brazilian place, specifically, that he liked on a Harvard Square back street—only to have his squad boss balk, suggest he settle for hamburgers at the red formica tables of Charlie's Kitchen behind the JFK School.) All of which is to say, the game was different now: Layton was *badly* needed, and sending Layton on an errand to yet another country was almost becoming routine by this time, 2003. Of course, what was called a "no objection" clearance to allow such foreign work was always applied for and always given, albeit begrudgingly, by CIA and State ahead of time. CIA did tolerate activity such as FBI bomb-squad investigations abroad, but, to repeat, it really didn't appreciate anybody horning in on their own foreign intelligence.

Khaled Khemir had been an informant while a student at MIT. Layton had already established that he was now living in Tunis, but the Bureau seemed nervous about using simple overseas phone or online contact with him, so this trip was arranged.

▮ ▮ ▮

On the other hand, Layton didn't like putting pressure on this kid—or a kid back when he had known him, anyway—and he remembered Khaled Khemir in Boston as a rather quiet, brainy sort. He had returned to Tunis and was teaching part-time at the national university in the city.

And in Tunis, Khaled Khemir himself was now reluctant, or so Layton detected in two brief local phone calls from the Hôtel Majestic. Then, to complicate the situation, Khaled Khemir announced that he was leaving Tunis for a few days to visit his ill mother now living with one of his sisters somewhere near Sfax, telling Layton they could get together when he returned. So the French girls from

Montpellier, having them around, became a way to kill some time for Layton as much as anything else.

III.

Two mornings later, speaking in French, the hotel manager came up to Layton. Layton was walking through the lobby, returning to his room after breakfast with the copy of Flaubert's *Salammbô* in hand. The manager said, "I must say, I admire your taste in women." The manager's name was Youssef, possessor of the nickname of El Bey—translated more or less as "The Ruler"—during his days as a striker with Espérance Sportive.

In his good French suits, Youssef was rather dashing. He exuded sheer confidence, like a former rock star or—better, here in football-crazy Tunis—somebody who actually *had* been a player for Espérance Sportive. He spoke to Layton in a man-to-man way now, practically congratulating him for what Youssef must have seen as Layton's conquest of the duo of sylphlike blondes. It was all humorous for Layton, who while still lean and athletic at his age, the short military lie-down haircut silver and a perpetual tan from so much travel lately, certainly wasn't the kind of guy for a conquest of the sort the manager was envisioning. Actually, after having seen the girls a couple of times at the cafés on Avenue Bourguiba, Layton was just sitting outdoors at the Café des Deux Avenues there one afternoon, the girls taking the table next to him. One of them, Véronique, eventually asked if he might have a light, an overt ploy to start conversation. There was something in their vulnerability. At first they did put on some about how the little jewel of a village on its cliff high above the sparkling Mediterranean, jet-setting Sidi Bou Said, had bored them and so they decided to move to the city, though before long in the talk they unabashedly poured out their predicament—virtually no money, definitely no return tickets, and barely able to stand another night in a hotel beside the patch of soot and dust that passed for a city bus terminal, a place called (Layton appreciated this connection) the Hôtel Salammbô. There followed much talk of the size of the roaches at the Salammbô, the lack of air-conditioning at the Salammbô; there was much talk, as well, concerning how their luggage had been confiscated by the expensive hotel in Sidi Bou Said, and how they had, in fact, left there with little more than the jeans and halter tops they were wearing, plus a couple of dresses and, of course, their cosmetic kits. Without return tickets they had no choice but to try to survive in cheaper Tunis for a while, hope something might happen. Perhaps Layton was the something.

In the course of the conversation, especially beautiful Jeanne-Isabelle, of the bruised-plum lips and high cheekbones, just started sniffling, then her eyes teared up, Jeanne-Isabelle peeling off her big wraparound sunglasses and dabbing those eyes with a paper napkin. Layton, feeling particularly avuncular, told them he would help; he accompanied them to check out of the dismal Hôtel Salammbô, and he booked them a room next to his at the Majestic. He knew how to play the expense account game lately, not as tough overseas even with the cheap FBI; it would be easy enough to claim that the girls knew Khaled Khemir, say they might be valuable on that front. But when asked about them now, Layton had to be honest with the hotel manager, "They are simply friends, I'm helping them out."

"They seemed tired when they arrived yesterday, *les jeunes filles,*" Youssef said. "They must be sleeping late. Tell them that tomorrow I can arrange for breakfast to be served here, or even in their room, beyond the regular breakfast time, right up to eleven."

"To be frank, I personally don't have any idea if they're still sleeping," Layton told him. "Though I imagine they might be. Remember, they do have their own room. They're in 219, and I'm in 218."

"*D'accord,*" the manager said.

Layton knew the manager must have been picturing what Layton himself was picturing—the single door, cream-enameled and ornate, probably dating back to the "1911" carved in the Majestic's whitewashed façade. It was locked, but a twist of the wrist on the tarnished brass knob and an unbolting of the latch would be all that was needed to combine as a single suite the two spacious old rooms; those rooms had long French windows (opening to balconies), grumbling air conditioners, and no shortage of a matching overdone floral patterning (exploding roses, ferns) for the drapes and spreads, even the upholstery on the chairs themselves, with the mismatching old furniture all freshly cream-enameled to give some sense of matching, too. The Majestic *was* a find, Layton had decided, no denying its authenticity.

Going through the lobby the next day around noon (he looked at those clocks above the desk for the time in different zones again, maybe he had even dreamed of them the night before), Layton thought he heard voices coming from what should have been the empty dining room, which he knew didn't serve lunch, only breakfast and dinner. He saw the girls with their freshly washed blond hair, loose and stringily wet. They were sitting at a table with Youssef; they were listening, laughing, hanging on every word in his talk surely documenting his legendary soccer exploits, as Youssef made good on that offer of keeping the waiters in their frayed gold jackets around for a very late continental breakfast for the girls.

Though for the moment the man Layton saw sitting there didn't even seem to be Youssef the hotel manager in the least, and with the girls—for the moment—this Youssef was entirely the star player again, El Bey, the Ruler indeed.

Meanwhile, Layton was beginning to suspect that this errand was maybe not going to be as easy as he had first thought, getting the information on some of Khaled Khemir's former grad-student teaching assistant colleagues back at MIT; they had been monitored closely for the last four months, were labeled as "chatterers," possibly linked to Palestinian resistance organizations. Khaled Khemir was still in Sfax.

▮ ▮ ▮

To be honest, Layton liked Tunis, liked it a hell of a lot.

He liked this newer part of the city, with wide, tree-lined Avenue Bourguiba and its cafés, the French district that surrounded it offering plenty more of the frilly white colonial architecture. He especially liked just letting himself wander in the older part of the city and the Medina proper. Dim walkway tunnels, twisting cobbled lanes so narrow you could spread your arms and touch the ancient walls on either side of you. And once you got away from the few main tourist venues and well behind the Grand Mosque, into the real Medina, it was a contained world in itself, with shops and little banks for the locals, always kids playing soccer against the houses, everything suddenly more Arabic—the workers in smocks and skullcaps, the women wearing head scarves—everything suddenly more dreamlike, too, Layton told himself. In a bit of reading beforehand of Flaubert's letters, Layton learned how on a trip to Tunis and the ruins of Carthage in preparation for writing *Salammbô* in 1858, Flaubert, when not out at the archaeological sites, spent his own share of time in the Medina, completely walled then, carousing with the French trade consuls and sampling the prostitutes, because Flaubert when young never failed to sample a foreign city's prostitutes, apparently. The Medina probably hadn't changed much at all since then, Layton thought: the same smells—sometimes leather from the sandalmakers or perfume from the nooks and stands selling their many essences, sometimes just the aroma of bread, the stacked fat loaves pushed in wobbly wooden wheelbarrows through the Medina often making for a traffic jam in itself—and surely the same sounds—the din of tambour and reed-flute music, from boomboxes if not from actual musicians now, or just the quiet tap-tapping of a silversmith's hammer in a particularly out-of-the-way alley, even the rhythmic rattle of a weaver working a loom for another fine exercise in the geometric artistry of the world-renowned carpets produced here. That afternoon, following the encounter with Youssef entertaining the girls, Layton lingered at a café in the Medina. He drank a strong tea and reread some of the lush sentences in *Salammbô* (often billed as Flaubert's worst novel, though for undeniable richness of prose it could have been the best, having served as almost the literary bible for French Parnassiens and Symbolistes, the Décadents later). When he returned to the Majestic, he detected the coconutty fragrance of shampoo even from the hallway, well before he got to his room. The girls had figured out themselves how to unbolt the door connecting the two rooms, or possibly Youssef helped them, and in Layton's room now, Jeanne-Isabelle was sitting, legs crossed at the knee, on the edge of the made bed while letting the window air conditioner blow-dry her hair, the cooling turned off and the fan on high. Naked except for emerald panties, she was thumbing through a French fashion magazine. She explained nonchalantly, without looking up, that she hoped Layton didn't mind, and she said that each of them, the two girls, needed a shower and a bathroom of her own to get ready for that evening. Youssef was taking the two of them to a disco.

She kept turning the pages, and, after all, toplessness was for French girls just beach etiquette, so she definitely saw it as no big deal. Her breasts were lovely, pert, her shoulder blades sculpted artistry in themselves, the line of her backbone a delicate chain; she lifted up a hand for one of those raking shoves through the damp mane of hair, chin held high, the gesture she and Véronique had nearly patented, and she continued on with the magazine. Finding her casualness more ridiculous than anything yet, Layton lightly slapped her smack on the *derrière,* smiling, telling her to scoot and close the door—he said that a phone message had been left for him at the desk and he had a call to make.

Jeanne-Isabelle stood up, pecked a kiss on each of his cheeks as if he were a favorite uncle, then did exactly that, scooted, the two dimples on her backside just above the low line of the emerald panties taking turns winking at Layton, emphasizing the pure absurdity of it all. At the doorway she slowed down, smilingly tiptoed like a kid making a show out of trying to be very, very quiet, the old walking-on-eggshells routine, and returned to the adjoining room, gingerly closing the door.

IV.

The next day Layton met Cunningham a second time at the couscous place on Rue du Caire. Once they disposed of the small talk about whether Layton minded eating at the same restaurant again ("Best fucking couscous of one's life," Layton told Cunningham, "why toy with a premise like that?"), the conversation did seem to be veering toward one tack. On Cunningham's part, anyway.

"What you want to do is see him," Cunningham said.

They were talking about Khaled Khemir, of course.

"Yeah, it's what I want to do, all right," Layton said." I don't think he's dodging me—that thing about his mother in Sfax sounded honest enough."

"But you have to see him. Talk to him."

"Of course I have to."

The lenses of Cunningham's horn-rimmed glasses reflected so that you couldn't quite see his eyes; he was wearing the same seersucker sport coat as last time.

"And not just talk on the phone," Cunningham emphasized.

"He's touchy on the phone."

The waiter brought more bread, Cunningham nodded. Layton got the feeling that Cunningham was a regular here, no doubt, knew it was a safe spot to talk.

"I wonder if it would have been easier," Layton said, "if I had come to Tunis more officially, if you know what I mean. There's a contact from the National Police Academy in the city *préfecture* here, I think, he maybe should have handled my visit, no?"

It was a program left over from the Hoover regime at the FBI. Hoover's National Police Academy trained a lot of cops from abroad, most of them hanging up on their office walls in police stations back in their own home country framed photographs of themselves with pals from that training course in the States, proud of it, Arab world or not. It gave the FBI, usually wielding only Stateside jurisdiction, international ties, and it was something CIA types considered way out of line. Cunningham didn't get into that now, but flatly assured Layton the "no objection" approval Layton had obtained from the CIA was a much better way to proceed in this particular case.

"You will see him?" Cunningham asked.

"Yeah, what the hell am I doing here otherwise. Soon, I hope."

Cunningham seemed satisfied with that.

"Harvard," Cunningham then said, as if plucking the word out of the heat of the restaurant.

"What's that?" Layton said.

"You're a Harvard man?"

Layton hadn't heard that term in years, and it appeared Cunningham had done a little background checking on Layton since they had last met, knew where Layton had studied. Cunningham talked of his own time at Brown, also emphatically used the term "Ivy League," as if it was supposed to install the two of them in some club with a complicated secret handshake perhaps, a shared understanding of life. For somebody like Cunningham in today's CIA, no longer the depository for fellow graduates of the Ivy League that it had once been, Layton's stock had apparently risen considerably—Layton not the usual FBI rube but a, well, "Harvard man."

Cunningham talked about how much he had enjoyed Brown, how the classes were small and you could design your own major, and how the education was decidedly top-notch. It was a standard, to-be-expected spiel from somebody from that so-called Ivy League who hadn't gone to Harvard or Yale and had to trudge through life with a pressing need (Layton had no idea why) to constantly explain why he hadn't gone to (which meant hadn't been admitted to) Harvard or Yale, or at least Princeton.

There was something Layton really didn't like about this guy.

Layton took the trip around Tunisia for several days because Khaled Khemir still hadn't returned from Sfax, also because of what was degenerating into the afternoon circus next door. The manager Youssef—El Bey, all right—was spending most of his own afternoons in that room next door with Véronique and Jeanne-Isabelle, keeping room service busy to provide for the ongoing party. Layton saw no harm in that, but the romping made it tough to get some sleep with a nap in the two or three p.m. heat, the kind of napping that Layton had been savoring lately, if truth be known—deep hammer-on-anvil slumber free of the phantasmagoric cinema of constantly dreaming, that playing out of reruns concerning Layton's admitted mess-ups in life.

▮ ▮ ▮

Layton traveled to Kairouan and then Sousse, making a loop from Tunis.

He relied on the long-distance *louages,* dented white Peugeot station wagons with seven others in the three rows of seats, not counting the driver. The passengers were usually all men, some in work clothes and some in robes and dressy *chechia* caps, "*Bonjours*" politely exchanged. The drivers liked to convert the dashboard into their own personal "space" with maybe a shag carpet on the deck, also an assortment of objects dangling from the rearview mirror (anything from wooden prayer beads to three—he saw this on one *louage*—empty American 7-Up cans, seemingly collector's items here); a beaded covering for the huge steering wheel was mandatory. The drivers drove fast and recklessly, never hesitating to dangerously swerve to overtake any top-heavy, wobbling lorry on bald tires out there on the otherwise deserted two-lane; Layton figured they were paid by the number of runs they could complete each day.

The geography was handsome, constantly changing as you got farther inland. First vineyards and olive groves laid out neatly on the hills, then fields of undulating golden wheat, then the sand flats of the oncoming desert in earnest, the first date-palm groves standing like islands and the occasional robed rustic on a mule gazing at the Peugeot speeding by in but a blur for him, surely.

An ancient city with a golden-walled medina, Kairouan was a place of pilgrimage, "The Fourth Holiest City in Islam," rising impressively out of the level plains. Kairouan was entirely different from, almost the direct antithesis of, the next city he stayed in, very modernized Sousse on the return loop; Sousse was a decided tourist trap of gleaming white hotels along the sweeping miles of Mediterranean beach. Different cities, no doubt, but the experience in each for Layton was quite the same. Layton found himself alone in a hotel room in each place. He found himself reading the copy of Flaubert's *Salammbô* in French, that epic of the passionate, star-crossed, half-perverse (the Flaubertian touch) love between the beautiful young Carthaginian princess Salammbô and the leader of the revolt of the mercenary troops against Carthage, the confused young Numidian general Mâtho, who should have been a lyric poet and never any combat commander whatsoever. Layton would be reading, yes, he would be caught up in the words, then he wouldn't be reading. He would be just staring at nothing, as it started again.

He found himself crying for no apparent reason, without the escape of the drugging sleep he had slipped into back in Tunis to ease any of it. And it was little use trying to make some sense or logic out of it, attribute it to a specific known failure, as he did admit to a lot of things—how he had never paid off on what should have been his promise in life, how both his career and marriage had gone nowhere (he *should* have done something like graduate study in French literature, he *shouldn't* have married a woman with whom he had so little in common), while his only child—his son, the one person in life he had always tried to believe in—ended up, if Layton was honest, bilking Layton out of his pension money and what should have been an easier life now, without having to hustle this way for what amounted to pocket change. But there was no reasoning, no cause and effect. It was maybe all one of those nail puzzles that looks like it conforms to the rules of geometry, as you want to believe that if you just concentrate, fully analyze it and slowly work the disentanglement, it will be miraculously solved, even prove miraculously revealing when it suddenly loosens in your trembling hands.

But this puzzle didn't untangle, everything remained locked hopelessly together, and there was just the overwhelming blank frustration that nothing but nothing made *any* sense, there away from Tunis.

▮ ▮ ▮

There was just stupid crying for Layton. There was just crying for no reason at all because he felt so goddamn sad. There was just catching sight of himself in a hotel room mirror again, a ceiling fan chugging through the feeble air-conditioning again, and the near disgust with himself. There was just the old message, "Get a fucking hold of yourself, man."

▮ ▮ ▮

"I used to dream so much when young of going to the States," Khaled Khemir said.

"I suppose a lot of people do," Layton said.

"No, you don't know what it's like. I mean, that's the problem with being an American, you have no idea what it's like."

The contact with the elusive Khaled Khemir had finally been accomplished, the purpose of Layton's trip to Tunisia, and, if nothing else, Layton felt good about that. They sat drinking leafy, mint-sweet brown tea from small glass tumblers at the outside table of a café up by the university, a cluster of new streamlined buildings on a knoll behind the Medina. Layton was doing what he had to do, and Khaled Khemir was doing what he had to do, too, Layton knew, even if Khaled Khemir didn't enjoy it. It was the old game, somebody gave you something because they needed something themselves. When Khaled Khemir had been a contact back in Cambridge and a grad student at MIT, his visa had run out and he wanted an extension. He had a German girlfriend he was head over heels in love with; the girl was working on a Ph.D. in philosophy or linguistics at Harvard, and Khaled Khemir couldn't bear leaving her. In truth, Layton had never gotten much important out of him in Cambridge; Khaled Khemir had known some Libyans in the States who had very vague connections with the Lockerbie bombers, and Layton was never sure whether Khaled Khemir offered the information on them that he eventually did then because he didn't approve of such tactics at the time or, more likely, there was a long-standing, bad-blood general rift between Tunisians and Libyans. Neither of them trusted the other; why, Khadaffi himself had once tried to *annex* the other country in another typically mad Khadaffi pipe dream, in 1980. Now it was Khaled Khemir's brother who needed something, and while the brother wasn't the scholar Khaled Khemir had been (the brother was taking courses not as a grad student at prestigious MIT but as an undergrad at a state teachers' college on the Cape to keep his student visa, and presently he had bad-check charges to deal with, about to be deported), Khaled Khemir wanted to see the brother finish his education in America. In other words, Khaled Khemir's cooperating now had more to do with family than anything else. Khaled Khemir looked different, too. He was no longer the skinny grad student with a reedy voice; he had always seemed so outright scared when Layton was full-time with the Bureau and they met several times amid those, indeed, red formica tables and gum-chomping middle-aged waitresses in uniforms at noisy Charlie's Kitchen, the Harvard Square hamburger dive. Khaled Khemir now had already told Layton about his part-time lecturing in mathematics at the university, which should lead to a regular appointment soon. He also told Layton of his marriage to a Tunisian woman whose family was a friend of his family (the German girl in Cambridge was only "a stage" he was going through, he laughed); he had two young daughters. His voice more sure, confident, his body having filled out some, yet he still seemed young, with the dark eyes too big in his skull and making him look perpetually startled, the soft smile. He continued with the story about growing up and wanting to go to America very badly, either Miami or Las Vegas, specifically.

"Always Las Vegas," Khaled Khemir smiled some more, "and Miami."

"Really?"

"In my village in the Tell, in the north, the old women used to have songs about it. That was the mythically exotic good life for us to which young men supposedly fled, it would even turn up as a romanticized theme at local bazaars, the wonders of Las Vegas and Miami. Not that anybody ever went there. It must have been the movies that gave us the idea."

"I would have thought it would be France," Layton said, "if you were looking for an icon for flight. Don't young Tunisians often go to France?"

Khaled Khemir sipped his tea, laughed.

"No, France was the colonizer, so there was no dream about them, or their country. France was almost a joke, something you'd see as a long trip that you really didn't want to take, but probably would take. When we were kids, if a kid took a long time going to the shop or whatever, you'd say to him, 'Where did you go? France?' "

Layton smiled. He liked this Khaled Khemir. He also realized, when they got to talking about specific people (the Bureau was involved in investigating a Stateside racket in which Arabs in America were apparently using the widespread wholesaling of knockoffs of brand names—designer handbags, car stereo systems, and such—to raise money for Palestinian resistance activities), yes, Layton also assured himself that when he returned to Boston and filed his own report, he wouldn't include everything he had been told. Layton had gotten to the point that in this time of a cowboy president and who knows what else equally as crazy, he wanted to believe in an America that was different from the internationally bullying one he saw today, 2003, an America that people still dreamed of, even if those dreams were merely envisioning the glitz of Miami and Las Vegas; Layton really didn't care about anybody *anywhere* selling knockoffs of *anything*. Actually, most of the last hour or so he just listened to Khaled Khemir speak about how lucky he was to have found his wife—she worked in the government Ministry of Women and the Family—how lucky he was to have two such fine young girls, three and five.

"Or five today for little Fatma," he said, "and I must go back now, the birthday, you know."

"I understand," Layton said.

But what was strange, certainly, was Cunningham from the embassy—and CIA—calling Layton for one last meeting at the couscous place, as if he simply wanted confirmation beyond any doubt that it *was* Khaled Khemir whom Layton had spoken to.

"Don't be crazy, man," Layton told him, "I dealt with the guy for a full couple of years back in Boston. I know him."

Which was about all Layton was going to give him, and Layton, granting he was abroad, had that "no objection" filed formally and properly, so he didn't have to play this self-satisfied—how should he put this?—"*Brown man's*" game any longer.

"Fuck him," Layton later thought, which made him feel good. "Fuck him, and then some."

V.

The trio of them were almost at the summit there at Byrsa Hill, the site of the gone main temple for what had once been ancient Carthage. Layton and the two French girls, Jeanne-Isabelle and Véronique.

The narrow suburban road was steep; it snaked up past fine white villas, the velvety black asphalt strewn with fallen orange flower petals. The temperature must have been an even ninety degrees. The girls exaggerated their trudging behind him, and though they had bought big liter bottles of mineral water at the tiny white-and-blue stucco Hannibal train station on this the commuter line (the girls halted every twenty paces or so now to take long chugs), they kept complaining like a couple of kids, in French, about how *hot* it was, and how *steep* the road was. That came with accompanying, and comically innocent, old emphasizers, including the functional "*sacré*" and the more classic "*Zut alors!*" They didn't look at all chic anymore, though they had retrieved their wardrobes; having taken the same train on their own farther up to the Sidi Bou Said hotel that they'd originally fled, they had managed to get their suitcases and clothes. Both of them had on simple white T-shirts and camp shorts now, Jeanne-Isabelle wearing sort of a clown's red-and-yellow socks with her tennis sneakers and Véronique, sweaty and poutier than ever, cursing herself in her whispery French for not having worn socks, red and yellow clown-style or otherwise, with her own chafing tennis shoes. They both wore their big sunglasses but no makeup, looked pretty scruffy by this stage in their travels, if truth be known.

The fun with the hotel manager—El Bey, now simply Youssef once more—had expired while Layton had been traveling. Apparently, Youssef's wife, a heavy woman in full traditional white robe and head scarf, by no means a typically docile Muslim female spouse, had shown up at the Majestic on the tip of a hotel maid, to cause a noisy scene. And though Youssef was now letting the girls stay a few extra days (he had taken over their tab from Layton), he made clear that it would be no longer than that; the girls had already persuaded Véronique's soft touch of a grandmother to wire them the money to get back to Montpellier. So they weren't just scruffy, but somewhat defeated, too, their jet-setting escapade over and both of them having to face the drudgery of their jobs back home—Jeanne-Isabelle a hair stylist and Véronique a secretary in an insurance company, *if* she could get the position back—there in Montpellier, where they claimed it rained and rained *all* winter. Layton had a day left in Tunis himself, and he had decided to, in a way, make good on his cover, a cover that he really hadn't needed, and go out to Carthage, which was now a suburb of Tunis. He wanted to walk through some of the scenes of *Salammbô*, possibly follow the route Flaubert did in 1858 when he visited, F. bumping along on a mule, to research the novel. Back at the hotel that morning, when the girls heard his plans for the day, they had insisted, again like a couple of kids, that he take them along, pleading that he couldn't leave them at the boring hotel with "*rien à faire*"—nothing whatsoever to do. And now, like kids, all right, they complained, but Layton didn't mind. It was funny. And he liked them, liked their dreaminess in setting out as they originally had and believing they both would meet playboy millionaires while on their confused trip, a jaunt to posh Sidi Bou Said in Tunisia, which they had hoped would solve their own problems back in rainy Montpellier once and for all.

The empty museum there at the top of the hill was housed in a former Christian monastery. And during a bit of strolling through its rooms now, the girls did relax, admiring the Carthaginian jewelry—gold, turquoise, and bursting pink coral—in the showcases. They lingered at the little model of Punic Carthage rebuilt to scale like something in a model train layout, and lingered longer, for the sheer yummy horror of it, at the displays of children's burial urns excavated from the Tophet—an infamous sacrificial burial site—located there; the children apparently had been offered to the god Moloch in ancient times, given in trade for divine assistance in war. On the other hand, maybe the girls were on good behavior at last because they were honestly grateful to Layton, their rescuer; he had also promised to treat them to a good late lunch at one of the seaside terrace restaurants back down the hill and on the other side of the suburban train tracks, by the beach and more of the elegant white villas there.

▮ ▮ ▮

Outside the museum again, the three strolled around an empty wide esplanade of broken columns set upright—all of that from the later

Roman settlement, rather than the Punic—above the tumbledown brown stone ruins of what apparently had been a residential quarter of the city of Carthage itself during Salammbô's time; not very impressive, and it was true that the original Punic Carthage had left little evidence of its existence—the most powerful civilization of the ancient world at one time had now become the most vanished of civilizations, the heaps of rocks for these unearthed buildings right below the esplanade about the only remaining trace of it, amid the clutter of weeds and giant sunflowers and an inordinate amount of crumpled plastic water bottles tossed about. Layton wandered off on his own, and Layton started feeling much better. No, not simply better, but really good, which is to say, better than he had felt in a long while.

In years, possibly.

He was at the edge of the esplanade. From that vantage point you saw the hill running down to the old Punic harbors, once within the gone, strong city walls, presently just a couple of distant ornamental ponds surrounded by still more villas next to the sea; across the flat Gulf of Tunis that striped alternatingly sapphire and turquoise in the distance, two jutting peninsulas of jagged mountains opened up to the huge Mediterranean. He looked at the sea. Then he looked down to the center of the maze of ruins only a few dozen yards below him, where Jeanne-Isabelle and Véronique now sat on a crumbling brown stone wall, in the welcome shade of a scraggly lemon tree. Véronique had her back turned to Jeanne-Isabelle, who was braiding Véronique's long and lustrous blond hair into a thick rope, the two of them humming a song together.

Most everybody had a dream, Layton knew, as corny as that sounded. The girls had their dream of the easy life, Youssef had his dream of remaining a soccer star forever. And Layton had once had his dream of maybe being a scholar, maybe actually going on a research trip like this in the course of a long and productive academic career of university teaching somewhere, giving his students something, and writing something consequential himself about a book as great as what was considered by some but a minor effort by the master Flaubert, that *Salammbô*. Ancient civilizations even had their massive collective dreams, of conquest and glory, and spreading out from this very hill, there had once been an empire equaled by none, what included not only this North Africa but much of Spain and Gaul, and almost the largest prize beyond that, as Hannibal marched his leathery elephants and his thousands of shivering, sandaled soldiers across the snows of the high Alps, with the City of Rome itself, for a moment, anyway, within his grasp. But maybe here was also the overlooked truth about the dreaming, that everything was gone before it started, and now contemplating what had once been triumphant, the scant rubble of Carthage corporeal, Layton realized that it yielded merely the message of nothing to nothing—or possibly nothing all along, the suspected void, because, when you thought of it, everything was inevitably heading toward nothing before it even started, before it even aspired to or had the chance to be something.

Yet the trick, Layton sensed, was to appreciate the few instants of clarity that you are afforded in the brief blur of it all, to be looking out at the most legendary sea of all seas, this Mediterranean that sparkled brilliant, to be looking down to the ruins that could inarguably lay claim to a past of the rarest of glory, though that past adding up to nothing didn't really figure into it either, didn't matter whatsoever. It didn't matter because there was the wonder of a reported here and now that *trumped* everything else, because there were two beautiful, living, long-legged girls in shorts and T-shirts, both happily humming some tune like a duet now, one braiding the other's hair in the shade of a crooked little lemon tree. Layton kept looking at the girls, almost a painting.

The day smelled of heat and flowers; a bee buzzed somewhere.

It was perfect, wonderful, and, damn, did Layton ever feel good. Not only this, but knowing that for once he had definitely bucked the FBI and its meaningless treading in circles, the constant lying and the constant hounding of people, which he had grown tired of. He had bucked, too, the smug CIA itself, gotten the better of the likes of that weasel Cunningham. Layton had decided that in his report he would tell *nothing* significant about information gathered from Khaled Khemir. Or he would tell as little as he had to, just to collect his own contractor's payment, always straight cash, as well as ensure a visa extension for Khaled Khemir's brother. Layton knew that Khaled Khemir himself, happy at last with a lovely wife and two young kids, simply deserved to get on with his life. (*Layton didn't know then, of course, how Khaled Khemir would disappear when he traveled to an international mathematicians' conference in the Czech Republic the very next month. Layton learned of that, and a lot else, only later. As it turned out, the real reason for dispatching Layton to Tunis was basically to confirm firsthand Khaled Khemir's identity, which was why Cunningham wanted to make sure that Layton did literally "see" Khaled Khemir. Cunningham, who kept pressing Layton for such identification, in the end was satisfied that this young man was, in fact, the Khaled Khemir the government had designs on, who knows why. And with that established, Khaled Khemir could be "taken out," to use the absurd term thrown about so lightly and casually even on the evening news lately, because that's the way "potentials" and "suspects" and especially anybody who—as Layton figured in this case—maybe had something on Cunningham's shadowy CIA was dealt with lately, quickly whisked off to somewhere and imprisoned without a trace or, on occasion, outright gotten rid of. Cunningham was in on it from the start, he was using Layton, and the assignment of Layton's gathering information from Khaled Khemir on Palestinian supporters was only the ruse needed to bring Layton to Tunis. Rather than finally asserting himself, bucking anybody, Layton would have to admit that he had been suckered, he was the one who actually fingered Khaled Khemir, dealt him what amounted to the classic kiss of death at a point in history when Layton's own country was bent on smooching the whole world to death, or so it sometimes seemed—but Layton surely wouldn't learn any of that about Khaled Khemir till later, much later, it coming out when Khaled Khemir's brother Hosni Khemir was quietly deported, Layton futilely protesting. Plus, to know all of that was getting ahead in time, was to realize how Layton would afterward look back on it, and right now Layton was almost outside of time, somehow absolutely free of its inescapable, persistent thumping.*) Yes, in the blinding sunshine on Byrsa Hill, Layton felt more than good.

He felt fucking great.

■ ■ ■

The girls were both standing now. Véronique twisted her neck to try to glance down over her shoulder, brushing off her skinny behind in the khaki camp shorts, and Jeanne-Isabelle put on an exaggerated studio yawn, extending her bare arms—which themselves looked pretty skinny in the loose, oversize white T-shirt—stretching those sticks of arms this way and that to make her point. Obviously they were ready for the lunch he had promised them.

They looked up to see Layton on the esplanade above, each saying in French something along the lines of, "Can we *please* go now?"

And Layton, smiling, called back to them in his own French that they all certainly could.

THE DEAD ARE DREAMING ABOUT US

Somehow, just sitting there on the sofa in the condo, by himself with the magazine at night, he remembered what she had said to him.

He remembered where they were and exactly how she said it, which was maybe odd in itself. After all, they had only gone out together for not quite a whole year back then in what was definitely the otherworld of Cambridge in 1967.

They had met at a mixer at Radcliffe in the fall. It was one of those usual deals where he told himself he would simply hole up in his bedroom on the top floor of Lowell House, sit down at the oaken desk under the flex-arm lamp and bang away at the light-green Hermes portable for a couple of hours now that his roommates were gone from their own bedrooms off the sitting room. He would see how he felt after finishing, decide then if he would take the long walk up Massachusetts Avenue and across the Square to Cabot Hall at Radcliffe. A friend at Radcliffe who graduated from his high school in Illinois a year ahead of him had run into him that week, told him he really should try to make it. (He did things like that in college, writing as hard as he could even on a Friday night sometimes, because he knew that he would become a famous writer, like his heroes, the cagey Irishman Joyce and, more so, that wizard of an Argentine, Borges. He had actually seen Borges led onto the stage just the month before—a grinning and somewhat shy blind man in a good tailored dark suit, his thinning silver hair combed straight back—to deliver the Charles Eliot Norton Lectures there at Harvard. He had no doubt everything would work out for him as a writer, and hadn't he already been admitted, on the basis of manuscript submission, to all the tough-to-get-into creative writing classes, wasn't he already genuinely known around campus for his short stories in the various student literary magazines?) And he did go to the mixer, rather preciously called a "Jolly-Up" at Radcliffe in those days, where, as always, there were a ton more Harvard guys than Radcliffe girls.

He tried to look as if he was enjoying the scarlet punch he ladled from the bowl—somebody had spiked it with something—and he was watching everybody else in the posh Cabot parlor with its purposefully dim lighting, the Kinks or Wilson Pickett or whatever booming. He was maybe thinking about how with only such scant light you could still see the fine oil paintings of murky landscapes on the wood-paneled walls, all of it reminiscent of a manor house and making that parlor, yes, altogether too posh, too dignified, for anything as frivolous by definition as a mixer. As it turned out, his friend from high school wasn't even there. Then he spotted a girl, looked at her talking with at least four other guys in sport jackets around her, and he could tell she was looking at him. Not especially tall, wearing a sweater and skirt and leotards, all black, delicate features and bow-like lips, hair glossily dark, there was no gamesmanship right from the start: Taking his hand when he asked her to dance, heading out with him to the crowd of bumping bodies where they had literally rolled back the old Oriental rugs for the mixer, she simply said, whispery, a little out of breath, "I was watching you, I was telling myself I hope that boy will ask me to dance."

She was from Connecticut, grew up in a family of seven hearty brothers in the modernistic redwood-and-plate-glass house her father the MD had designed himself; she was an art history major, a junior like him.

Within a month they were spending most of their time together, during the week studying in the evening, with leisurely breaks at the old Hayes-Bickford cafeteria (she would have cinnamon toast and tea, he would sometimes order two of the thirty-five-cent baked custards in their tan crockery bowls, a specialty the Bick was close to famous for), then on Saturday night going to a movie or showing up for a party in Lowell House or at the gray triple-decker in Central Square. A trio of his buddies from creative writing classes had managed to move into the run-down apartment there, each using his own specific ruse to get out of a dorm before senior year despite it being almost impossible to get out of a Harvard dorm—one of the Houses—before senior year; they were a good bunch, a literary set who made a lot out of him because he was known the way he was in the creative writing classes. (While he wouldn't become a famous writer, he would go on to a long career in journalism, in Boston and then New York, respected in his field, and now he was an editor in Dallas, where he certainly never expected to end up, sort of bought away from New York by the Dallas newspaper when it changed hands and the swashbuckling new owner actually thought that with top-notch talent he could challenge nationally the established newspapers in places like Boston and New York.) They missed each other terribly during Thanksgiving break, missed each other even more during the long Christmas break. There were long-distance calls from Illinois to Connecticut, when long-distance calls were so expensive—an extravagance his father regularly pointed out to him—and when you sometimes could actually hear the satellite's beeping in the transmission, reminding him yet again of all that cost.

And it might have been after a party or a movie or just a dinner that particular Saturday night in one of the Square restaurants that could seem exotic back in a time when most of the Square wasn't yuppified, was more working-class, with its diners and dim all-men's bars (always the local Trinity on the wall in those little cubbyholes—Ted Williams, Jack Kennedy, and Bobby Orr, in that order of importance); there was the cheap French place up by Radcliffe, where it felt daring merely to say the rolling word *Beaujolais* to the waiter, and there was the cheap Spanish place behind the clapboard clubhouse for the *Advocate* literary magazine (he was an elected member of the Board of Prose Editors, though he stopped going to the meetings after a while, bored), and there was the old and very cheap, but somehow exotic, too, German Wursthaus. At the Wursthaus they *never* checked ID's, and the tough local waitresses in their comical Bavarian dirndl getups didn't mind if you lingered too long in one of the dark wooden booths, took your time and also took up valuable customer space even after the meal was over, snuggling some with your date before maybe facing the heavy snow outside, everybody bundled up out there and moving almost somnambulistically this way and that, the Yellow cabs pawing tentatively along in the quiet whiteness.

They probably *were* at the Wursthaus that Saturday night, and they maybe decided to skip going to another party thrown by his literary pals at the gray three-decker in Central Square. Late March was absurdly late for snow, and the best way to survive it was just to get a little messed up on bourbon and relax listening to some albums at Lowell House, talking and drinking and smooching in the sitting room, then, of course, moving to the bedroom for the hungry lovemaking of twenty-year-olds convinced they were more than in love, very much so.

In bed after the lovemaking, they lay there talking, shifting their bodies now and then to get comfortable, drinking out of cafeteria glasses the Old Crow with ice cubes from the little grumbling second-hand refrigerator in the sitting room. She'd certainly experimented with a lot more marijuana than he had, but was coming around to see his arguments for the physical high of bourbon as opposed to the airier high of pot, which he conceded had its good points, though for him it really didn't compare to bourbon, he would tell her.

His roommates, two of them, were gone again that night, and therefore she and he could listen to the component KLH stereo (that was the big word for it then, a "component" stereo) with the door of the bedroom wide open. And remembering it, he liked to think that maybe it was the Donovan album that she had first brought over one afternoon after classes; it was something she had got him to eventually appreciate, the spooky, slowly echoing electric harpsichord, also the way that if you listened close you could clearly discern, distinct, what was coming from the left speaker and what was coming from the right speaker, another marvel of the day. He could listen forever to her talk about painting. There was the stuff she hated (for her, Monet was overrated, "all those pastels fit for a tissue ad") and the stuff she loved (while on that subject of Monet, she had a secret theory that perhaps, just perhaps, the whole of Impressionism was nothing short of a *haut bourgeois* sell-out, innovation easy enough for said class to accept as daring, but still safe enough for them in their set *haut bourgeois* ways; she said that maybe the "real action" of the nineteenth century in France, though overshadowed by Impressionism, was French Symbolism, beginning with the influential experiments of Delacroix and his ultra-true colors, and giving way to the twin ultimately haunting masters of the mode itself, strange Gustave Moreau and stranger Pierre Puvis de Chavannes). Or, as the Donovan played, possibly it wasn't art she talked about, and there were always the hilarious stories of the seven brothers she had grown up with, each in his own way as loopy as any of that same number of dwarfs, she the only sister lost amongst them but always very happy, surely the beautiful Snow White in that castle of the modernistic redwood house in Connecticut. And what the little plastic clock on the night table had to say didn't matter to them, together there on the tangled sheets of the steel-framed bed, up on the top, fourth floor under a sloping ceiling and the single window's many panes frosted at the end of the dormer alcove like that; they drank more of the iced Old Crow, pungently aromatic and Listerine-strong on the palate, made love another time. And afterward, with the silver radiator clanking out its own contentment, the snow still falling steadily, they lay on their sides for a long while, facing each other and looking *right* at each other. She maybe had her flattened palms together under her ear, childlike, he maybe reached out to lift a strand of her lustrous dark hair from where it had fallen in a ribbon across her forehead, placing it back atop her head again, as she smiled and as she finally said it, serious, but soft and gentle, too; he always remembered it:

"The dead are dreaming about us."

He kept looking at her. Hesitantly smiling like that, her bow lips seemed a little unsteady, a little frightened, because sometimes, it was true, she herself could seem a little frightened about a lot of things. She told him:

"That's what it is to be really, really alive. It's to know that it probably isn't real, that it's unlike most things that are real, but it's so special, so right, that if the dead could have anything at all, it would be to be alive, of course, and that's what the dead are dreaming, they're dreaming about us right now, probably in their minds dreaming up everybody right now. We're here only because of their dreams. That's what being alive is, that's the easiest way to understand it."

But the relationship didn't work out. There was the predictable amount of arguing and awkwardness the following fall when they broke up; she cried and he felt quite lost. Before long, however, each was dating somebody else, and even when they ran into each other around campus during senior year, they chatted, laughed. He took pride in telling people that they had remained good friends, and from what he had heard, she more or less did the same.

And picking up the glossy alumni magazine now in his condo in Dallas, thumbing through the endless ads for not only expensive German automobiles but this time an actual double-page spread for a bona fide Bentley (the alumni magazine attested to what Harvard seemed to be about lately, by and large too much money, and he had lost some of his affection for the place—understandably, granting this was petty—when neither of his own sons from his marriage that was over years ago had been admitted to Harvard), yes, thumbing his way through more reports on more new construction at the university, some general articles, too (one on a breakthrough in DNA testing, with research being done at Harvard, which he did read around in), he found himself at the obituaries in back. He saw her name, there among the fine print for the Class of 1969.

What it reported was pretty much what he knew about her later life. She had married a guy from their class who went on to become an ethno-musicologist, the two of them adopting a couple of African kids to add to the three of their own while living in Africa, where her husband did his dissertation research; despite her never pursuing a career with the art history degree, the time in Africa had given her the impetus to get as involved as she had been—housewife or not—in refugee relocation programs over the years, the names of the many organizations enough to constitute a genuine list here. He read over the write-up once, then did so again, the initial jolt of seeing it subsiding. He noticed it had been cancer, the variety undisclosed. He told himself it was good to see how the two boys with African first names were listed among her own children and her husband, a professor at Middlebury, as survivors.

So, as he sat alone on the sofa at the glass-topped coffee table this night, back from the newspaper's downtown offices now that the morning edition had gone to press, he closed the magazine, placed it on the table. He remembered again what she had said, what he had, in truth, thought about often in his life, what did stick with him more than anything else from the several months they were together. Strangely, it wasn't a real sorrow that hit him now, but rather how what she had said, what he had always remembered exactly, put him on the brink of realizing now something very important, something that made him a bit woozy just to almost grasp the idea of it—though he didn't *quite* make the jump, *quite* grasp the idea of it, and the more he thought about it, tried to grasp it, the more the realization of it all receded. Until, turning practical in his picturing, he remembered the way she looked the very first night at that Radcliffe mixer, her smile, the black sweater she was wearing, the short black skirt with the black leotards; the skirt was surely what was daringly called a "mini" in 1967, he thought. And he remembered again how she told those stories about her brothers with such animation, how she loved to talk about them as he lay in bed with her in Lowell House, she seemingly the one and not he—as he looked back on it now—with a born narrator's instinct and skill.

"The dead are dreaming about us," he repeated it aloud, if only a whisper.

He stared at the closed magazine on the table, then stood up from the sofa.

He headed to the large back bedroom and pushed aside the sliding glass doors opening onto a terra-cotta patio balcony, the cushioned wrought-iron furniture illuminated by the strong moonlight on a very balmy night in Texas. The darkness of the wooded park beyond the balcony railing smelled sweet with late April's fresh budding, cicadas clattered softly.

He sat out there for an hour or so.